THE PUNCH LIST

RICHARD NEER

A RILEY KING MYSTERY

OTHER TITLES BY RICHARD NEER

FM: THE RISE AND FALL OF ROCK RADIO
SOMETHING OF THE NIGHT
THE MASTER BUILDERS
INDIAN SUMMER
THE LAST RESORT

for Jim Del Balzo

TROIKA: A GROUP OF THREE, ESPECIALLY IN A RULING CAPACITY

I

Moses Ginn sat in front of me at the diner, or the closest approximation to a real one in Charlotte, North Carolina. It had a laminate lunch counter, sassy bleached-blonde waitresses who smoke, some stainless steel and an extensive menu of fried food, but that's where the authenticity ended. Oh, and the owner could have been Greek, or from somewhere in Europe/Asia/Africa proximate to the Mediterranean.

"So, Mr. Riley King, you free in the middle of the afternoon on a business day? And here I was thinking that you be some big time private dick."

I used to love friends who try to push boundaries with me. There was a time I'd take the bait and jump right in. *Oh yeah, mine is bigger than yours, fool.* But these days, I just let it pass. Besides, in Ginn's case, I wasn't sure I'd measure up. Although he had to be more than ten years my senior, his six four frame had me by two inches and his sinewy physique would be impressive on a man three decades younger.

"Hey Moses. You call, I'm here. Nothing so urgent I can't help out a friend in need."

He nodded. "We friends? Hope we'll still be after we talk some business."

Moses Ginn was neatly turned out in a linen guayabera shirt and sharply creased cotton blend trousers. Italian loafers, no socks. Even seated, the man projected a formidable presence. His voice was a deep rumble, his eyes blazed with quiet intelligence. Given his age, he had undoubtedly weathered the slings and arrows facing a black man coming of age in the South, although a man as impressive as he would have had few individual challengers.

I said, "You were pretty vague as to why you wanted to meet. I know we haven't worked together in a while. Business has been slow."

Ginn and I had made an informal agreement a year or so ago. He'd be my first call when I needed assistance of the muscular variety. I recently had asked him to play nursemaid to a client on Hilton Head Island. It turned out his presence wasn't necessary and he never sent me a bill. Perhaps he had emailed it and it had been relegated to my junk file, necessitating an in-person dunning.

I said, "Let's get down to it then. What can I help you with?"

"You and me got some unfinished business needs taking care of."

"Okay, I got it. I owe you for that gig on the island that never materialized. I never got a bill. Just tell me how much and I'll take care of it. I never welsh."

He chuckled at the archaic term. "That ain't it but thanks anyway. You remember a man named Johnny Serpente?"

Johnny was a Russian who had ripped off the mafiya in Brighton Beach in a past life. The authorities were content to write off his murder as payback by the mob, but I wasn't so sure. In any case, his ex and I had a torrid affair that ended over a year ago.

I played dumb. "Why would that name mean anything to me?" I wanted to find out just how much Moses Ginn knew and why he would bring up the late gangster's name. Only a handful of people were aware that I had any interest in Serpente. The first time I laid eyes on the man, he was room temperature on his newly renovated bathroom floor.

"Oh, I don't know. Word be that you was living with his widow 'til recently."

"That's not a state secret." My relationship with Charlene Jones (her maiden name) was not something I advertised in the Charlotte Observer, but people in my circle were aware of it. I didn't recall talking with Ginn about her.

Moses said, "I knew Mr. Serpente very well, you might say."

"Let's cut to the chase. What do you getting at?"

"How about the name Randee Blankenship? That ring a bell?"

Another name I had never discussed with him. Randee was a friend, a New York school teacher who had retired to North Carolina. She was a force of nature for causes affecting the downtrodden, and when she discovered that Serpente was ripping off public money with his shoddy building practices, she set about to hold his feet to the fire. She had done it rather recklessly and was lucky that Serpente's past had caught up with him before he struck back at her with all his force.

I gave Ginn my best tough guy squint, he gazed back in amusement. This reeked of some sort of shakedown. Although I didn't know much about him, I had sized him up as a righteous dude not given to blackmail. Subtlety wasn't has forte. He came at you straight on. It was out of character for him to issue veiled threats.

I said, "Yeah, I know Randee. Again, Moses, what is it that you want?"

"You know what I do for a living, Mr. Riley King? When I ain't working with you, that is."

"No idea. I thought you might be retired. From what, I don't know."

"I'm the senior clubhouse attendant at Mecklenburg National."

I tried to hide my surprise. The Nat was an upscale country club. I doubted they'd be tolerant of his side profession as hired muscle.

I said, "Okay. Serpente was a member of the Nat and that's how you knew him. And maybe he bitched about Randee and you overheard. I still don't understand what this has to do with me."

"Did I mention I was Special Forces, back in the day?"

Ginn was slowly feeding me information, perhaps seeing if I'd make a connection. It had eluded me so far, and if this was a test of my deductive powers, I was failing it.

Some quick math told me he was likely a Vietnam vet. "Forgive my ignorance but I would think that the skills you picked up in the service would qualify you for a more advanced position."

Ginn said, "You would think, coming from a white man. But flash on being black, coming back from 'Nam. Not a popular war. Not a popular color in the Carolinas those days. Things has changed some, but mid-seventies, that was truth.

"Yes sir, the only job there for me when I came back was the one I left. The powers that be at the club thought they was doing me a favor. But what they didn't know is that I learned me some skills that could be useful to them."

Strategy, stealth, infiltration, even wet work ---
these were the skills that came immediately to mind. How
would that benefit the old money sachems at Mecklenburg
National? Despite the sometimes fractured grammar, Ginn
spoke with homespun eloquence. I waited for him to
enlighten me but he just sipped his coffee and stared right
through me.

I said, "Let me guess. The bigwigs at the club lost
one of their own and aren't satisfied that the mob put out a
hit. The local cops went along with the gang thing and the
feds had bigger fish to fry. But your guys aren't convinced.
Randee Blankenship knew a crusty PI who was willing to
do the dirty deed. That about it?"

Ginn smiled. "I guess that high end pussy went to
your head, King."

He had described my ex-girlfriend, Charlene Jones,
rather crudely but the characterization was accurate. Once
Johnny Serpente no longer presented a threat to Davis,
Randee or me, I was more than willing to sample the high
end, uh, rewards Charlene brought to the table.

I was losing patience with the dance. "Rather than
waltz around this until I guess what your game is, why
don't you lay your cards out. What can I help you with?"

Ginn said, "Not who aced Johnny Serpente, that's
for sure."

"And why is that?"

"Because I did."

2

Years ago, the late Australian song and dance man Peter Allen wrote a refrain: "Just ask me I've been there ... I've been through it all." After over thirty years in my line of work, I feel that way. Nothing can surprise me.

But in the last five minutes, Moses Ginn had shocked me twice.

Confessing to the murder of Johnny Serpente, unsolicited, constitutes a first. When I was with the FBI, I saw countless felons, even when confronted with irrefutable proof of their culpability, vociferously maintain their innocence. Even on death's doorstep --- when you would think confession would be good for the soul, or at least a last ditch attempt to set the record straight, it was no-go.

No longer in law enforcement, I have no power to arrest Moses Ginn. The best I could do would be to inform my Charlotte/Mecklenburg cop buddy Peter Shabielski. Depending on departmental politics, he might agree to look into it or bury under a mound of unsolveds. Most likely, he would tell me what I already knew --- that his department believed the circumstantial case made by the FBI that a Russian button man had done the deed and then vanished, as they are wont to do.

It wasn't that *he* bought that neat little scenario: he thought Charlene was responsible and I should watch my back. But since I was now out of her clutches, he would probably suggest that we both should spend our efforts on something more worthwhile than the perp who rid society of a destructive rodent.

Mr. Ginn had an agenda and in his own good time, he would reveal it. Surely I wouldn't be the vehicle he would use to turn himself in, if that was his intention.

I said, "So what do you want me to say? Kudos for a job well done?"

He laughed, showing perfect white teeth. The V.A. dental plan must be good one.

"Aren't you curious as to how I came to be the instrument of his demise?" He pronounced it da-mease.

"I'm always entertained by old war stories, apocryphal or not."

"Oh, I can assure you, this ain't fiction. Everything I'm going to tell you is the Lord's truth."

"Okay. But why now? It's been almost two years since Charlene and I discovered Mr. Serpente's mortal remains soiling his smartly renovated master bath. The world is at peace with the story that the Russkies did it. Why are you telling me this now?"

"To avoid more blood. That's the simple answer."

"Explain."

"Randee Blankenship got her nose again in matters some powerful folks would prefer be let alone."

"What powerful folks are we talking about?"

Moses grunted. "Johnny was just the point man for the building scam. You know the deal. Serpente got contracts. Minor league corruption and the public had no clue. I'm sure you figured that out."

"And you're working for these people? Who are they, Ginn?"

"They call themselves the Troika. They decided that Johnny had done them wrong and I was the man to make it right."

"And this is something you had done for them before, given your special forces skills? I've used you as muscle in the past, but I assumed you drew the line at murder."

"I never did anyone didn't have it coming."

"You know my friend, that's what every unrepentant killer tells himself. *They had it coming.* You rationalize it that way so you can play judge, jury and executioner."

I failed to get the intended rise from him. He answered calmly, in his James Earl Jones voice, "Like that author your friend Rick Stone killed? Or the lawyer that you shot in New Jersey? The one killed your girlfriend. Where was your justice system then?"

He'd done his homework on me. Touché.

I said, "So Ginn, cut to the chase. Your bosses have sent you to deliver a message. And if I don't deliver it or if Randee disregards it, we'll have deserved what comes next? You're a hired gun for this Troika, is that it?"

He had ordered coffee shortly after we'd arrived and although it had to be ice cold by now, he took a long drag. "No, that ain't exactly it. When I got back to the States and took back my old job, it was like I was invisible around the locker room. Some of the older gents even called me the 'house nigger' and didn't care if I heard. So I picked up on a lot of shit that told how things work in this town.

"These men were pulling the strings. Even though I seen things that opened my eyes in 'Nam, I thought that it was different here in the land of the free, home of the brave. Back then, I never liked much what Muhammad Ali done, but truth is, the man was right."

Ginn didn't seem particularly proud of the course he'd chosen. It was what many did in that era, trusting that the government had their best interests at heart.

He continued. "After I got out of the service, I heard 'em talking at the club about a vexating problem they had. I approached one of them, a man more kindly comes to black folk, and I suggested that I might help find them a solution, which I did. Gradually they started trusting me. Made use of my talents when they be needing them."

He took another sip of coffee. I used the moment to interject. "So, you were now on the road to perdition."

"A road you're familiar with. I come up with solutions."

"Listen to yourself, man. You're working with men who take bribes, rip off the public and you say you do their dirty work. Really?"

"They ain't that far off from what you do. You need to get something done in our fair city --- they the ones make it happen. They grease the wheels. They pour money back into the community. They all made their own fortune long ago. They see this like community service. They got they own rules. When there's a project makes the town better, they make it happen. No bullshit gets in the way."

"Yeah, well, that's nice. But they worked with Serpente. This bastard used asbestos ductwork, years after it was banned as carcinogenic. Substandard wiring. Dangerous fire hazard. Lead based paint and solder in the plumbing. Potential brain damage."

"That's why Serpente met his maker. These men didn't know the gory details. They just knew that Johnny paid on time and got the job done. But when they found out he was ripping them off and hurting people, they voted what they be calling a sanction. And they made sure Johnny's replacement knew why he was gone and that they wouldn't be tolerating no repeat."

"Damned upright of them. So now what?"

"You made note of them skills I learned. One of them was how to bug a room. Didn't use it so much in country, but comes in handy here. The Troika met the other night and decided that your friend Blankenship was getting too close. They let her be after Serpente because she seemed okay that he paid for what he done. And since they rigged it so he willed most of his money to Habitat for Humanity, she was believing that justice prevailed."

"Wow. I always wondered why a creep like him would donate all that money to charity." Charlene expected to be his sole beneficiary but all she got were leftovers. She didn't take it as kindly as Randee had.

"Like I say, my bosses aren't monsters. A few changes to that will and Johnny seems like some kind of misunderstood saint."

So Johnny hadn't been crying out for redemption with his bequeath to charity. I don't know how the lawyers managed to alter his will, but it did stop Randee in her tracks back then.

Moses said, "But now, your Ms. Blankenship is digging again. Starting to look in some folks' mind like there's no alternative but to make sure some harm come to her. By accident, of course."

"An accident that you create. Right, Ginn?"

"No. I don't hurt no old women. Your ex-squeeze Charlene Jones may be on the to-do list, too. I talked them out of doing anything yet. I told them there're better ways and they went along with it. But that ain't gonna hold forever, if she keeps on digging."

I had misread Ginn all along. With his brawn, I'd judged him as a simple but decent man. It turns out he'd been playing me all along. "Hey man, you and I have worked together for a while now. Were you spying on me?"

"I admit that when I got word you needed some muscle, I jumped right in. I knew about you from the Serpente deal, and I liked what I heard. Figured we think alike most times. I wanted to steer you away from any more digging into the Troika's business. In a friendly-like way, you understand."

"Jeez, with friends like you..."

"I'm on your side, King. Trying to keep you from making a big mistake. See, in the past, the Troika men gave me my head because I always delivered. But things be changing. There's new blood in the group. He's trying to convince the others they got to act first, ask questions later. He thinks I'm getting soft."

"Damn, my man, that's age discrimination. You need to take that up with human resources, not me."

"Laugh all you want Mr. Riley King, but the Troika ain't men to be trifled with. I'm the only thing standing in the way of them taking some action against you and your friends. Do I got your attention now?"

After issuing his warning, he tossed a five on the table and bolted. If this little trick was designed to leave his last words echoing, it worked.

Charlene probably wouldn't take my call. She was in the cocoon of country music stardom now. No doubt she had some personal assistant screening her messages, with explicit instructions to delete any coming from me.

As much as I had issues with Charlene, she was highly motivated by self preservation. Randee Blankenship posed another problem. Tell her that she's being threatened and she'll respond by threatening back. She is fearless, even up against bigger battalions. I need to convince her to back off until I can assess the danger level more fully. The odds of that working are small. It will only make her more determined.

3

My friend Charlotte/Mecklenburg Detective First Grade Pete Shabielski has been a great asset over the years. Our history goes back to New Jersey, where he was a straight cop in a crooked system. Not that he wasn't above bending the rules a little to get the job done. Or helping me nail someone who had escaped their just desserts when quirks in the legal system gave them undeserved refuge. Pete and I usually saw eye to eye over what lines we were willing to cross to achieve our goals.

So I called him the morning after my conversation with Ginn and he agreed to meet me at Four Mile Creek Park, a bucolic little trail that meanders through the marshlands of south Charlotte. Shabielski was waiting at the trailhead when I arrived, leaning against a wooden bridge support.

The town had taken what was once written off as a worthless swamp and turned it into a picturesque nature trail, frequented by dog walkers, cyclists and runners who appreciate its scenic beauty and abundant wildlife. It weaves across a marshy creek and its surrounding wetlands over long boardwalk bridges and paved walkways. It is a popular morning destination for fitness minded women of all ages, but especially young mothers pushing their newborns in ergonomically designed rickshaws, as they try to regain their pre-pregnancy shape. I sometimes walk my dog Bosco there, more frequently when I'm between girlfriends.

"Baristas just jacked up their prices or I would have brought you one," he said, Starbucks in hand. No fancy lattes or frothy concoctions for him, only the high test dark roast meets his standards. "You look like you could use a jolt, kemo sabe. How's Jaime?"

"Fine. She's off to L.A. this weekend. Half the time she's with me in Charlotte --- then a week in New York, a week on the coast. That's the business she's in."

"Best of both worlds. She makes major bucks, leaves just when she's starting to get on your nerves, comes back in time to keep your gonads from bursting. Sounds like a perfect arrangement."

"Spoken like a man who's been married for twenty five years and has two daughters in college."

Peter gave me a wistful grin, probably wondering how he'd have fared as a footloose bachelor. "I don't suppose you called me to discuss our respective domestic arrangements. I guess the grass is always greener. You still planning on leaving Charlotte?"

"House will be on the market soon. That big oceanfront pad in Hilton Head beckons and I can't see keeping two places. I know some people there already and I can work as much as I want on the island. But the reason I called was I wanted to run a couple things by you."

Although Pete has been burned in the past by blowing against the empire, he is a natural born iconoclast. His maverick ways had gotten him banished from Jersey, albeit with a financial settlement that allows him to work in Charlotte for considerably less money. With family a major consideration, he is now careful to pick battles he can win without leaving fingerprints.

I gave him a highly edited version of what Ginn had told me, leaving out the big man's name. Peter had been on the periphery of the whole Serpente affair, becoming aware of the details after the fact.

He said, "And here I thought we'd wrapped that hot mess into a neat little bundle. So what do you want to do? Use some of that dough you scored to hire security for Randee? I was you, I'd let Charlene take care of her own protection. She's doing well enough."

Even though Charlene and I did not part on great terms, I didn't want anything bad to happen to her, other than for her music career to totally tank and as a result, eat herself into an extra forty pounds. Lately the opposite was happening. She looked better than ever and her new album was making her an even bigger star.

I snapped back to the present after a moment of nostalgia about lost love. "I can't babysit Randee forever, even if she'd agree to it. I need a more permanent solution and that means going proactive."

"But that means taking on this little cartel, and you don't even know exactly who they are."

I said, "My source told me that these men are members of Mecklenburg National. I've never played there, but I hear it's pretty exclusive."

Shabielski snorted. "It's a tougher layout than Quail Hollow, where they played the PGA in '17. The membership list is more tightly guarded than Augusta. Women only play Wednesdays and with each other. Strictly old school, in good ways and bad."

"How do you know so much about this club? If it's so exclusive, how can the likes of you get anywhere near there?"

"They're very pro-cop. They throw a big shindig once a year for the department. We hold a lottery to see who gets to play, same guys can't go two years in a row. Goody bags, silent auctions with the proceeds going to the local Fallen Officers Fund. But it *is* hard to get on. The fellow who owns it personally screens anyone applying for membership and runs a tight ship."

"So since Johnny Serpente was a member, this guy had to clear him. Automatically makes me think he's a part of this cartel. What's his name?"

"Whoa, dude, don't jump there so quick. Daniel Wright is a pillar of the community. Old money. Great grandfather built railroads. Worth billions. Whispers are he has a lot of pull in our department. I can't imagine he'd tolerate the kind of thing you're talking about. Why would he?"

"Let's walk," I said, pointing down the trail. We were careful not to let any of the joggers or cyclists get close enough to pick up even a sliver of our conversation.

"That's just it, Pete. Why would any of these guys do it? Apparently, they're all rich old lions in their professions. Sounds almost like this is a hobby. Like a shadow government. Shape the city into what they want it to be."

Peter removed his lightweight sport jacket, revealing a sweat soaked white shirt clinging to his tight abs. He hates ties and only wears them at funerals and other occasions when the brass insists.

He said, "So let me get this straight. We're talking about taking on an invisible group of powerful men who make this city go. You know my history in Jersey when I tried to expose the chief of my little department for overlooking the vig. I was lucky to find a job six hundred miles away after he got through with me. I still look over my shoulder to this day, case he decides he wants a little revenge."

"I know that, Pete. I'm not looking for a partner, just a little help, is all."

His clear blue eyes were a wonderment at this early hour, when mine were fogged from lack of sleep.

He said, "I can do that. Let me start with this little nugget. Get back to this source of yours and tell him that you'll handle Blankenship. I'll even help you there if you want, meet with her as a courtesy. Then walk away from this. You're talking about leaving the area anyway. You've got a good thing going --- a great lady who only has eyes for you. A nice chunk of change from your last job, whether you deserved it or not. Life is good for Riley King these days. But don't push your luck, dude. This ain't the Jersey shore and if you're bent on taking on the guys who run a town this size, you're going to need a lot more help than I can give you. A small army would be a good start."

4

I respect Pete's opinions. He has been in law enforcement for over twenty years, working his way up from beat cop to his current detective first grade status. He bucks the system when he feels it serves the greater good. But since his forced exile from New Jersey, he's been loath to challenge antagonists directly when he doesn't see a clear path to victory. At the very beginning of the Serpente investigation, he gave me the same advice he was giving me now --- *don't mess with boys who are out of your weight class*.

Unlike him, I have no immediate family to protect, only friends. At least two people I care about are in peril. Randee Blankenship is someone I've only known for a few years, but I admire her determination and moral compass. She has a huge heart. She also has a great deal of courage, which sometimes intrudes on her better judgment.

And then there is Charlene. Although we are anything but close now, at one point not that long ago, I was seriously thinking of buying her a ring. She left me suddenly and I still don't know exactly why. In my kinder moments when my thoughts drift to her, I accept my share of the blame for not being as supportive of her singing career as I might have been. In my less generous analyses, I think she's always been a heartless vampire who uses people up and casts them aside after she's sucked them dry. To this day, I vacillate. Although I'm happy with

Jaime, no woman has ever incited my passions like Charlene. Unfortunately, that makes me a member of a sizable club.

After emailing and texting Charlene that we needed to talk, I dialed Randee and she answered right away. Dispensing with pleasantries, I got right down to it.

"Randee, there's something involving you and the Serpente situation a couple years back that we need to talk about."

"I was wondering when my little probes would reach your ears. I wanted to develop the evidence a little bit more before I spoke to you, handsome."

"Reaching my ears isn't the problem. It's who else's ears it's reached."

"Great. I'm glad I rattled some cages."

Typical Randee. Charging ahead, without thinking of the personal consequences or who else might get hurt in the crossfire. She has the naiveté of a true crusader --- who trusts that her adversaries' tactics will be as honorable and above board as her own. I had hoped that the experience with Serpente taught her a lesson about recklessly tilting against greater forces, but her revolutionary zeal goes on unabated. She is a child of the sixties.

Whereas these well heeled country clubbers might not be complete sociopaths, willing to eliminate anyone in their way, they do seem capable of doing what they *deem necessary* to preserve the status quo. It would not be an unrestrained bloodbath like the mob wars of yesteryear. It would be more like --- a surgical strike here, an untimely accident there. These seemingly unrelated incidents could accomplish their goal without attracting undue attention.

"Randee, before you go any further, I need to explain some things to you. When can I see you?"

She was reluctant to hear me out, afraid that I might deflect her from her charted course. She knew I had her best interests at heart, but she believed she was willing to martyr herself for her causes. I wasn't eager to put that to the test.

"I'm pretty tied up right now. How about next week?"

"Can't wait that long. Tomorrow."

"I'm busy."

"Get un-busy." I wasn't in the mood to fool around.

Silence. I thought for a moment that she'd hung up but she came back, answering in a monotone. "I'm doing my daily three miles around the lake at seven a.m.. Get your lazy ass up here then if you want to talk."

She hung up. Three miles at seven it was. Moses Ginn had not issued a deadline, but that gave me no comfort that one did not exist.

5

It is way beyond my powers to hack into the Nat's membership rolls. I'm pretty good with a computer, but I know enough to realize that my expertise is eclipsed many times over by those who have made it their mission in life to defeat any type of security.

This was an assignment for what I call my "Baker Street Irregulars", or "BS", so named after Sherlock Holmes' bevy of street urchins that he engaged to spy on his foes. In my case, they are comprised of computer nerds who can watch major motion pictures a month prior to their release, steal any piece of music ever recorded and serve up rough justice to those they judge unworthy.

I am frightened by their abilities and know that someday they could turn against me. I'm careful, but I also know that I'm kidding myself. Anything on my computer is fair game for these trolls, even if I employ the most resolute firewalls.

I use them sparingly. I've never met any of them. They have different preferences to initiate contact. Some respond quickly, others are more guarded. For payment, they generally provide me with routing numbers so that instant remuneration magically appears in their pseudo-named accounts.

For this task, I need to be extra vigilant. I'll be dealing with the secrets of rich, powerful men. A disenchanted teenager working out of his darkened bedroom might see this as a golden opportunity to rip off whatever they call fat cats these days. The whole thing could be traced back to me and all the financial security I now possess will be consumed in lawyers' fees. There's that --- plus the fact that it's just *not right.*

When I got home, Jaime was working in her makeshift office, harnessed to her smart phone. She shushed me and scribbled *conference call* on a pad after I pecked her on the cheek. She was listening intently and obviously didn't want the other parties to know she wasn't alone, so I wrote, *Dinner?*

She scratched out *not yet --- half hour.* I wrote, *I got it, is pasta ok?* to which she nodded. You'd think she was a Trumpista dealing with Putin the way we were communicating so surreptitiously, but I understand how paranoid some of these Hollywood clients can be.

Still in shorthand mode, I gathered up my laptop and contacted my most trusted "BS Irregular". His reports were the most concise and professionally delivered, never exceeding the parameters of the job with extraneous gossip. He was always reachable through *Google Hangouts*, which most of the others eschewed as too 'old school'.

> "Can you call me?" I typed.
> "Why?"
> "Sensitive subject. Prefer to meet in person."
> "Not possible."
> "Double fee."
> "I will make exception. Is this legal?"
> "Is any?"
> "Half in advance of meet."

I generally don't pay for anything in advance but he (or she or it) has proven trustworthy, plus if they screw me, they know I'll never work with them again. I agreed, forwarded the payment and shortly thereafter received a time and place for the meet.

Satisfied that I was making progress, I set about making dinner. I picked a bunch of basil leaves from the garden just outside the kitchen, and combined them in the processor with pignolia nuts, garlic, sea salt, Parmesan, Romano and olive oil. My culinary skills aren't diverse, but I can whip up a mean pesto on short notice.

I started water boiling and tossed in some fresh linguini. The pasta would be ready within the half hour Jaime had allotted. With a minute or two remaining until al dente, I stuck my head into her office, just as she was finishing up. The timing couldn't have been better.

"Be right in, Riles. Thanks for taking care of dinner. I've been swamped."

I headed back to the kitchen and my golden retriever Bosco, who had been dutifully lying at Jaime's feet, caught a whiff of the food cooking and bolted from the office, following me. He usually has his designer kibble an hour or so before we eat, but a few strands of linguini for dessert are always welcome. He waited while I poured the pasta into the colander and sighed with impatience as I shook the water out.

"Here you go, buddy. Just a little, that's all."

Jaime had insisted more than once that dogs don't understand, "that's all" and expect more where that came from. Bosco isn't a beggar, but when he sits at attention and looks at you with those sad brown eyes while you're eating, it's hard not to slip him another sample.

"No pesto. Your breath is bad enough," I scolded. He looked back at me in puzzlement.

Jaime set the table, jabbering away about her day. I was preoccupied with my own problems and heard only every third sentence or so, but my eyes weren't too tired to appreciate what stood before them.

Jaime radiated the energy of an adolescent. She was forty one, more than a few years my junior, but in most ways, more mature than I. Auburn hair, green eyes, full mouth. Slender, athletic body, not much on top, but as Spencer Tracy once said about Hepburn, "what there is, is cheerce."

She was barefoot, wearing crimson running shorts and a Pearl Jam tee shirt, one of the benefits of working from home. I watched her smooth movements with silent appreciation and wondered again how I'd almost let her slip away. Unfortunately our dinner conversation was likely to reopen some old wounds, but I couldn't risk her finding out about these issues after the fact. Issues that caused her once to lose trust in me.

She said, "Dad is resisting giving Spicer a young sidekick in the next screenplay and the producers are insisting on it for the umpteenth time. I keep fighting the same battles and neither side wants to give an inch. That's going to take up my all my time out in L.A. next week."

"Dad" was John Peterson, multi-millionaire, bestselling novelist whose Elton Spicer mysteries involve a seventy five year old protagonist busting villains a half century younger. His books have spawned two movies so far: the first starring Clint Eastwood and the last, Harrison Ford, who Jaime refers to as H. Apparently, another is in the development phase and as usual, the moguls want Spicer to take on a young stud assistant, male or female, to carry the physical load and, oh by the way, attract a younger audience. It was either that or the septuagenarian accidentally ingests something that endows him with superpowers, so that he can fight crime from the rooftops at night while napping in his rocking chair by day. Actually, that last is my idea, but I don't think it's a bad one.

I said, "Sorry, babe. I'm sure you'll find a way to keep the wolves at bay. I have to admit, that last flick where your boy H outmuscles that WWE guy strained credibility just a little."

"Spicer knows many ancient Far Eastern martial arts moves. These wrestlers are just 'roid rage freaks." She opened a bottle of cabernet, sniffed it before pouring like Bosco would, and took a tiny sip. "How was your day? Anything develop with that client from yesterday?"

I dished out the pasta, keeping the pesto on the side for Jaime. If she puts on six ounces over the course of a week, it causes her to increase her workout load exponentially or starve herself for a few days. An extra ten pounds wouldn't hurt, but she meticulously records everything she eats and is careful never to exceed her self-imposed caloric limit. I think it a bit obsessive but I can't argue with the results.

"Yeah, well, we need to talk about it." I explained what I'd learned from Ginn. I tried to minimize the immediate danger to me, but stressed how others might be in the line of fire.

"Johnny Serpente, eh," she said when I was finished. "The gift that keeps on giving. Have you talked to Charlene? Do you have to?"

"I haven't but I should. Look, she has an entourage now, no doubt with security. So she's probably covered. I just need to make sure she knows what's going on. Problem is, I don't know if she gets my texts or emails. She's got layers of people between us now, which normally doesn't matter to me, but in this case, I need to be sure she understands the threat."

"Can't you send Stone or somebody?"

Charlene was the reason I'd lost Jaime. Rick had interceded on my behalf and convinced Jaime that I had only let Charlene stay with me to protect her from her gangster husband. The mistake was that I neglected to tell her about the arrangement beforehand. She found out on her own and broke up with me.

Charlene and I became intimate shortly after that. Jaime now professes to understand that she had voluntarily given up her exclusivity, but she still isn't happy about the whole chain of events. Charlene Jones is ravishing, capable of seducing any man she sets her sights on. Even though my relationship with Jaime is in a good place now, she doesn't savor putting it to the test with Mata Hari. Neither do I.

I said, "Jaime, I promise I'll exhaust every other possibility. But I have to make sure she knows. That's the extent of it. If I do have to see her in person, don't worry. I'm all yours."

"I know that." Another sip of wine, followed by a long sigh. "Look, I understand. That woman Ted McCarver had you find for him, Stevie Perry, wound up dead. I know you take these things as personal failures, but think about it. My mother was killed right after she hired you and I don't hold you responsible in any way. You're not the entire female gender's personal bodyguard."

In my mind, I know she's right. But that doesn't stop bloody images of her mother and the sad death of Stevie Perry from haunting my dreams. Responsible or not, I can't let the same thing happen to Charlene Jones.

6

At nine thirty that evening, I kissed Jaime goodnight and lit out for SouthPark, the city's premiere upscale mall. My "BS" had instructed me to meet him on the second level of the adjoining parking facility at ten. I asked if he needed to know what I'd be driving, and he simply replied, "Really?"

Point taken. I know nothing about him/her and he knows everything about me. Usually, the roles are reversed, and it makes me uncomfortable when I don't have the edge involving knowledge of the opposition. It's happened twice recently, most disturbingly during my encounter with Moses Ginn.

I pulled into the garage a few minutes early and drove through all three levels before parking on the middle one. There is no gate or mechanism for collecting a fee, and the security guards they employ resemble Paul Blart. The stores had been closed for almost an hour, and I didn't detect any patrons lingering near their cars.

The night had cooled considerably, so I was content to sit with the roof window open, listening to The Highway on Sirius/XM. It seemed that Charlene's new country album was being featured at least once an hour. I was a little curious if any of the songs were about me, but not curious enough to actually seek it out or God forbid, download it. It might stir up some memories, or worse, whatever hell Jaime might rain on me if she caught me listening.

Ten p.m. came and went and no one tapped on my hood. There were a few cars still in the lot, night workers. Custodians, stock personnel or window dressers. There might be a smattering of VIP shoppers who have the juice to command private showings of the forthcoming season's fashion, given the opulence of some of the remaining vehicles. It struck me that my "BS" might be someone who worked at the Apple store or one of the other tech shops. I was tempted to get out of the car and snoop around, but my instructions were to stay put and he would find me.

At quarter past the appointed hour, a minor annoyance cropped up. A homeless man was approaching. My Audi isn't exactly pristine, but I didn't fancy finding an open car wash this time of night to rid it of vomit or urine. I pulled out a ten, then considering my newfound wealth, made it a twenty. I hoped that the handout wouldn't encourage a rambling conversation that might drive my assignation awry.

The man looked filthy, but he didn't smell bad. He was wearing shabby clothes and a greasy ball cap, pulled down to just above his eyes. There was scraggly gray hair protruding from the back and sides. Food and tobacco stains adorned his shirt, and his jeans were torn off at the knees.

My Beretta was in the center console. I lifted the latch and laid the gun on the passenger seat, covering it up with an old newspaper. This man could be a harmless beggar, or an artfully disguised hit man acting at the Troika's behest.

As he drew closer, smiling, I noticed his teeth. Expecting yellow, rotting incisors, I was taken aback by how well kept they were. And the glasses he wore under the cap sported designer frames. I eased my right hand toward the gun, holding the twenty in my left. I was covered both ways.

"Riley King. Your pictures do not do you justice." The voice was nasal and high pitched but the words were crisply articulated. It was an obvious attempt to hide his real voice.

This was no homeless man. This was my BS.

I said, "The disguise wasn't necessary. Give me some credit. If I really need to know who you are, I can find out."

He laughed. His voice dropped to a more normal register, a downy tenor. "Let us not get off on the wrong foot. I must be careful. Some of the things you have me do are not exactly according to Hoyle. And when you insist on finally meeting face to face, it makes me worried that I am being set up."

"I share those same concerns. How about I get out of the car, pat you down for a wire and then you can do the same to me."

"You are still a dinosaur in so many ways, Riley. May I call you Riley? I could have a parabolic microphone aimed at you right now in a place you would never find. But... if you insist," he said, raising his hands.

"Never mind. You do have the advantage of me. What should I call you?"

"How about Deep Throat? I have always admired how one man with a conscience brought down a corrupt administration. Maybe I could do likewise in some small manner."

This was no kid. Most teens these days have never heard of Nixon, much less know any details of Watergate. He was tall and slim and there was something vaguely familiar about him --- as if I had met him in a previous life.

Close up, I could tell the long stringy hair wasn't real, but some skill had gone into the disguise. To the casual observer, he might appear as a street person. But to a pro, seeing him from a few feet away? This man was a talented amateur to be sure, but he had overlooked a few details. Details that could get you killed by someone who did this for a living.

I said, "So, I'll admit, I was expecting a kid. How did you get into this line?"

"As much as I admire the work you do, I am not given to chit chat at the moment. Perhaps someday I can be more forthcoming but at the moment, I need to know what you need me to do so I can proceed with it."

There was something forced and unnatural about his speech. No contractions. Overly formal. Aspergers? Genius in his field but socially awkward. Or was this another aspect of his disguise, one more sophisticated than I'd given him credit for? Maybe the overlooked details were intended to make people underestimate him.

I said, "Are you familiar with Mecklenburg National? It's an exclusive country club."

"I have heard of it. I have never been interested in golf. What about it?"

"I need a list of the membership. Shouldn't be more than a hundred twenty five from what I could gather on my own. Names, addresses, occupations. Particularly interested if any have roles in city government or special connections, although I would assume most of these guys are movers and shakers."

"When do you need it?" Deep Throat asked.

"ASAP. Look, my friend, I appreciate that in our dealings to this point, you've never questioned *why* I need certain information. But in this case, I want you to know that lives could be at stake and the sooner I get the list, the better equipped I'll be to help some innocent people. That's all I can say now."

"Do you want detailed financial reports on each of them?"

I'd considered that. The membership list was small for such a well appointed facility; usually a club needs upwards of three hundred members to be viable. But for me to thoroughly check out over a hundred names? Shabielski was right, it would take a small army. Too much information can be more daunting than not enough. When lawyers want to hide something in discovery, they often flood their opposite number with documentation, which makes finding the damning evidence like the proverbial needle in a haystack.

I said, "Get me the basics. If anything pops a red flag in your mind, let me know."

He scratched his chin in thought. "What sort of red flags are you referencing?"

"Maybe someone who holds a position at the club who doesn't meet the pedigree. Or someone whose net worth seems far in excess of what it should be, given their income plus any inheritances. That sort of thing."

"Vague. Mr. Riley King, very vague indeed. I will do what I can."

"I appreciate it. Oh, and one more thing. I want everything you can find about the senior clubhouse attendant. A man named Moses Ginn. And I do mean everything."

7

MOSES GINN

Moses Ginn was up late nursing a Macallen, his beverage of choice. He owned a well appointed condo on the twentieth floor of the finest building in uptown Charlotte --- free and clear. His name was not on the deed. It was consigned to one of the holding companies they had set up for him. He considered his lifestyle understated but elegant, down to his neatly pressed wardrobe and impeccably shined shoes.

All of this bounty came from his benefactors at the Nat. Although his salary was in line with what attendants at private clubs were paid, the benefits were otherworldly. He was careful not to flaunt his wealth around his few friends outside the club. When one of them noticed a particularly posh article on his person, he had a ready-made story as to how fortune had gifted him. He never showcased that item in public again.

He had marked his sixty seventh year a few months ago, a milestone he never thought he'd reach. His years at the Nat had taught him hard lessons about how the world worked and who really controlled it.

The group called themselves the *Troika,* a name he assumed had vague European origins, probably Russian. These three gentlemen seemed to wield more power than any elected official in the city, maybe even the state. The fact that they did so without the knowledge of the government, the media or the populace was unbelievable, given the scope of their efforts. In the past, it was a heady experience knowing that he was an influence on such men, and at times able to bend their goals to a shape more compatible with his own.

After tonight, he wasn't so sure. The meeting at the club earlier had not gone badly on the surface. They allowed him to explain his strategy. When he was finished, he received a tepid vote of confidence. Something told him that it was like the endorsement an owner gives a baseball manager the week before he fires him.

One of three was a city councilman from a safe district --- short of being photographed in bed with a farm animal; his perennial reelection was a certainty and had been for fifteen terms. This man was the oldest and Moses saw him as the conscience of the group. Anything that violated his Christian code of ethics was unacceptable, but occasionally he could be coaxed into giving in to what the others deemed necessary.

The second was an attorney --- successful, but not recognized by the outside world as particularly brilliant. He'd been a member for twenty years, succeeding his father, the genius who had founded the group. He was more pragmatic than the councilman, more prone to ethical compromises to achieve ultimate goals. Both men had been steadfast supporters of Ginn, until recently.

The turning point was when the third member of the inner circle came aboard. He had been groomed for the Troika position by his recently demised father, a member of the high command in the police department. A burly man in his early forties, the man had risen to captain on the Charlotte/Mecklenburg force, largely due to his father's patronage. Ginn saw him as a blunt instrument, an advocate of swift action without considering the consequences. Right from the start of his tenure in the Troika, the man was Ginn's natural enemy.

The group had evolved over the years with different faces, but only when an original member died or became too incapacitated to continue. Up until now, other than Serpente, no egregious missteps had been made. But this new guy rubbed Moses the wrong way and there was little Ginn could do. Whereas the other two were enchanted by the younger cop's vigor and fresh ideas, Ginn came to regard him as a personal threat. The caution Ginn advocated during their occasional crises had served them well, but the new entry saw his reluctance to take drastic measures as a sign of weakness, and he was turning the others in his direction. It had happened again during their informal meeting tonight.

"So Moses," the attorney had asked. "You're convinced that this Riley King will stop the old lady from going any further?"

"I wouldn't put it quite that way," Ginn said. "More like a shot across the bow. King was fine to let the whole thing die with Serpente. And that old bird Blankenship let it go when she found out that Johnny's will donated a big number to Habitat for Humanity."

The attorney said, "Your idea. At the time, it made a lot of sense."

The cop said, "But it's not holding up. She's got a bug up her ass again. She needs to go away."

Moses pretended to give the idea consideration before responding. "Yeah, but if anything happens to her now, Riley King comes at us full force."

The newest member of the group challenged him. "And you can't handle King?"

Ginn said, "Why poke the sleeping bear? He got money and connections with some big media folks. His friend Stone works for a radio station. And his girlfriend is hooked up with heavy writers and movie dudes. Something happens to him and we got us a boatload of problems."

The cop stood up. "Bring 'em on. You think a bunch of Hollywood pussies scare me?"

The lawyer interceded. "Now, wait a minute, gentlemen. Let's not escalate this any further than we need to. Moses, you told us originally you thought King could be reasoned with. You stand by that assessment?"

"I'm saying I planted some seeds with him. We need to give some time to see if they root. From what I know of the man, he ain't out to change the world. He's willing to let things be if it don't affect him or someone he's tight with. But you fuck with one of his friends, he's like a dog with a bone. He won't give it up."

The cop wouldn't back off. "So how about a preemptive strike? The tragic accident happens to King. I doubt anyone will tie it to us if it's done with some skill. But if you have cold feet or you're scared, I can make it happen."

The councilman, who had been feigning a certain amount of indifference said, "I don't see the need to go there. Moses has always come through for us and I'm sure he will again. Won't you, Moses?"

The meeting ended shortly thereafter, but the tone lingered. The cop was getting more brazen and the others stood by and let him wail with little protest. The tide was turning against him. And he might be powerless to stop the waves.

8

When I got back from my clandestine meeting with BS or Deep Throat as he now wanted to be called, Rick Stone called. He was living in Hilton Head at the oceanfront house we owned together. He only came to Charlotte when he was bored with the women on the island. It was unusual for him to call this late, so something was up.

I said, "How'd the golf go today, Ricky?"

"77. Could have been a 73 if I had a couple breaks and putted better."

"Yeah, yeah. Funny how nobody ever says it could have been an 81 if I hadn't gotten a couple of good bounces and drained some long putts."

"Well, since you'll never shoot in the 70s shankasaurus, I guess that point will be academic to you."

I gave him a quick rundown on Ginn, a man he'd played golf with once. They had gotten along well but it was that round with Ginn that had sent Stone adrift. He had always hoped to join the senior tour when his radio days were over. But playing one round with Ginn had convinced him he'd never make the grade.

I could go on ragging him about his game, but I could tell he was troubled by something having nothing to do with a couple missed shots.

Stone said, "So Riles, where were you? I tried you before and it went to voicemail. You've been moaning about how bored you were with no big cases. Why out so late on a school night?"

I told him about my get together with BS that was inspired by Ginn's meeting. He peppered me with questions. When we finished, he said, "Anything I can do to help?"

"I was thinking if no one from Charlene's camp gets back to me, maybe you could try to see her in person. Might be easier for you to get through than me. She might actually listen to what you have to say."

"Maybe. Only problem is, I need to be on the island tomorrow. McCarver's doing a big station sponsor party and I need to be there."

"Okay. But you seem a little off. Everything all right?"

"I'm a loser and I'm not what I appear to be." Stone had been a fixture at WJOK in Toms River, New Jersey for many years, ever since Ted McCarver had bought the station and turned it from a sleepy suburban FM into a major sports talk entity. Ted had sold the station a few years ago, and the conglomerate that bought it fired Rick as soon as his contract expired. McCarver had since tried to duplicate his Jersey success in South Carolina, by purchasing a small FM daytimer. Rick was now his mid day personality.

He said, "I'm cool. Just a little bored at WPHX. I thought that free form idea Ted had for the place would be cool, but so far, it's frustrating. Ratings are up a little, but it's a slow process. And most of the listeners are from back when the Dead Sea was still sick."

I don't know the radio business that well, just what I know from Rick. The digital age which now affects my business has taken an even more devastating toll on his. At least he doesn't have former Special Forces dudes threatening his life.

He said, "So, Riles, you might have to man up and deal with your ex all by your lonesome. Jaime okay with that?"

"Not. I can't see that I have much choice. Unless one of Charlene's underlings gets back to me and we don't have to worry about it."

"Why would these guys target her anyway? She's a hot act in country music now. Only thing I can think of is they think she may be able to identify these Troika guys. Even if Johnny didn't tell her outright, she might know who he hung out with and connect the dots."

"She always told me that Johnny never talked much about his affairs. Like Michael Corleone. *Don't ask me about my business, Kaye.* When I first met her, she claimed Serpente wasn't into anything shady down here. She thought he left that all behind in Brooklyn and was totally legit. I think she really didn't know or just didn't want to know. She's a survivor and she's smart."

"Smart enough to dump your ass. Sorry, couldn't resist. But you're better off with Jaime anyway. She's great."

Jaime will never quite give off the sparks I had with Charlene, but her day to day temperament is more simpatico to mine.

Talking things through with Rick often sent me along new paths and today was no exception. I hadn't given much thought to how she could identify Ginn's inner circle. It might even be the men in his regular foursome at the Nat. As much as I don't relish opening old wounds, her casual remembrances might be the key to our mutual survival.

9

I was up at 6. I told Jaime's semi-conscious form where I was going, but her drowsy "uh-huh, have a good time," indicated it hadn't registered. She was probably dreaming of accepting a producer's Oscar for Best Picture or some such Hollywood honor. For good measure, I left a note on the coffeemaker, explaining that I had not fed or taken Bosco out. He was dead weight on the bed beside her and my mention of breakfast held no sway with him. There was a dreamland squirrel he had to catch.

Randee Blankenship lives in a condo on the eastern shore of Lake Norman, a vast manmade body of fresh water just north of Charlotte. My house borders the western side. She had bought an outdated apartment from an estate and turned it into the nicest residence in the complex. She loved the area and got along well with her neighbors, most of whom were retirees who liked to have an early lunch and drink wine all afternoon.

As promised, she was stretching in front of her building when I pulled up shortly before seven. As I parked the Audi, she lit out down a path that bordered the lake, almost as if she hadn't seen me. I got the message --- she was annoyed with my summons. It took me a quarter mile to catch up with her, sprinting faster than I like to run while warming up.

"Breathing kind of heavy there, King. A little out of shape?" were her first words.

"Lovely to see you too, Randee. No, I usually take it a bit more leisurely first, but no problem. I'll drop down to your level now."

She snorted, "Wow. Big man. You might actually be able to outrun a seventy one year old woman. Impressive!"

"Is this what passes for trash talk in the geriatric set?"

That was a cheap shot but I wasn't too happy with her at the moment. I'd left the bed of a fine-looking redhead to trade silly barbs with a grumpy New Yorker, who was giving me no credit for trying to protect her ancient ass.

Actually, that ass doesn't look so ancient. Randee is in terrific shape, dresses fashionably, and is considered a real hottie by the widowers in the complex. She could easily hook up with one of the wealthier ones if she were so inclined, and travel the world first class, luxuriating in five star hotel spas with chilled cucumbers over her eyes. Knowing Randee, she would rather take her morning jog barefoot over jagged gravel.

I said, "So Randee, truce? I'm sorry I insisted on meeting with you right away, but it's for your own good."

"And who appointed you my keeper, King?" She wasn't ready to lay down her arms just yet.

"Why so belligerent? Why can't you just listen to what I have to say?"

She stopped running but kept moving away from me. "Because I'm on to something and you're going to try to talk me out of it."

She was wearing a pale blue Adidas jacket and matching nylon running shorts, which set off her eyes. She once admitted to me that she colored her hair, but the light brown tint was subtle and age appropriate.

"Randee, hear me out and then do whatever you want. You will anyway, no matter what I say. I'm not sure why I bother."

There was a rock outcropping just ahead that formed a natural resting spot for joggers. With the dexterity of a gymnast she climbed onto a flat surface and reclined. "You've already spoiled my run. I might as well listen. Go."

At least she didn't pull out a stopwatch and announce I had sixty seconds. "Why are you digging into Serpente again?"

"Who says I'm digging into Serpente, big boy? He's been dead for almost two years now."

"Okay, Randee, cut the crap. I'm trying to help. You got lucky two years ago. If Johnny had lived it's likely he would have come after you full force. You may not have survived it."

"Speculation, my dear. If Kennedy had lived, we may have been spared Vietnam. Or not."

"Remember when your cat was poisoned? That was Johnny's way of letting you know he could get to you. You charged ahead anyway and his next move would have been more direct."

"You said at the time we couldn't be sure that my late tabby didn't just get into some chemicals I had around the condo while I was working on it."

"All right, be stubborn. Since you're into revising history, let me bring you to the present. A man who works for me on occasion told me that some dangerous people are concerned that you're digging into their affairs. He said that he had been ordered to make you stop. With no restrictions."

"I knew it. So I'm close."

"Only counts in horseshoes and hand grenades. Wherever you are is as close as you'll ever get. My little conversation was a warning. This guy didn't have to do that, he could have just struck. They let it go two years ago when you backed off because of Serpente's will. They're not inclined to be so tolerant again. They mean to kill you, Randee."

"Not if I expose them first."

"And who's them?"

She pulled a small towel from her jacket and wiped a trickle of perspiration from the corner of her eye. "I don't have names yet. But I know what they're doing. Were you aware that Serpente was just the front man, a lower level operative? And that after he died, the corruption continued."

"Randee, these people killed Serpente, not some Russian hit man. The man who warned me did it, and he's got the credentials to back up his story. The men he works for want you gone. He wants to give you a chance to retreat. For your own good, you should take it. "

"And if I did do that, what makes you think they wouldn't just kill me anyway? Just to be sure."

"No guarantees. But if you keep charging ahead, he'll have no choice. My only job then will be to avenge your death."

I was hoping putting it in such blunt terms would scare her straight, but Randee Blankenship never quit anything in her life.

"As much as I appreciate the sentiment King, I'm not oblivious to danger. I'm taking a concealed weapons course at a local firing range. My best bet is to get them before they get me."

I'd known Moses Ginn for a couple of years. I read him as a man who keeps his word. He didn't have to put us on notice --- he could have just done the deed. The warning was a bloodless way out if I could convince Randee to pay it heed.

But from what he'd let on, the Troika's trust in his effectiveness was waning. If he didn't show instant results, they might put their murderous plan in motion without consulting him.

"All right, Randee, think about this: Whoever is feeding you information might be playing both sides. The bad guys know you're after them, and that information coming from somewhere. Give me the leads you've got so far. I'll try to find out exactly who these men are and where they're vulnerable. In the meantime, I'll arrange some security for you."

"I'm not going into hiding like we did the last time. And if this killer is as good as you say, how can anyone protect me?"

I hate dealing with stubborn people who are smarter than me. I was trying to come up with a plan on the fly and she was batting down my arguments like 90 mile an hour fastballs to Mike Trout. But it still stuck in my mind that Ginn had come to me first --- if he really wanted Randee dead, he would have just done it.

I'd move heaven and earth to find her killer if that happened. I needed to talk to Ginn again. Friend or foe, he might be our only hope.

10

I am actually acquainted with a longtime member of the Nat.

Problem is, he hates me.

His name is Jack Devereaux, father of Liz Devereaux, the woman my friend Derek Davis married a few years ago. After we had eliminated Johnny Serpente as Derek's tormentor, I thought that Jack had ordered the beating. I flat out accused him face to face, ambushing him in the stable on his ranch. Despite his many other transgressions, he was innocent of that one. The Bible-thumping rancher now regards me as a Satanic messenger, or maybe the Devil himself.

I wasn't above using Jack's name at the sentry gate of the Nat. It seems silly to have an armed security guard in at a country club, but I guess it keeps the riff-raff out, meaning anyone who isn't worth eight figures. Are they afraid the less well-to-do will swipe their balls from the fairway?

I drove up in the freshly washed Audi, sporting my spiffiest Ralph Lauren golf shirt and slacks, hoping that the car and my apparel would pass muster. The overweight gatekeeper looked like one of the Cossacks guarding the Wicked Witch of the West, attired in a ridiculous costume that the club elders must have deemed intimidating.

In my best mid-Atlantic tone, I informed him that I was late for a tee time with Mr. Devereaux. He waved me through and no flying monkeys gave chase.

Great security. He probably carried a rapier, instead of a gun. I plan to sneak out to the eighteenth green later and relieve them of a few balls. That'll teach 'em.

The club's circular cobblestone drive empties onto a shaded parking area. From there, I walked to the stately clubhouse, (established 1912, as a bronze plaque proudly states). The building has undergone many expansions and renovations since, but it reeks of the quaint charm that old money grants. There was nothing flashy about it --- every detail is underplayed, but the overall impression upon entering through the twelve foot arched doors is spectacular.

The white Carrera marble floors in the entry give way to hand scraped hickory planks in the elegant dining room. The reception area resembles that of a fine New York hotel. The entire lobby is wainscoted with dark burled walnut, beneath hunter green wallpaper with heraldic crests. Gas lit sconces of oil rubbed bronze dimly illuminate the room. The soaring coffered ceiling displays a massive crystal chandelier.

A small embossed sign pointed me toward the men's locker room. I was lucky that the two blondes staffing the reception area were too busy discussing last night's *Scandal* to notice that I wasn't one of the regulars. I affected a casual swagger: if you look like you belong, most guardians will leave you alone.

Moses Ginn was seated in a small booth outside the green carpeted locker room, staring at a computer screen. If he was surprised to see me when he looked up, it didn't show.

"Welcome to the Nat," he said, as if I was an honored guest at his invitation. "How may I be of service to you, suh?"

"Cut the act, Ginn. You can't have been expecting me."

He smiled his most gleaming smile. "Oh, but I was. We got unfinished business. Step into my humble office. May I offer you anything? Coffee? Tea, perhaps?"

Ginn's little room did not reflect the grand scale of the building, but it was just as well furnished. The pass-thru to the locker room was trimmed with birds-eye maple and blue pearl granite. His desk chair was surfaced with what I like to call *rich Corinthian leather*, thank you Ricardo Montalban. The desk itself wasn't large, but looked like it dated from the club's establishment. He motioned me toward a wing chair, festooned with crossed golf clubs and what I assumed was the Nat's coat of arms.

"Let's get right to it, Ginn. Don't just drop little hints like you did the other day. I spoke to Randee Blankenship. She's afraid that even if she stops her investigation that your people will come after her anyway. How do I know you won't?"

"There be no guarantees in life, Mr. King. But we do go by an honor system. You give me your word she'll quit, I *will* vouch for you."

"How can I be sure these men won't go over your head?"

"Like I told you, I still have sway here. Long as they're convinced that there's nothing to fret them, they'll trust me. But one false move by Ms. Blankenship and all bets are off."

If he could be blunt, so could I. "Why did you kill Serpente?"

"I told you. The men I work with don't fancy being double crossed. They pay liberal wages but they don't cotton to any skimming. Mr. Serpente was endangering folks with his shoddy materials, old asbestos and the like. That wasn't part of the deal."

He took a sip of tea from a black china mug. "These aren't bad men. They don't wish nobody harm. Long as folks stay in line, it's all good."

"You hear yourself? Folks stay in line? Just because you've done well, you forget your heritage?"

Ginn almost spoke in anger at the accusation, but he caught himself. "Ain't talking, black, white or brown here. These men got a vision for this city. Things working all orderly like. And if you want to use old clichés, yeah, where everybody knows their place. Look, they ain't got nothing against a man improving himself. Look at me. But they don't abide folks taking what ain't theirs. And they don't abide nobody messing with their grand design. I don't know how much more plain I can put it."

"How many men are in this inner circle? Just three?"

"Only three, like I said. And don't waste your time asking me who they are."

"What if they betray you, Moses? You said you caught them with your monitoring system talking with this new guy. What if it's gone beyond talking?"

"I can take care of myself, don't you worry none."

I gave him a wistful smile. "You know, I don't think I ever lost a fight when I was younger and given to such things. But I'm not a kid anymore and you're older than me by a goodly margin. What happens if you run into some young punk trying to make his name? You won't even see him coming, Ginn. He won't be observing

Marquis of Queensbury rules. Won't even know what that means."

Moses Ginn rubbed the top of his shaved pate and looked down at the desk, shuffling a couple of papers to one side. "I'm aware of that."

"I'm saying you can't trust these guys. Look at Serpente. Did he see it coming?"

"Can't say as he did."

"Exactly. They didn't send him a memo. Like, 'the executive board has decided that your services will no longer be required. Your choice, Johnny --- open a vein or someone will do it for you.' No, they just dispatched you and you did what you do."

"S'pose I did. But I ain't never skimmed. Never turned on them. They got no call to come after me."

I stood up. It was my turn to leave him hanging.

"And you're sure that goes for this new blood, as you call him? Well, I hope you're right." I exhaled.

His turn. "I got work to do. Where you be tonight?"

"Don't know."

"Number I call you on the other day good?"

"It is."

"Mr. King, you have a nice day, sir. And take some good advice from a friend. Enjoy life, like every day be your last."

II

Despite his poker face, I came away from Ginn knowing that he was concerned about his expiration date with the Troika. I had advanced those fears. He hadn't fully committed to helping my cause, but the intimation of contact later was a good sign.

The dynamic of the small group had changed recently, causing them to doubt the resolve of this stalwart fellow who had never let them down.

Upon parting this morning, Randee had given me a flash drive containing her research to date. That and the fact that she was attending lessons aimed at obtaining a concealed weapons carry permit told me that she was taking the threat of physical harm seriously. With this stubborn old broad, that was probably all I could hope for. Being that Ginn would have been my first call to guard her, I'd have to dig up an alternative. It would have to be someone who could best him if it came down to it. No one came to mind.

I found a Starbucks in South Charlotte and settled in with an apricot scone. I opened up my tablet and signed on to Hangouts. I contacted BS, and as always, he responded immediately.

"Need to talk," I wrote.

"You're unsecured. Public access. Dangerous."

"Not near home. Important."

"How?"

"150%"

"$ are not everything. Answer your phone."

How this man knew my phone was buzzing was beyond my ability to comprehend. I'm clearly not at his level, but I'm not a naïf when it comes to technology. Amazed by his prowess, I followed his instructions and it soon became apparent as to how he knew. He was the caller.

"Hail, King. What is so urgent?"

He was making no attempt to alter his voice, although I was sure he has the ability to distort it electronically beyond recognition. Was he starting to trust me?

I said, "For someone as careful as you are not to reveal your identity, I'm shocked that you'd just dial me up."

"Do not underestimate me. I am on a burner routed through so many connections that it would take a team of experts a year to trace, provided I would stay on the line that long. Now speak."

I had the feeling I was talking to some form of artificial intelligence. If I hadn't actually met him in person last night, I could believe that, give his staccato delivery

"Okay, Throat, if I can call you by your last name. I've discovered that there are three men in this little group at the Nat."

"And I have obtained the membership list. It stands at 96 who are currently active."

"Smaller than I thought. Good, but still pretty unwieldy."

"This is true."

"I may be able to help you winnow it down. Something has changed recently. Someone died recently amongst the three and another took his place."

"This is fact or speculation?"

I said, "Fact. To put it in terms you'll understand, there's been a disruption in the force."

"Do not belittle me. Soap opera fantasies set in space, while entertaining, do not guide my philosophy. Treat me as an adult please."

As his voice rose in impatience, there was something about it that rang familiar. Did I actually know him from another time? "Sorry. The best way I can put it is that there's been a change in the dynamic of the group. If it's coming from within the membership, the ball's in your court."

"Sports analogies are as worthless as popular culture references, but I take your meaning. How is that apricot scone, by the way? I am more partial to cranberry myself."

Somehow he had triangulated my location through my phone or tablet and hacked into the shop's database. He had to be guessing that I was the one who had purchased the scone.

Or not, since I had used a credit card. Nothing is private.

"The scone is delicious. Would you like me to pick up one to go for you? Just tell me where to deliver it."

"I have already eaten, thank you. I will assume that was a clumsy attempt at humor, rather than a juvenile trick to reveal my location."

I said, "I yield. Just play along with me. Can you narrow one phase of your search to recently departed members or those recently added? Let's say within the last six months."

"Easily done. I will send you the results shortly. And I assume you still require my observations on any anomalies within the group."

"Yes. And have you come up with anything on Moses Ginn yet?"

He was silent for a moment. "I am embarrassed to tell you that I can find no records of a man by that name in Charlotte."

"Could be in any of the surrounding counties. But he definitely works at the Nat. I just was with him there. How about their HR department?"

"There is no one employed by the club under that name. I would question if this man exists outside of your imagination. The film *Fight Club* comes to mind. However, if he is not a hallucination brought on by extreme stress, he has skillfully obliterated all evidence of his existence. As you are aware, I have taken great pains to obscure my identity. At the very least, he is my equal, or in all modesty, my superior."

12

"This sounds like a terrible time for me to be away. Especially since Rick won't be around either," Jaime said.

We were having dinner at home. Somehow, Jaime had found enough time to break away from making deals with the stars to rustle up a meal. Well, kind of. She had squeezed in a phone call to a Chinese place that delivers. To her credit, she had set it out with a flourish, and found a wine that paired nicely with the take-out.

Bosco lay obediently under underfoot, aware somehow that the spicy Asian dishes would upset his digestive system. He was also mindful that neither Jaime nor I particularly enjoy fortune cookies, and that if he bides his time, they'll find their way into his bowl. Jaime insists on that, rather than feeding him from the table. But every once in a while, when she isn't looking, I manage to slip him some contraband.

I said, "Actually, hon, I think this is a great time for you to be away. You know, I have to get this house spruced up to sell. With that oceanfront house in Hilton Head, it makes sense to move down there full time. I'm a solo act now, and you can fly out of Savannah as easily as you can here."

"It is paradise there, I'll grant you that. And that house is fabulous. But you're changing the subject. We're talking about you being alone now. I'll be worried the whole time. And if anything happens..." She left the rest unsaid.

"Look, if it gets bad, I'll go to the mattresses." She had no interest or expertise in the history of organized crime, but she is a film buff and can recite practically every line from *The Godfather,* so she got the reference. It's one of the things I love about her. What American male of my generation wouldn't?

Jaime said, "You really think it'll get that bad? Now I'm even more worried. Maybe you should come with me."

"Can't cut and run. That would only postpone the inevitable and besides, I need to do whatever I can to keep Randee safe. Hey, as they say in Texas --- I'm not always right, but I'm never wrong."

Jaime didn't find that amusing and had lost interest in her food. "And Charlene, too. Am I right in assuming that she's part of the mix?"

Pause.

We will soon be residing full time in a magnificent oceanfront house on Hilton Head. We have a devoted dog in good health. No financial worries. Jaime's career is going great guns and she is loving it.

But the fact that she wanted to hear more about Charlene's story is troubling. It told me she doesn't fully trust me. Given our past, am I kidding myself that I could ever regain that trust?

Now three women were plowing into ground best left untilled --- Randee, Charlene and Jaime.

I said, "Jaime, if this man hadn't threatened her, she'd be out of my life totally. But you know my history with female clients. If anything happened to her, I'd feel like I hadn't done enough. I just need to be sure she knows what's going on."

"I wish you had told me about Charlene moving in with you before I found out on my own."

"Do we have to go over this again? I admitted that it was a mistake. I thought you understood I was just trying to protect her back then. It never would have gone as far as it did if I didn't think you were finished with me."

She rose abruptly and in doing so, knocked a container of white rice onto the floor. Bosco sprang from under the table and began lapping it up. I shooed him away before he could eat much, but his tongue is quicker than my reflexes. I bent down to clean up what was left.

"I'm sorry," Jaime said. "I'm so clumsy. I didn't mean to spill it."

She started to sob. I stood up and held her. Bosco sensed there was something wrong and slinked away, thinking that his unauthorized food run was responsible for her anguish.

"Jaime, I'm sorry. I handled things very poorly. It's been over for a long time now. But if she's in danger, I need to warn her. You get that, don't you?"

She had burrowed herself deeply into my shoulder. She wept for another moment and then slowly pulled away. Awkwardly attempting to gather up the remaining rice, she avoided my eyes. I knelt to help and took her hands.

She finally looked up at me, mascara running from tear stained eyes.

"I know," she murmured. "It's just that Charlene is so gorgeous and talented. And then there's plain old tomboy me. All I do is exploit other people's talent. My mother left me a great business. What have I done on my own?"

No matter what our station in life or however grand our achievements, are any of us truly content with who we are? Is that little boy who was bullied on the playground, or that overweight girl with acne and no prom date ever far away from our present, more accomplished selves? Or are they always lurking, ready to pounce at a weak and unguarded moment of self-doubt?

But rather than chalk this up to her insecurity, might I be giving off signals that I'm not aware of? As hard as I've tried to put Charlene Jones in the rear view mirror, I still think about her. The way things ended with us didn't make sense. I've almost succeeded in convincing myself that it doesn't matter now, that I am happy with Jaime and that Charlene represents just a few glorious months of my past.

I said, "Jaime, you are far from a plain looking tomboy, you're a great looking lady. And you took your mother's little boutique agency and turned it into a force in the industry. Your dad's books became a major movie franchise because of you. Lots of people have the skill to write or act. Not many can recognize talent like you can and nurture it."

"But I keep picturing her with you. I can't get that image out of my mind."

"Come on, you had boyfriends before me. No one better looking maybe, but still."

She forced a smile at that. "Matter of opinion."

"Ouch. Look, you're headed out in the morning. Maybe a little time away will be a good thing. I'll let you know when the coast is clear. Don't worry. Things will work out. Just will take time, is all."

Time, and pre-emptive action. Randee was in the crosshairs, and I was too. Again, the irony was that a few times in the past, when there was a threat, I had turned to Moses Ginn. I had trusted him and he had always come through with flying colors. But he was working undercover all along and I hadn't picked up the slightest hint. He was working for the opposition and as such, represented a formidable foe.

Knowing Jaime would be safe, a continent away, was one less complication to consider.

13

MOSES GINN

Moses Ginn had graduated from high school, but in the five decades since, he realized that he hadn't learned much of use while there. It would have been easy to blame the pitiable schools and incompetent teachers that children of his color were relegated to, but he attributed most of his academic failure to his own indifference. Despite his native aptitude, he did not seek out more illuminating reading than the hand-me-down, outdated textbooks that were mandated. Back then, he was more interested in girls, music, and sports, like most of his classmates.

His education was informed mainly by his observation of the Troika's founder, an old southern attorney who taught him how politics worked. After the old man had died, his son became the group's leader and senior member. The lawyer still seemed to be Moses' supporter, but the city councilman had become more of a trusted confidant.

The Troika's newest member was his most dangerous adversary. The police captain made no bones about his opposition to Moses patient approach. Unaccustomed to such vocal opposition, Ginn chose to let the man win small battles, hoping that one of them might backfire and cause the others to lose faith.

This time was different --- it was no small battle. The Troika had never given murder consideration as an first step. But this new man was advocating the cold blooded murder of Randee Blankenship and they didn't reject it out of hand. Blankenship was a crusader for the downtrodden, a path Ginn might have chosen had his personal history been different.

But even more troubling to him was the dominoes that would start to fall after Blankenship was eliminated. Forces would be set into motion that could not be easily halted.

Next, Riley King would be targeted, and maybe Charlene Jones.

The world could surely live with one fewer country music babe, and the accidental death of a retired school teacher would hardly cause seismic eruptions. What he knew of Charlene would not qualify him for membership in her growing fan club, but her libertine escapades were not worthy of a death sentence.

But King would prove a tough adversary, a challenge Ginn did not relish. Moses' qualms were more than just worry that he might not emerge victorious. He respected King as a brother-in-arms. He had more in common with the former fed than he had with the ruthless local cop who had recently become a thorn in his side.

Moses decided to sound out the councilman, apart from the others. He asked for a moment of his time in the club's private dining room. Unlike the cavernous main space, this smaller room contained one large table that seated sixteen. Also, unlike the larger area, it harbored one of Ginn's listening devices.

"I don't have a lot of time, Moses," the man said. "I'm meeting a donor for drinks and dinner and I need to shower and change. Awfully muggy out there."

Ginn smiled. Not one white hair on the man's luxuriously thick mane was out of place, and his golf outfit would be perfectly acceptable as dinner garb. But the meticulous politician always sported a jacket and tie while dining, even a tuxedo when he felt it was called for.

"I won't keep you long, sir." Moses was careful to play his subservient role when he could be observed by others.

"Well, out with it, man. I can see that something's been on your mind of late."

"Yes, it has. I'm just a little afraid that we might be losing our way."

The elder raised his shaggy eyebrows. "That sounds pretty strong. How exactly are we losing our way? In your estimation, that is."

"With all due respect, when this group started, it was with goodly intentions. To cut through the politics and special interest types to make this a world class city. When we start knee-jerk reacting to an old school teacher and be fixing to kill her, well I'm sorry sir, that don't sound like us."

The man nodded as Moses made his point. He said, "The simple idea was to have three wise men who have the gift to see what is needed and the will to make it so, even if the winds of popular opinion blow against it. Over the years, despite the occasional stumble, we've lived up to that promise. I firmly believe that, Moses."

"That's what I signed up for. But now we got a new member, youngest we ever had. I'm not sure he understands our ways."

"That was by design, my friend. We were afraid we had gotten too stodgy, too resistant to change. We needed to hear fresh ideas and approaches. Understand, my old friend, that I share some of your trepidations. Change is always disrupting to the old order."

He looked quickly at his Rolex, signaling his time was short. "Let me assure you of one thing. In order to take extreme measures like the one you're describing, the vote must be unanimous. I'm not in favor of anything so drastic, as of now. I believe my old colleague is in agreement.."

"Would you think of maybe making me a voting member?" Ginn had not intended to bring this up, but he had been part of the circle longer than anyone and until now, his guidance had been heeded.

"Problem with that Moses, is that then there would be four of us with a vote. When we decide on lesser situations, the majority rules. We don't want any tie votes keeping us from acting. And the very term Troika means three. If we gave you a vote, we'd probably need to add another member, making it five. The more chefs, the more the soup gets diluted. So as much as I think you deserve it, I'm afraid it's a non-starter. Now I really must go. I hope I've addressed your concerns. Thank you for bringing them to my attention."

"Yes, sir. Thank you, sir," Ginn said.

Moses was left adrift. He had one more arrow in his quiver, but he was reluctant to use it. He had hoped to resolve things on his own without escalating the case to a higher power. He could not afford to burn favors at that level unless there was no alternative.

The councilman's words were gently spoken and there was no intentional condescension; no outright dismissal. But that's not how Moses heard it.

Can't let the black man vote. We love you folks but it would upset the delicate balance of things. Know your place, boy, and someday, when you're ready, we'll allow you to be more than three fifths of a man.

The more things change, the more they stay the same. *There's always an excuse, isn't there?*

14

Charlotte Douglas International is a pleasant place, as airports go. The terminals are clean and modern. Parking is plentiful and reasonably priced. There's even a bit of old Southern charm --- sturdy white rocking chairs dot the concourse and the smell of comfort food wafts from the kiosks.

That said, the less I see of it or any other airport, the better. Even though they have streamlined the vetting process, it is intrusive. There's nothing I hate more than waiting in line to shed my shoes, belt, wallet, computer and anything metallic to be frisked like a suspect in a crack house bust. Jaime is in the sky at least three times a month and she has all the *TSA pre* perks befitting her frequent flier status, but I couldn't do what she does. It makes me appreciate her even more.

We'd made up after our little spat the night before. I scrambled her an egg white and cheddar omelet and deposited her luggage into the trunk of the Audi. At the airport, she dashed through the security line, while looking back and mouthing kisses. I lingered a bit longer than usual, apprehensive that it could be some time until I saw her again.

Ginn hadn't called --- perhaps he'd rejected my offer. Slightly depressed, I drove back to a house that no longer contained Jaime. Only Bosco greeted me at the door, but even his normal exuberance was dampened when he realized that Jaime wasn't with me. He didn't follow me into my office, retreating to her spot on our bed instead. Jaime didn't approve of him napping on her pillow, but since she was eight miles high over Kansas by now, what the hell?

I checked out the flash drive that Randee had given me. The first file told me what I already knew: two years ago, she had become interested in Serpente when one of his complexes came up for auction. She asked my builder friend Derek Davis to inspect the place before making an offer on a potential flip, and he uncovered numerous dangerous violations.

From there, she found a young plumbing inspector who told her that Serpente had offered him a bribe to overlook these hazards. But he vanished before substantiating his charges. She carried on nonetheless, and with Davis' help compiled her own evidence, including a damning video. She tried bringing it to the attention of the local television outlets and the Charlotte newspapers, but they regarded her proof as too thin to pursue.

So she started a blog, hoping to use social media to "out" Johnny Serpente. Her website attracted a great deal of traffic when a right wing radio host named Patrick Henry blasted it on the air. His intent was to humiliate her *Liberal Yankee* sensibilities, but his vicious rant only succeeded in making her a sympathetic figure. When people saw the abuses Serpente had perpetrated on the taxpayers, she became a lower case heroine.

Charlene and I discovered Johnny's body the next day. The local media was rife with speculation that he had taken his own life rather than face imprisonment. The tale that the Russian mafiya had exacted their revenge got a short bump, but within two weeks, the story faded from the public consciousness when a prominent local politician underwent a sex change. Later, when it came out that Serpente had bequeathed a large share of his fortune to Habitat for Humanity, even Randee was satisfied that he had made restitution for his sins and she moved on.

She still blogged on a regular basis, but nothing she unearthed matched the Serpente affair. Now she had a just few hundred loyal followers.

So why was she back on the Serpente case?

Rather than sift through all the material, I called Randee. I asked her directly what had inspired her to re-open what had seemed like a dead issue and she answered without hesitation.

"The plumbing inspector."

"You mean the guy who disappeared?"

"The very one. You know me, I'm always looking for properties to renovate and flip. I heard about a possible opportunity just across the border in South Carolina. As I was checking it out, I ran into that young inspector. He's working with a group of investors looking for rundown buildings in good locations. He pretended not to know me at first, but I cajoled him into letting me buy him a couple of drinks. After a few adult beverages, he opened up about Serpente."

"You *do* have a way of bending men to your will, lady"

"Hasn't worked very well seducing you, big guy. Anyway, he reported Johnny's bribe attempt to his boss, who said he'd investigate. After a week, his supervisor told him that he'd looked into it and that it was all an innocent misunderstanding. When he protested that there was no way that the offer could have been misconstrued, he was told the matter was settled and to shut up and do his job. He was never assigned to inspect another Serpente project."

I said, "So someone in the building department had ties to the Troika. That stands to reason. That's when he disappeared?"

"No, that was later. He was an idealistic kid and wouldn't let the matter drop. But the day before our next meeting --- when he was going to flesh out the details for me --- he was visited by a large older black man who told him that he was being monitored, and that if any word leaked out, his wife and daughter would pay the price. The alternative was to accept an out of state job offer that paid very well. I guess Johnny's death was proof he'd picked the right option."

Moses Ginn. It fit his modus operandi. Use the carrot before the stick and in this kid's case, it had worked temporarily. "So this chance meeting brought it all to the surface again. But how did you convince him to help you, given the threat to his family?"

"He had always felt conflicted about not exposing a corrupt system. I admit, I made it personal, asked him if that was the kind of world he wanted his daughter to grow up in."

"But did he give you any names? The guy in the building department who told him the bribe was a mistake?"

"He said that man retired last year and moved to the Virgin Islands. Good luck finding him and getting him to talk. Every man has his price, and whoever is behind this is very good at finding out what that price is. They seem to have limitless resources. I've been poring over columns of figures on the public record for two weeks now."

"Look, be careful. As I told you yesterday, I don't know how, but these guys are onto you. You might get a visit from a mysterious black man soon, and I'm afraid it won't be a just a threat."

"I have a bunch of lessons at the range scheduled. I'm getting really good at this. I'll be ready."

Good at this? Against a Special Forces vet? She'd have no chance. I repeated my words of caution and rang off.

The logical place to go next was the former plumbing inspector, whose identity was on the flash drive. This kid had proven vulnerable to intimidation, which normally isn't my default mechanism but if I need to employ it, I will. I don't have time to fool around with vague hints.

The other side was playing hardball and not observing niceties. They had set the rules and we had to play the game on their turf.

Sometimes, a strong offense is the best defense.

15

Green Mansions, LLC works out of a half empty strip mall in Fort Mill, South Carolina just a few miles south of Charlotte. Their online mission statement was to restore and repurpose solidly built old buildings rather than demolish them. The website was replete with platitudes about saving the planet's resources and high minded principles about green building practices, reducing waste and saving our heritage. The flowery language was similar to what the late Johnny Serpente used to hawk his services. If Green Mansions had ties to the Troika, maybe they share the same ad agency.

The *about us* page only listed a president and CFO, so it was difficult to determine if they were a modest start up with great aspirations or a front for something else. It smelled like a shell corporation and a money laundering outfit --- more grist for Randee's mill someday. I'm sure that Deep Throat could provide more information but I had all I needed for now.

The storefront was not impressive, but it did jibe with the concept of responsible building practices. The reception area had dark painted walls with minimal casing. Black and white posters of old cityscapes were the only adornment. The floors were bamboo: they resembled more costly material but were renewable. The company logo was simply its name --- white block letters on a black background, encased in a cheap aluminum frame on the back wall.

The reception desk was a repurposed dresser, whitewashed with milk paint. The woman behind it was overweight and an obvious smoker. She must have cosseted her habit during breaks outdoors, since the scent in the small room was as neutral as the decor. She was dressed casually in a low cut navy tee shirt, revealing too much of her enormous breasts. A long floral skirt, open toed sandals, black varnished nails. She was probably around Jaime's age, which was all they had in common.

"How may I help you, sir?" she asked in a Georgia accent so thick that I had trouble understanding.

"I'm looking for Bill Flores. Is he in the office today?"

"He's out at the moment but he's due back in real soon. Did y'all have an appointment?"

I was dressed in business casual. Dark cotton blazer, white polo, light brown Dockers, tan loafers. Spiffy. Jaime would approve.

I said, "No actually, we have a mutual friend who told me to look Bill up. Said we'd have a lot in common seeing as I've flipped a few houses in my day."

"Well sir, that's not really what we do here. Bill is out looking at a property but said he'd be back before lunch. Should only be a few minutes."

There were two shabby-chic upholstered chairs across from her desk, but she didn't motion me toward them. "We all like to eat at the Rusty Ribbon. It's just a few doors down on the left as you go out. It'd be a whole lot more comfortable for you than waiting on him here. When Bill gets in, I'll shoo him your way, Mr...?"

"Riley. Randy Riley." I like alliteration.

"And who is your mutual friend?"

I'd come prepared with a name from the building inspector's office in Charlotte, Jimmy Bailey, who had worked there around the same time Bill Flores had. I gave the receptionist Bailey's name and trekked to the Rusty Ribbon.

A few minutes before noon, the place was fairly empty. The bar was mottled by greasy circular streaks --- a quick wipe down with a dirty rag and then pronounced sanitary. Old beer stained coasters, half eaten bowls of peanuts and stray corn chips were scattered about. The joint had they call a "sweet mop" smell, meaning the utensil hadn't been properly rinsed and the cleaning solution had become stagnant.

I'd sooner drink from a toilet than at this place.

Luckily, the timing worked out. Before anyone of the staff in the back noticed I was there, a small Latin man walked in. It had to be Flores.

"Bill Flores? Randy Riley." I rose, extending my hand like a used car salesman welcoming a sucker. "I've heard so much about you. Jimmy thinks the world of you. I think we may have a lot in common."

I grimaced as if passing a Port-o-John. "Look, my friend, let me buy you lunch. But this isn't my kind of place. Let me take you someplace nicer."

Flores looked perplexed. I'd overwhelmed him. A total unknown was offering to buy him lunch in a nicer place than he was used to. Like a child offered candy from a friendly stranger in a black sedan, he was suspicious.

"Pleased to meet you, Mr. Riley. Sorry, but I've got a full schedule today and I just came over out of courtesy. I don't really have time for lunch."

William Flores was a compact man. He wore jeans and a pre-faded denim work shirt, proper attire for poking through old buildings and examining their bones to determine if they are worthy of reclamation. His close cropped black hair gave way to a neatly trimmed goatee, alert brown eyes giving me the once over.

"Just a drink then," I countered. "I know a good spot a few minutes away. I'll drive if you like and have you back within the hour."

I frowned as if I'd be hurt if he didn't accept my generous offer.

"How well did you know Jimmy Bailey? I wasn't on the job very long there, but he was nice to me," Flores said.

"*Beetle* Bailey? We go way back. Coincidence. I mentioned to him I had some business in Fort Mill and he said I should look you up. He was curious to see how you were, seeing as how you left the building department so quickly."

"I didn't know he knew where I work now. I had a great offer in the private sector. Somehow they came looking for me and I couldn't say no."

"Hey, you can tell me all about it over a drink. Come on, my treat. Old Beetle will be mad if I don't give him a full report."

I hoped I wasn't laying it on too thick with the "Beetle" business, but the blurb on the department website called him Jimmy "Beetle" Bailey. I didn't think anyone reads the funny papers anymore, although the Charlotte Observer still runs *Beetle Bailey, Blondie, Dennis the Menace*, and a few other oldies, some of which should have died with their creators. But I always appreciate the gams and bosom on Dagwood Bumstead's wife.

Flores said, "Okay, Mr. Riley. But like I say, my time is short."

"Cool. My car's the black Audi over there. Just hop in and relax. I think you'll like this place."

Flores smiled faintly, shrugged, and got into the passenger seat. The place I was taking him was a vacant lot, a mile off the highway. And I seriously doubted that he'd like it much.

16

Another example of how age has imparted wisdom. Either that, or it has turned me into a spineless vacillator.

My original intent was to take Flores to a vacant field, shove my Beretta into his Adam's apple and make him talk. It's usually not my first choice, but time was of the essence and it is an effective tactic with most civilians.

But as I drove the Audi toward my pre-selected spot, I began to see William Flores in a different light. It turns out he was what some have uncharitably called an "anchor baby", meaning that his parents had come to this country illegally but he was born here and thus, is a citizen of the United States. His father worked unskilled construction jobs for substandard wages, until he gained a master's expertise in finish carpentry. High end builders sought him out for their most demanding clients, and eventually the Flores family achieved the American Dream --- a nice Cape Cod in the suburbs, and the ability to send their offspring to college.

William became interested in building, but unlike his father, did not possess the talent or patience to excel in fine carpentry. But he knew what to look for when it came to craftsmanship, so he took courses to become an inspector, charged with judging the efforts of others.

His father fell victim to inadequate safety measures, precautions that his wealthy employers did not care about or felt would be cost effective. Inhaling the carcinogenic construction dust took its toll --- his final year was spent bedridden, strapped to an oxygen tank.

Flores was just over jockey size with classically handsome features. He spoke with the slightest lilt of an accent. I could never share such personal recollections with a stranger, but his stories of growing up poor but beloved made it impossible for me to execute my original plan. Maybe that was his intent all along.

Some hardboiled detective.

I drove him to a nearby tavern as I told him I would. I hadn't scouted the place out, but lucked into a suitable venue. I couldn't care less about the quality of the food and drink, just that the din didn't overpower what I had to say.

Texitos was clean, dark, and not crowded. Its few patrons were neatly dressed and looked respectable. Flores and I were shown a booth toward the back and we ordered drinks --- he a ginger ale; me the house Vinho Verde.

"I couldn't help but be touched by the story you told me in the car about your dad," I started. "Sounds like he was a fine man."

"It took me a while to appreciate everything he was trying to teach, but I now try to school my daughters as he did me."

"I'm sure you're doing a fine job."

"I try."

If I handled this awkwardly, he might just storm out and I'd be left with nothing but a glass of cheap wine and the check. It helped that I had driven him here. Cabs were scarce in this part of the world, so he might be a bit more tolerant.

"Mr. Flores, I need to confess something. I don't know Beetle Bailey. I used his name as a ruse to get you here. There's something we need to talk about."

His face darkened. "Did the big Negro send you? I did what he asked. Why can't you people leave me alone?"

The *big Negro*? Moses Ginn. I played along, switching roles again. I didn't think my preppy attire made me look intimidating, but sometimes my size alone does the job. Flores liked to talk, and with a little gentle coaxing, I figured I could get what I came for.

"Look, Mr. Flores, I don't want to cause trouble over what could be a misunderstanding or poor communication. What exactly did the big man ask you to do?"

"I called the number he gave me a long time ago. He said to keep it if anyone started asking me questions about Mr. Serpente."

Flores was the double agent, not out of guile, but out of fear. I said, "So you told him that this Blankenship woman was at it again."

"Yes. And that I told her nothing."

"That's interesting because apparently after she met with you, she started digging into records at the building department."

Fear crossed his face. Again, I could imagine how someone Flores' size viewed a bruiser like me. "I said nothing. She knew all about what Serpente had done. I didn't tell her anything she didn't already know. On my mother, I swear."

Of course. One of Randee's little tricks. She insinuates that she knows more than she actually does, and he confirms her suspicions unintentionally. She is good at that game, far more practiced at it than the frightened young man sitting across from me.

"What did she already know that she confided in you?"

"She said that she knew that Serpente was not at the top of the chain, that others were pulling his strings. I said that may or may not be, but I have no idea who these people are."

The restaurant was still quiet. Two or three couples drifted in, older men with younger women. Bosses taking their secretaries out to lunch? Or a prelude to a quick stop at a nearby hot sheets motel?

"So if you didn't say anything, that leaves the man who hired you. Your boss. He would have been Blankenship's next stop. He must have spoken out of turn. Do you know where he is today?"

"Please. He has treated me very well, very generous. He has never mentioned the name Serpente. I'm sure he knows nothing of this matter and if he does, he would not betray a confidence. He is an honorable man."

"I'm sure he is an honorable man. As Marc Antony said, they're all honorable men."

He gave me a puzzled look. What did a Latin pop singer have to do with honor?

The waitress came by and asked if we wanted another round. I nodded.

When she left, I said, "I just need to cover all the bases. Hey, I can locate him without your help, but the sooner I can put all this to rest, the better it will be for everyone. You're certain you didn't give the old biddy any names? Anything she can trace back?"

"I don't know any names. Even the big Negro you work with, sir. I have no idea who he is."

Flores was a decent man, trying to make an honest living. He'd seen the working conditions Serpente promulgated kill his father, and he felt obliged to report them. But he lacked Randee's relentlessness when it became clear that there were larger forces at work, forces that could destroy his family.

I was guilty, as well. I had been willing to settle for the story that Serpente's Russian mafiya past had caught up with him. Even if Charlene was involved, as Shabielski suggested, I didn't really want to know. I wanted to believe that Serpente's corruption died with him, although I always suspected he must have had masters.

William Flores couldn't point me toward those masters, but the man who hired him was a step higher on the chain and more privy to their secrets. Flores grudgingly told me where his boss was working that day.

As we finished our drinks, I forced small talk with my hilarious observations about the other patrons. He merely grunted in response. Bad audience. I drove him back to work in silence. The normally loquacious Flores had absorbed the lesson about loose lips sinking ships, even though he didn't possess enough evidence to wreck a kayak.

I hoped that the "big Negro" knew that. If he didn't, I would tell him.

17

Spero G. Youklis, CEO of Green Mansions, LLC, was attending an auction. A hundred and sixty years ago years ago, on this very site, human flesh might have been the subject of bidding. Today, the item for sale was a decaying mansion that over the centuries had housed Revolutionary War patriots, Civil War rebels, and antebellum carpetbaggers. On what once had been an expansive front lawn, a dozen or so denizens gathered in front of a makeshift podium to pick over the remains.

Peeling, mold clotted paint, boarded windows flanked by dangling shutters and tall rotting columns on a blue stained concrete porch were the final insult to the handsome colonial architecture. Tall weeds had taken over the yard, providing a shady sanctuary for snakes of the reptilian variety. The human breed sought no such refuge.

My friend Derek Davis had told me of such events. I was surprised that the grand old structure had not been ticketed for preservation. Somehow its antique presence had escaped the state's notice. A one-sheet handout informed me that the main building had been erected in 1760, burned to the ground by the British in 1813, and rebuilt ten years later on the footprint of the original stone foundation. It had been bought and sold many times since, the current owner being a local bank that had foreclosed it from an amateur rehabber. Likely some fool who watched reality shows that promise exponential profits for --- as

Stone might quote Springsteen --- "*a little touch up and a little paint.*"

Youklis had orange skin, a high forehead and black-dyed hair arranged in tight curls. An upturned nose that had been broken more than once. He looked like he needed to shave more than once a day. Dressed in a tropical weight tan suit which was straining in the wrong places.

Flores had told me that the auction was scheduled for three and that prospective buyers were accorded two hours prior to check out the premises. I asked him why it wasn't his job to do such inspections and he replied that normally it was, but that his boss had insisted on taking the lead on this one.

As advertised, festivities began promptly at three. This ramshackle proceeding bore no resemblance to classic automobile auctions that I occasionally watch on the Velocity channel when I can't sleep. Unlike Charlie Ross and his highbrow, British accented colleagues, this dude was pure cornpone, probably working the tobacco and hog futures circuit if those things still exist. Bald, ZZ Top beard, bold red plaid shirt, jeans and cowboy boots. Thick Texas drawl.

"Howdy, howdy, howdy ladies and gents, Oops, no ladies present and by the look of this crew of the S.S. Motley, very few gents."

Indulgent guffaws.

"No reserve on this fine edifice so's we'll be moving it today, no matter what. We'll start at ten thousand U.S. government greenbacks, Confederate currency sadly not accepted. Who'll give me ten, ten, ten...."

This nutty sideshow was worth the trip as I watched a combination of the well heeled, the naively ambitious and the desperate --- amateurs and pros --- stake their ground. The obvious bargain hunters dropped out at fifteen grand.

Youklis had yet to bid.

Two nicely dressed older men went back and forth in small increments until they reached twenty, then one of them shook his head and backed off.

"Have, have twenty thousand dollars, twenty, twenty who will give me twenty five?"

No one responded. The high bidder stole a anxious glance at Youklis.

"We have twenty, let's make it twenty five, no? Twenty one then...twenty one, twenty one who'll give me twenty one thousand for this marvelous tribute to our Southern heritage?"

I hadn't arrived early enough to walk through the place and I didn't take note of how many acres it came with or if a mule was included, but twenty grand seemed awfully cheap for a decent sized building not far from Charlotte.

"All righty, twenty thousand is bid, twenty thousand, going once, twenty going twice."

Youklis spoke for the first time. His voice was high pitched, maybe a little New York in it. "Twenty thousand two fifty."

"Twenty thousand two fifty it is. Going once, twice, and hammer down, sold for twenty thousand two fifty. Congratulations sir, this fine property and the acres surrounding it are yours. Well done, sir."

Something didn't sit right. Unless this was a toxic waste site or there was some draconian government restriction on what could be done with the property, this was the deal of the century. And the auctions I had seen on television were quite unlike this one. Here, the bids grew only in tiny increments, then stopped abruptly at twenty. Suddenly the auctioneer asks for a five thousand dollar jump, scaring everyone else away. He was about to pound the hammer when Youklis spoke at the last second. The bidding was quickly closed before anyone else could jump in.

It reeked of a setup. Everyone else dropped out almost on cue. I had never seen an auction where a last minute bidder jumps in at the end and wins for only a few dollars more, especially for a house and prime suburban land, ripe for development.

Rather than approach Youklis cold with some flimsy story that he might immediately recognize as contrived, I'd contact Deep Throat and get background. Spero Youklis in some ways reminded me of Serpente, a tough little Yankee who was merely a middleman for something greater. Throat could find his Achilles heel.

It was even possible I could skip over Youklis altogether and jump to the next link, if I could establish his ties to someone at the Nat. I could always find Spero if I did need to follow up. Unless Moses Ginn was the ultimate insulator, the man who keeps all the links at a distance from each other so that no one could tie them together.

Something else regarding the auction was nagging at me. Something Randee had told me years ago. I couldn't remember exactly what.

Randee would know. She never forgot anything.

18

"And I thought I had problems with memory loss" Randee said.

Cell reception in South Carolina is sometimes spotty, but I caught every sarcastic word, and pictured the sneer that went with them.

I said, "You know, I have other things to think about occasionally other than keeping your butt safe."

"Well, smartass, before I start looking into assisted living for you, you may be of some use. What do you want to know, King?"

Although there might be an edge to it, trash talk from this old broad was a sure sign that she was no longer angry with me and was onboard with the mission. She should be, since I had adopted *her* proactive strategy rather than my own inclination to let sleeping dogs lie.

"So, Randee, refresh my recall about you and auctions with Serpente."

"Two years ago, when I met the late Mr. Serpente for the only time, he tried to buy me off. He said that the property I was interested in re-habbing with our friend Derek could be had for a song if I played ball with him. I hadn't really given it a second thought until you just brought it up. Why?"

I was driving home from South Carolina on I-77, cruising northbound at 70, cars flying by me like I was on a bicycle.

I said, "I was just at my first property auction and it didn't seem kosher. This little Greek guy got an old mansion on ten acres for twenty grand."

"Holy shit."

"Nice language, coming from a grade school teacher."

"A hottie of advancing years, teacher no more. That's an incredible deal. Where is this place?"

I said, "Fort Mill. West of 77. Can't be more than twenty miles from Charlotte."

"Do you have the lot and block number?"

"It's on the one sheet. I can scan it and email it to you when I get home." Bosco hadn't been out since I left this morning, and I didn't want to bother my neighbor Mrs. Keegish to stop by and walk him.

She said, "Please. I'll look into the history of the property and check out the tax rolls. From there I can trace ownership. It's obviously a foreclosure but I'd be shocked that a bank would accept so little."

"Absolute auction, no reserve."

"Bulldoodie. I've been interested in a few of those. The auction house says no reserve but they talk to all the prospective buyers right after they get the deposit. If they get the sense that they're a bunch of bottom feeders looking to steal the property, they'll cancel the auction at the last minute."

"And that's legal? After they advertise that it's absolute?"

"I'd think a former fed would know the answer to that. All they have to do is say that the seller changed his mind and has decided to hold on to the property. If they really, really need to sell it, they'll call any seriously interested parties back and try to make a deal under the table, implying that there are multiple bids."

The machinations wealthy people go through to avoid taxes or government scrutiny never fails to amaze. When I grew up, there was such a thing as *false advertising* and I believed that it was prosecuted. Whether I was just a unenlightened kid then and it has always been like this, I'll never know. These days every other commercial on Stone's radio show represents a scam. The most honest spots are for used car dealers, which should tell you something.

I didn't express my naiveté to Randee. "Understood. But this auction actually came off and there *were* several other bidders. Thing is, they all seemed to defer to this one guy."

"Interesting. So this obviously was a set up. Why were you at an auction in the first place?"

"Following a lead you gave me. Okay, here's an assignment for you, teach. Look into the laws in South Carolina about this sort of thing and see if they could pull this off legally. If not, maybe we can nail someone lower on the ladder and get them to rat on the higher-ups."

"Are we getting sidetracked here? Or are you just giving me busy work to keep me out of trouble, King?"

"Not at all. My lead was your plumbing inspector, Flores. He told me he was given this job at a big salary boost. That essentially makes it a bribe to keep his mouth shut. His boss was the man who won the auction. He didn't do this to help a young Latino he took a liking to. He was asked, or more likely ordered, to take Flores on. If we can establish a link to that person or persons, we're closer to our goal. Capisce?"

"I get it. So you think that the bank's involved, too?"

"Could be, wittingly or unwittingly. I need to find out who's pulling this Greek guy's strings."

"And you can't just beat it out of him?"

I laughed at that. "You have me pegged all wrong, Randee. I'm a gentle man. Hell, I go to the Charlotte Symphony every few months, just to prove how couth I am."

"You need to build a bridge. To get over yourself. All right King, as they say in the Bible, I will devotedly do your bidding."

"Thanks. How's the shooting going?"

"It's great actually. And it's not just shooting. They teach you proper care of your firearm. How to clean it and re-assemble it. I must say, for someone who thinks the second amendment should be repealed, I'm impressed."

"Hey, to me Randee Blankenship constitutes a one person militia."

19

I called Throat's burner next and got a recorded message, not his voice. I was about to check in with Stone when my phone sounded through the car's speakers. It was Throat.

"Yes, King?"

"Hope I didn't violate any protocols, using that number."

"Hardly. It is my hotline, so to speak. I decide the urgency of returning the call and act accordingly."

Techies have always been weird. Stone had told me some stories of strange behavior by the engineering staff at stations where he had worked. But this guy was too much.

I'd branched off I-77 and was now on the newly laid Highway 16, which most Charlotte residents hadn't discovered yet. I was no more than a few minutes from home and my dog's full bladder.

"I'm honored you prioritized me. I called you for a couple of reasons. First, you got anything on Moses Ginn?"

"Your phantom nemesis? Is this a test? Because I can uncover no record of his existence at Mecklenburg National. You are not wasting my time and your money to evaluate my skill sets, are you?"

"Hell, no. He's real, for better or worse. His number didn't come up on my caller ID, but I figured you could crack that."

"It is not that simple. He is probably using TOR relays to bounce his actual location all over the world. I do it all the time. Someone who doesn't want to be found can run fake Google searches and mislead even the most diligent searcher with things such as a phony Facebook account."

"You're speaking another language. TOR relays?"

"I did not think you would understand. Simply put, most people *want* to be found online. They are selling something or want to be accessible to their childhood chums or unfulfilled fantasy romantic interests. So they leave a trail. Or take action to promote their profile for reasons of commerce. But those who wish to stay anonymous and still use the web can leave false trails. Dead ends. Since the internet only exists electronically and is not really a place, it contains infinite corners where one can hide."

"I never knew there were corners in time, until I was told to stand in one."

"Very good. Grace Slick sang that in the 70s with Jefferson Starship before they sold out. Although I thought your friend Stone was the one who quoted song lyrics."

How the hell did he know that?

I said, "Well, Throat, rest assured that Moses Ginn does exist. I'm not bonkers yet. The more information I have on him, the better. But for right now, I need you to find me some links. There is a company called Green Mansions, LLC in South Carolina. I need to know if any of their directors or employees have any ties to Mecklenburg National. It's a small company, probably less than ten workers altogether."

"That should take five minutes. Are you in a position to receive email?"

"I'm driving now. I'll be home soon. Why?"

"I have narrowed the list at that golf establishment to the most likely candidates. I will send you a list of their names and a brief précis on each. I now will research any ties to this other new entity prior to sending, so as to narrow the list further."

This man was strange but boy, he was good. "Great work. And if you have any hunches as to who the big three may be, I'd appreciate it."

"I never play hunches King. You should know that about me. But I will give you percentage based probabilities on each man. No women made the list since this club has no female members. I will email you the list and you can call or hit reply if you have questions."

With that, he hung up, not bothering to say goodbye. It was just as well, since I was pulling into my driveway. I rarely use the front door but since I probably would be going out again, I decided to leave the car out and go in that way. Bosco usually greets me, knowing he can usually guilt me into giving him a cookie if I've been out too long.

I wondered if he'd be industrious enough to head for the main entry, or if he'd be lazy and wait near the garage door, making me find him with his treat.

The front door was unlocked.

Jaime.

I had loaded her luggage and picked her up in front. She must have forgotten to lock the door behind her. No big deal. There was not much crime in my area and a lot of the residents leave their doors unlocked.

"Bosco," I called. "Hey boy, where are you?"

No response. No scrabbling claws on the hardwood floor. No squeals of delight celebrating my arrival.

"Hey, Bosco, buddy. Cookie." That always got his attention.

Had Jaime forgotten to lock the front door or had someone else been in? Mrs. Keegish has a key. When work detains me and it's past Bosco's dinner or walk time, I call her. She doesn't consider it an imposition. She loves the dog and she is happy to feel needed. But she never uses her key unless I call. I think.

I pulled the Beretta. Terrible thoughts crossed my mind.

Bosco was lying sick somewhere in the house, unable to answer. Or somehow had pushed open the unlocked door and run off.

Best case --- his doggie bladder was aging and he couldn't hold it in. So he was hiding, knowing his dad wouldn't appreciate a pool of urine in the kitchen.

I gave the house a quick once over. No dog. Looked under the beds and by his bowl. Near all seven of his dog beds that were scattered throughout the house.

Nothing. My best friend was gone.

20

Some tough guy I am.

I've kicked in doors, fully aware that a loaded weapon aimed in my direction was waiting on the other side. I've confronted gang bangers, mobsters of various ethnicities, and bad guys whose bulk dwarfs mine. I wouldn't say that there weren't some anxious moments, but I was able to remain cool and focused on the task at hand.

But I was in a full blown panic because my dog was AWOL. I didn't know where to start or who to call. I ran through the house, screaming his name and hoping he'd emerge from some cranny I hadn't searched.

I finally calmed to the point where I was able to think more logically. I called Mrs. Keegish and asked if she had taken Bosco out. She could be forgetful at times and it was possible that she had responded to an old message on her answering machine. She told me that she hadn't seen the dog in days, but offered to alert the neighbors. I thanked her but asked that she hold off for now.

Next, I tried to think like Bosco. If he had somehow escaped through the unlocked front door, where would he go? He always liked playing near the lake, and wasn't shy about taking a dip on a hot day. I discourage him from swimming. My fear is that he'll venture out too far and be too exhausted to make it back, or that a reckless boater might not see him. In his doggie brain, the forbidden allure while dad was away might have been too tempting to resist.

The last possibility was too horrible to contemplate: that I had brought this on myself and had been careless in leaving him unattended.

Randee's cat had been poisoned during the Serpente affair, and although we could never prove it, we suspected that the unscrupulous builder or one of his minions had used the feline to send a message to its owner.

Although Bosco is a large dog, he is exceedingly gentle. His presence might scare away a potential burglar, but anyone having experience with dogs could easily buy him off by offering anything that smelled like bacon. I went out the front door and circled toward the back, hoping to find a discarded chew toy or some evidence that Bosco had come this way. Sometimes he carries one of his toys with him when we go out, dropping it if he catches the scent of a squirrel who has the temerity to invade *his* yard.

My yard slopes down toward the water. At ground level in the front, I can't quite see the shoreline but I heard shouting from near the lake. I couldn't make out the words, but the timbre was deep and masculine.

I crept down to a point where I could see what was happening on the shoreline. Along the narrow stretch of white sand, stood Moses Ginn. He was tossing a yellow ball into the water, and my wet Golden was doing what he loved best.

Retrieving it.

21

I resisted the urge to blow Ginn away right then. Clearly, he hadn't heard me pull up. He was focused on playing with Bosco, and my dog was enjoying the attention.

I have a theory that you can tell a lot about a person by the way they treat so called inferior beings. That covers a wide range of creatures from the lowliest rodents to humans deemed *less than*. If a person considers everyone else an equal, they can't be incorrigible no matter what their other sins may be. However, if they treat those beneath their station with contempt or worse, then their heart is black and irredeemable.

It works as a clue to help read people, which is a large part of what I do for a living. And the hints I was getting from Ginn were positive. He had a broad smile that never flickered as he tossed the ball into the shallows, teasing Bosco into dropping it when he brought it back. He praised the boy lavishly and rubbed his ears between fetches. I didn't know how long they had been playing, but observing them for a couple of minutes, neither showed any signs of boredom.

I had to balance my relief that Bosco was safe and having the time of his life with the fact that Ginn had entered my house uninvited and taken my dog. Was this intended to show me that I was vulnerable and that if the

Troika voted for my removal, it could be accomplished with a flick of the wrist?

There was only one way to find out.

So I shot him.

Well, I shot *at* him. Ginn was wearing a billowing nylon windbreaker that trailed behind him in the lakeside breeze as he wound up for his next pitch. The round ripped through the back of the jacket and landed harmlessly in the lake. It served its purpose.

He looked up and saw that it was me. "Holy shit, King. What the hell? You could have killed me."

"I could have. The *Stand Your Ground* laws in the state would call it justifiable, too. You broke into my house, stole my dog and if I don't find a weapon on you right now, I'm sure there's one in your car, wherever you left it."

"Motherfucker, I come in peace. What the hell's wrong with you? I told you I'd be in touch, and I am. I ain't packing."

Bosco was not a gun dog. Although his breed make excellent hunting companions, I've never trained him as such and I was pretty sure this was the first time he had heard a weapon discharged in close proximity. He gripped the ball tightly in his mouth and cowered on the beach, a safe distance from the humans.

I said, "Good to know but let me see that for myself."

He raised his hands and I patted him down while holding the Beretta. He was clean.

I tucked the gun away. "You could have called."

"I did."

Sure enough, when I extracted my phone, there was a missed call. Probably came when I was in a bad cell zone in South Carolina.

"Sorry. I never got the message. But still, breaking into my house, taking the dog out? Not cool."

He shrugged. "Hey man, didn't know when you'd be home. Decided to wait in comfort rather than hang outside. Maybe watch a game on that monster tube you got. But your dog needed to go out and I figured he could use some exercise, too."

"You got a dog?"

"Died last Christmas. Had to put him down. Cancer. Hardest thing I ever had to do."

This, coming from a man who had killed Serpente and God knows how many others. But I could relate.

"Well, it seems Bosco likes you. No accounting for taste. Sorry I ruined your jacket."

"I'll just boost another one from the pro shop. Guess I lucky you such a lousy shot."

"No, you're lucky I'm good. I hit exactly where I aimed, bozo."

Offering a hand, he said, "Peace?"

"Maybe. Make you a deal. We'll go back to the house and discuss this on the deck. Glenlivet rocks, okay? But since you got Bosco all sandy and wet, I'll get you his towel and you dry him off. C'mon boy, we're late for your dinner."

The dog's ears perked up and he led the way back to the house. The sun was sinking low down, casting long shadows across the lake and painting the sky with pale orange tendrils. Bosco scampered up the deck stairs and waited at the French doors.

I held up a hand to keep the dog from entering, and tossed Ginn a towel. I came back with drinks for us and a bowl of kibble for Bosco. Ginn had done such a nice job cleaning him that the dog hesitated before attacking his belated dinner. But not for long.

"Okay, Ginn, why the visit? Let's get down to it."

"You into Disney?"

"When I was a kid. Born a little late for the original Davey Crockett but I was a card carrying member of the Mickey Mouse club and caught the reruns. Fifty years ago. Look man, I know you think you're like Jesus or something, speaking in parables but can we just cut to the chase here? What does Disney have to do with anything?"

"Everything and nothing. You see, Disney was the inspiration for the Troika."

"What, they traded their mouse ears for automatic weapons?"

"Not hardly. Old Walt was a visionary. He wasn't just about cartoons and white American history. Right before he died, he designed EPCOT. That was supposed to be the city of the future. Everything organized around a circular grid. The original members of the Troika was boys during that time. You know, IGY, International Geophysical Year. Charlotte was just a village then. They saw it like a model city. A grand experiment. So they formed this little group of rich dudes who had a vision for the future and the bread to make it happen. With me so far?"

"I suppose, but if these dudes were so high minded, why didn't they work through the system, run for office? Why this secret society and why only three?"

"They tried other ways but they didn't work. They thought the system was broke even then and couldn't be fixed. So they took a indirect route, sorta like the Wizard of Oz --- the men behind the curtain. And they had to keep the circle tight, because if word got out what they were doing, powers that be at the time would shut 'em down."

I said, "So three men thought they could control a city. Come on, no matter how small Charlotte was then, that can't work. How do you get big things done and keep it a secret?"

"Of course there was false starts, King. Mistakes made. But like they say about the devil. The key is to make you think he don't exist."

He took a sip of Scotch and smacked his lips in approval. "They didn't come by all this sway all at once. They usually had the same gigs --- a lawyer, politician and a cop. The politician to influence the city council. The lawyer to massage the rules. And the cop to dig up dirt on the folks they be blackmailing to do what they wanted. Course, they had people working under them that got no idea 'bout the master plan or where it be coming from. Folks like your man Serpente. A few years after they started, I came aboard. Only reason is I heard things I wasn't supposed to and made myself useful to them. Otherwise, I just shining their shoes and fetching them drinks."

He took in the scenery for a second. "Good Scotch. Maybe someday, I'll turn you on to something even better."

The late summer sun was almost down now and the air was taking on a chill. With a full belly, Bosco was content, curled up in a corner of the deck. I got up and brought out the bottle and some more ice, pouring us both another round.

I said, "All this is interesting stuff, Ginn. A few years back, a friend of mine, builder by the name of Derek Davis had a dream like that. He bought a big parcel of land not far from here and was going to start a village like what you're describing. Call it New Hope. Lost it in the housing crash. I don't know, maybe he liked Disney too. But he didn't envision killing anyone who got in the way of his plan."

"To make a tasty omelet, you got to break a few eggs. I told you, I believe it's all for the best at the end of the day."

"Yet you started this whole thing by telling me that Randee and I are next on the hit list, just because William Flores told you that Randee was on their scent again. Flores reports back to the *Big Negro*. Had to be you, right?"

"I been called worse. Yes sir, that's how it started. I had to let the others know what Flores said, though now I see that was a mistake. Shoulda handled it myself, got it all wrapped up and tell them later or not at all. But see, that there is the problem. Up until last year, I got wind of little brushfires, I'd handle 'em and no one said boo. This time is different. Balance of power shifted. Men getting older. New blood be more aggressive. Why I warned you to nip it in the bud."

"And who determines if I *have* nipped it? You?"

"Used to be. But now, I'm not so sure."

"All right. From what you sketched out, seems your problem centers on one man, this *new blood*. You have a political problem, Ginn. Maybe you need to deal with it the way you dealt with the others. Like you said, reason with them, use your leverage with them."

I raised my glass. "My advice, not that you asked."

Ginn gave it some thought, then said, "Ain't that simple. Man never would have gotten power in the first place if the other two didn't want it. Problem is, they see it slipping away. Black wards electing independent folks. Folks the Troika can't control. Maybe they see it leading the city down the wrong path."

"Obvious question. You're black. Don't you feel you're betraying your people?"

"The Troika ain't racist. They do more good for my people than the politicians they elect. Half of these new elected black guys got their own scam going. The Charlotte mayor that the feds nailed couple years back in that bribery scandal. What was his color?"

"Paternalism versus self determination. Fought a war over that. You hungry, Ginn?"

"I could eat."

"I'll get the menu from a place near here that delivers. Dinner's on me. I got a feeling we're in for a long night."

22

Ginn and I talked into the wee hours. My bottle of Scotch was nearly spent by the time we finished, well after midnight. I almost invited him to stay in my guest room rather than drive in his condition, although he showed no signs of intoxication. I toyed with the idea of calling Shabielski and setting up a DUI arrest. Bottom line, I still didn't fully trust Moses Ginn.

It was analogous to a first date. He was charming in his homespun manner. Modest, self-effacing. His stories revealed a lot about his code of honor. Our values seemed to match up, mostly.

But like a first date, we were both on our best behavior, my shooting at him aside. Neither talked much about our regrets, our shame. Men of our age have committed many missteps along the way, some intentional, some accidental. Ginn glossed over details about the men he may have dispatched for the Troika --- he never dealt with his murder of Serpente.

So as hopeful as I was that Ginn might prove an ally, by cold morning light, the flaws in that thinking were evident. Try as I might to persuade him, he refused to name names. In essence, he was saying, *Trust me, I'll manage the politics of my situation with the Troika on my own.* Given what I knew about his character, he'd only call for my help as a last resort.

I was wrestling with his "greater good" concept as it regarded his colleagues. Maybe these three men had been a positive force for the city's growth, but the whole idea of a *hidden hand* is troubling. How could anyone ever say for certain that their influence has been totally benevolent? Who could tell if they were adding to their personal fortunes by steering the city toward properties they had an interest in? They were unaccountable to anyone but themselves, since the public was unaware of their very existence.

Either way, the key tipping factor was that these men were willing to sanction murder if their power was threatened. Elected officials on a local level don't kill their enemies. If a bond issue is defeated, the mayor doesn't execute those who vote against it. As bad a man as Johnny Serpente might have been, two slugs to his medulla oblongata does not constitute due process.

And the man who I had downed half a bottle of expensive Scotch with last night had carried out this death sentence and had justified it within his own conscience. He implied that I had been traveling down that same path.

But there was an important difference.

Randee Blankenship had compiled damning evidence against Serpente and we believed that the authorities were about to pounce. There would have been a trial and it was very likely that Johnny would have spent his remaining years behind bars. If he somehow skated, would I have been willing to mete out justice as Ginn had?

The short answer is no.

Might I have played Robin Hood and ripped off whatever I could from him and given it away? Yes.

Stolen his wife and ravaged her every night while she lived with me? Well, I did do that, but after he was not around to object.

But cap him from behind while he was showing off his newly remodeled bathroom?

No.

And that was the gulf separating Moses Ginn and me. I had enjoyed our evening together. We had much in common. But whereas I live with ambivalence, Ginn is certain about right and wrong and is willing to follow through on his principles, wherever they lead --- his unshakeable belief that he is acting in service to lofty goals. And to do whatever it takes.

Powerful men, kings and conquerors throughout the ages have these characteristics. But eventually, their good intentions always become corrupted under the yoke of absolute power. Oft told accounts of historical figures who believed that the ends justify the means are cautionary tales. The human race learns these lessons slowly, if at all.

For now, I will treat Moses Ginn as a friendly adversary. I'll use him and he'll use me when our interests coincide, but I can't help thinking that one day, it will come down to him and me.

23

I made some coffee, ate some cereal, walked Bosco and checked my email. Throat had come up with a list of names who were likely candidates for the Troika. I didn't recognize any of them. Each one had a connection with Spero Youklis. They were on the same board or served on the same committee or had some social media contact. He still was at a dead end with Moses Ginn.

It was too early to call Jaime on the West Coast. I had neglected calling Stone last night, which I would have done had Ginn not intruded. He answered on his hands-free, obviously on a highway somewhere.

"Hey, Riles. What's happening?"

The connection was crystal clear. I said, "Lots. Sorry I didn't get to you yesterday. Crazy stuff going on here. How did you make out at the function?"

"Boring. There were a few cougars there, but way over my legal age limit."

"Sorry to hear that. You might try someone closer to your own vintage once in a while. For variety if nothing else."

"You're one to talk. How old is Jaime again?"

"That's your default answer, I know. Anyway, even though your new audience tends be closer to the grave than the gravy, it's a living."

"Yeah, welcome to my world. At least, I'm on good terms with Allie Middleton again and it's fun working with her. Sometimes I even stay past my time to go back and forth with her on her show. And I even have a beer with Wally Josephs once in a while. He's still a punk, but he's a lot better than he used to be. Even seems like he's grateful we saved his life."

As much as I like to rag on him for what he does for a living, I always liked his show. Stone has a way of elevating dialogue, above the mindless talking point prattle the others of his ilk indulge in. Today, Rick wasn't looking backwards to his glory years on WJOK --- hooray for him.

I said, "So things aren't so bad after all?"

He said, "It's funny. I'm like you. Got enough money, half a great house in Hilton Head. Don't have to work. But something's missing at WPHX. It's free form all right, but it meanders all over the place. The show needs some kind of structure but I don't know what. I'll figure it out."

"Where are you now?"

"Near Columbia. Thought I'd hang with you for the weekend if that's okay and then maybe head back to Hilton Head Sunday night or crack of dawn Monday."

"So you went home alone last night?"

"Uh, no. Went out later for drinks with Wally. Met a waitress and was up shagging her most of the night. "

"You'll never change, will you? Tell me she was at least half your age."

"You'll be shocked. She was mid thirties. Divorced. Hard to imagine any man walking away from that poon-tang. Se--weee-t!"

"You're hopeless. I'll wait to fill you in on what's been going on until you get here. I'll make lunch."

"Ooh, you are so domesticated. You see, why do I need a wife when I have you?"

24

THE TROIKA

"Is the counselor joining us or is it just you and me?"

"He's tied up. But I got him up to speed earlier and I can speak for him."

The two men were sharing an early brunch at a place called Toast in an upscale area of Charlotte known as Ballantyne. Although one of them had been a city councilman for nearly forty years, no one in the small bistro recognized him. He liked it that way. His companion was a police captain, dressed in a manner that belied his position. He wore baggy plaid shorts, Timberland moccasins, and a paint spattered work shirt.

The councilman spoke quietly. "So you put a man on Ginn. I wasn't aware of that and I should have been."

"Sorry. I talked it over with our associate and I assumed he'd mention it to you. It's really not a big deal. I just thought that we should be aware of how Ginn is handling this, see if what he reports squares up with the facts."

"And you can trust this man who's following him? That Ginn won't find out he's under surveillance?"

"He's fine. He's good at tailing people and if Ginn finds out, he's not to let him know that I ordered it. Nothing to worry about."

"Still. Why does he think he's following Moses?"

The cop made an elaborate show over scraping a sizable ball of butter from the top of his French Toast. "You know, I realize this isn't exactly a low cal option, but this butter is overkill. You'd think since I asked for sugar-free syrup that they might get the message that I didn't want the extra fat. And I asked the bimbo serving us to hold the home fries. Dumb shit. They're yours if you want 'em."

The councilman had no such caloric concerns. His metabolism ran hot, he was a nervous sort. The type of man who looked great in a suit --- in his late seventies, he still had a thirty three inch waist. But beneath the elegant trappings, he was a pale, emaciated specimen. He never wore shorts, even on the hottest of July days, his legs were so scrawny. The arms were pipe stem thin and the only area of his body that sported even a hint of color. He had a magnificent head of silver hair. He sometimes joked that the hair had gotten him elected in the first place. There was some truth to that, because even decades ago, he looked the part of a patrician.

He said, "No, thank you on the fries. Gave up greasy foods a long time ago. Back to my question, why does he think he's keeping tabs on Ginn?"

"I said that it had to do with some missing items at the club. Ginn was a suspect, might be dealing with fences. Just told him to report where he went, when, who he met with. General stuff. No listening devices or big zoom lenses. Just a small hi-res camera in case there's something that I might need to see."

The councilman squeezed a small dab of catsup onto his western omelet. He wore a pale yellow cotton sweater, over gray worsted slacks. This was as casual as he allowed himself in public.

"As much as I enjoy your company and the cuisine, what was so important that we needed to meet on a Saturday morning?"

The cop didn't answer right away, his mouth full of French Toast. "Last night, your boy Ginn spent eight hours at Riley King's house. He played with the man's dog, drank his liquor, ate ribs. Now does that sound like someone he's warning to keep his nose out of our affairs?"

The policeman stared at his colleague with hard eyes. He dropped his fork for emphasis. "I've been telling you guys for a while now that I don't trust Ginn. He's old and soft. He may still look like he can take care of himself, but he acts like it's the last thing he'd ever do. Is this the kind of man you want watching your back?"

"Now wait a minute, Richard. We have a long history with Moses. He's never let us down in the past. And you're forgetting that when Serpente became a problem, Moses took care of business and it never was traced back to us."

The police captain knew otherwise but chose not to reveal that information yet. He played along for the time being, waiting for the right moment. "And you're forgetting my role in that. I was the one who smoothed everything over in the department and pointed the feds toward that Russian. And that was before I even joined our little cabal. I just did what my daddy told me, didn't ask why."

"And we're grateful for that and now you can see *why* you did it. You are a full-fledged member of our group, partially in acknowledgment and gratitude for your role in that unfortunate caper. But you can't act on your own without the approval of us all when it comes to existential matters like this."

"Well, excuuuse me." His voice rose above the hushed level at which they had been speaking. "I don't wait around for danger to smack me in the face before I protect myself and my people. I know that you're cautious men. You operate in the shadows and I'm down with that. But in this day and age, you have to be proactive. It's like *stop and frisk* in that cesspool they call New York. It pisses the liberals off but it works."

The councilman had relatives up North but he didn't disagree with the characterization, a pejorative term he dearly wanted to avoid for his own fair city. "There's a difference between imminent threats and undermining a man who's served us faithfully for decades. We've only applied a sanction this one time. Our attitude toward extreme violence is not just a matter of morality. It's a question of exposure. You did a great job diverting attention from what happened to Johnny Serpente but things don't always fall into place so neatly."

The police captain's face turned red and he had all he could do to keep from throwing the remainder of his brunch in his companion's face.

"Fall into place? You think it was easy. I had to lie to a big time fed, Dan Logan. The guy who busted those terrorists on the Jersey docks a few years back. Who by the way, is a friend of Riley King. Do you have any idea what could have happened to me if he found out?"

"I never diminished your role in that, Richard. But the whole affair was orchestrated by Ginn. We all acted under his guidance and it worked. That's my point."

"Let me tell you something, Mr. City Councilman. Yes, it all did work out two years ago. But it's like the first war in Iraq. We left before the job was finished. So ISIS and all those other radicals could take over. Yeah, we diverted the feds and Riley King and the old lady. But we didn't wrap up the loose ends. We left a punch list. One by one, over the months that followed, we should have eliminated anyone who could do us harm."

"You mean murder them."

"You say you only ordered a sanction once. Well, my friend, that means you finally saw what needed to be done and you did it. You want to pussy-foot around? Okay, get the old bat to move to Arizona. I'm human, I don't like killing an old lady. But King? He's a loose cannon, ready to explode in our faces."

"A loose cannon that Moses seems to be befriending. Maybe it's part of his plan. Gain King's confidence so he'll get the Blankenship woman to back off. I don't understand this sense of urgency you have. Why can't we let things play out a little?"

"She's been buzzing around the building department. Going through old permits and records. What if she finds a link to us? You're sure that every little detail is cordoned off? And maybe if King wanted to stop her, he might not be able to. She can publish stuff instantly on her website. Are you willing to let fifty years of your life's work to go up in flames because you're too lily-livered to do what needs to be done?"

"I take your point. We're fully aware of the problem. But we need to discuss this at a full meeting, and I'd like Moses to be present."

"And what exactly will Ginn say to do differently? Nothing's changed except maybe he's in bed with the enemy now."

"He's been with us for forty years. He deserves the chance to explain himself."

"If he can. Good day, councilman."

With that, the captain stood, mock saluted his associate and stormed out, almost toppling a waitress struggling with a stack of dishes and a coffeepot.

The councilman dabbed the corners of his mouth. He took a sip of coffee, a bite of his omelet and acted as if nothing had happened. He extracted yesterday's Wall Street Journal from his leather briefcase and tried to focus on an article, but the events of the last few minutes kept disrupting his concentration.

Since their inception a half a century earlier, the men who comprised the Troika had changed, but in that time, only a handful had served. Four had passed away, one was near death in a Florida hospice.

There had been disagreements. What group could claim otherwise? But their singular purpose had always been to serve the city the best way three wise men deemed appropriate. Not every decision had worked out. They were still paying for their misplaced faith in Serpente. But at their core and to a man, they believed that the city was a better place, thanks to their ideals and efforts.

He couldn't sleep peacefully through the night, riven by his role in Serpente's death. He'd played golf with the man, considered him a friend. The Snake had crossed a bright line, betraying them out of greed and endangering the very people the Troika wanted to help. Even though that behavior could not be tolerated, killing Serpente was proving to be a bridge too far for the councilman. He wished there had been another way.

Now, one of their ranks was advocating murder merely for self preservation. Although he didn't consider himself a pacifist in his dotage, the councilman was starting to believe that the wisest course of action might be to disband the Troika and wipe all traces of their existence away.

His wife had died last year, and coupled with the Serpente sanction, his zeal for the group's causes and indeed life itself, had diminished. The daily grind was becoming a long slow march toward death and he wasn't enjoying the journey.

25

Stone pulled in around noon. I had some pre-formed frozen burgers that claimed to be ready within five minutes of hitting the business side of my Weber grill. Stone, hungry and tired from his ride, didn't complain that I hadn't gone to greater lengths, especially when I threw some nicely aged cheddar on top.

After I'd filled him in, he said, "So Riles, in the end, you trust this Moses Ginn? Hard to believe he's a paid assassin. I only know him from that time we played golf on the island. I really dug him. Seemed like a solid dude."

"I'm not sure. I mean, if he was determined to kill me, it would have been pretty easy to accomplish yesterday. Given how much Scotch we drank, he could have gotten me nice and mellow and boom! One less PI in Charlotte. And at that point in my cups, I wouldn't have cared."

"Damned decent of him. You still want me to talk to Charlene? She's playing in town tonight, then hitting the road for a bit. I looked it up. This might be our best shot."

"Did your homework, eh? Or should I say *my* homework."

"*Don't know much about history. Don't know much biology.* James Taylor or the original Sam Cooke version? Instant answer --- Cooke wins."

It took a moment for me to get the reference. I said, "Damn, man, between you and Ginn, I need a translator.

He speaks in parables, you talk song lyrics. No, I think I need to talk to Charlene myself, much as it pains me. Jaime's out of town working on movie stuff so she won't be giving me the third degree about it. I think if Charlene doesn't have me shot on sight, she might have some clues as to who these Troika guys are."

"Just trying to help, is all."

He looked a little hurt. He needed to feel useful and needed. I'd been in that same place the other night.

"I want you to come along, Ricky. Cover my six as they say in all those hip cop shows."

"Be happy to if you can spare another one of them burgers. I'm powerful hungry."

"Coming up, cowboy."

While Stone downed his second slab, I took Bosco out to do his business, although for some reason, I had to drag him outside. He wanted to sit next to Rick, just in case some of his cheeseburger happened to fall to the floor. It had been known to happen when Jaime wasn't around.

The Belk Theater is squarely in the center of Charlotte's compact uptown area. Comfortable seats, classy decor, excellent acoustics. It holds about twenty four hundred and hosts the Charlotte Symphony for a couple of dozen concerts a year. I don't know a lot about classical music, like whether the quality of the orchestra is up to world class standards. But whenever Jaime coaxes me into going, it's an enjoyable evening. I marvel at how this large ensemble meshes together so perfectly when I can't even play rudimentary guitar chords competently over the course of a three minute ditty.

Charlene was in the middle of her sound check. She was headlining tonight with her band: pedal steel, keyboard, violin, drummer and two barely dressed female backup singers. Roadies were flitting about, adjusting lights, tweaking amps and equalizing the audio console. Hours before the performance, Stone and I walked in through the front door. Standing off stage right was a muscular dude, SECURITY stenciled on his blue tee shirt, arms crossed like Mr. Clean. He actually resembled the figure on the disinfectant's label. Bulging biceps, shaved head, white eyebrows and goatee. His build alone would scare away most who might wish to accost the lady onstage, but would hardly be a deterrent to an old lover accompanied by an ex-Marine pal who happened by uninvited.

I nodded toward the big guy and Stone got the message --- occupy him while I attempt to get Charlene's attention. She was wearing boots, tight cut-off jeans and an ultra-snug tee shirt, shimmying to the beat and using a hand held microphone provocatively enough to evoke erotic memories of our time together. Although she played well, a guitar would block two of her most outstanding assets. She might strap one on for an acoustic number, but this number was kick-ass country/rock.

Rick was trying to engage the big man, perhaps using his insipid habit of quoting obscure lyrics, but the security guy was having none of the distraction. As I crept closer to the stage, he cast a wary eye in my direction. Stone tried to obstruct his view as surreptitiously as possible, but the big man was resolute in protecting his meal ticket. He brusquely shoved Rick aside.

My friend had just driven five hours to reach Charlotte from Hilton Head. He never said as much, but his all-nighter with the waitress probably hadn't ended well when he bailed on her at zero-dark-thirty. In short, he wasn't in the most tolerant of moods.

So when the roadie shoved him, he didn't turn the other cheek. He landed a haymaker to the bigger man's jaw. The man looked stunned but unimpressed, as if to say, "Is that all you got?" But Stone's reply was already on its way, a vicious knee to the groin. The man crumpled, moaning in pain, as Stone's forearm caught him flush on the chin for good measure.

"Teach you to lay your hand on a Marine, punk," I heard him say to the now prone figure.

The ruckus had created enough noise to attract the attention of the other roadies, who immediately dropped what they were doing and ran to the man's aid. Rick could handle himself, but would soon be outnumbered. Even me joining the fray would do little to even the odds, so I shouted, "Charlene."

She squinted through the stage lights toward the auditorium and recognized me. She shot me a dirty look and hesitated before yelling, "It's okay, boys. I know these two. Just a misunderstanding. Back to work."

Fortunately her magnificent set of lungs carried the day which made me think that she could do an acoustic set in this place without a microphone. The roadies followed her orders and backed off. Stone helped the moaning security guard to his wobbly feet and assisted him into a second row seat.

"No hard feelings, mate," he said to his victim. I walked to the stage and boosted myself up.

Charlene is a tall drink of water and with three inch heels on her boots, she can look at me eye to eye. There was nothing but disgust in those eyes as I approached, so a friendly air kiss was out of the question.

"I'm rehearsing, King. What do you want?" she said in a hushed voice that didn't carry over the proscenium.

"Lovely to see you, Charlene. We have a little problem we need to talk about."

"There is no *we*. Maybe *you* have a problem."

She was the one who had left me. This hostility was hardly warranted, unless she didn't appreciate Rick's attempt to de-ball her roadie.

"Look, I only need a couple of minutes. And the problem does involve you more than me. Has to do with friends of Johnny."

That worked. She looked skeptical, but clearly was curious how her ex-husband could reach out from the grave and cause her harm.

"Look, I'm in the middle of a sound check. Time is money. Can you sit out in the audience like a nice boy? Listen to a couple of songs we're rehearsing, then I'll see you backstage? Can you do that, Riley?"

"If refreshments are served, sure." I crow-hopped off the stage and parked myself in the first row, waiting to be entertained.

26

And entertained I was. Charlene's band ripped through two songs, stopping once during each when a discordant note or a false beat betrayed the tune's integrity. Her leadership was impressive. She gently but firmly called out the offending member and asked if there was anything she could do to fix the problem.

I didn't know the songs and since the sound man was still adjusting the mix, the vocals weren't always clear. The choruses, which usually contain the song's title, seemed to indicate they were entitled *There When I Needed You* and *Absolute Power Over Me*. They could have been about me, Serpente or her bass player, who clearly had something going on with her. I could tell by the way they looked at each other when she sang a come-hither line. Of course, it could just be good showmanship --- I doubt the Boss and the Big Man ever slept together.

The bassist was at least thirty years her junior. I am hardly in a position to knock that given Jaime's youth. His wiry right arm was sleeve tattooed, a limb of many colors. He had long, dirty blond hair and wore elaborate earrings. I couldn't see any other piercings but he was the type who had them in unknowable areas.

In short, she couldn't have rebounded with anyone more unlike me. I did feel a small pang of jealousy as they shared a microphone during one of the refrains. Despite my hopes that she would eat herself out of a career, she was fitter than ever. She looked great, closer to late thirties than her real age, which was fifty something.

After she was satisfied with the performance, the band began to break down. Stone sauntered over and asked, "What did you think?"

"Wish I was collecting some of her royalties. Sounded damn good to me."

"*She's so many women, he can't find the one who was his friend.*"

"Yeah Zevon, thanks. But she already told me to *hasten down the wind.*"

"She is a *credit to her gender. Worked you over good, just like a Waring blender.*"

I said, "I think she just nodded to me to meet her backstage. Wait here. I shouldn't be too long."

"Take your time. I think one of her backup singers digs me. I'm gonna check her out."

"Hopeless," was all I could mutter as I climbed the stage. The girl couldn't have been older than twenty five. Again, my own situation made it unconstitutional for me to censure him.

I followed Charlene through a maze of ropes, cables and rigging to her dressing room, where her bassist sat, arms crossed, unhappy to see me.

"Darlin', could you give us the room for a minute. I'll be right with ya." She put on her sweetest Southern drawl, an affectation she had never used on me. It worked onstage and in interview situations. The country music scene is very territorial and resents any faux rockers trying to slum in its genre.

The kid pouted but followed his mistress's orders.

"Nice lad. Have you adopted him legally or is that still pending?" I asked, after he left.

"You said this was business, King. If it ain't, I'll be calling security."

"I think security is in the bathroom, upchucking his lunch. You look great. And I'm no music critic but those songs were pretty great, too. I guess your writer's block is gone."

I don't know many women who are immune to flattery and Charlene was all woman. But I meant what I said, and it did soften her harsh facade.

"Thanks. You know what was going on with me. My suburban housewife life was too cush to give me anything to write about. But once I moved on, I had new experiences to draw from, some tough times. Maybe it's true that artists don't do their best work when they're happy."

Now she was flattering me? Two can play that game. Charlene is smart.

The room was small and spare --- normally it was used by the first violinist. The conductor and concertmaster had grander quarters, but there was nothing shabby about these digs. It was painted a pale green, there was a six foot quartz counter under a lighted makeup mirror. A small sink in the corner and a mini-fridge for refreshments, none of which were offered to me. There was a short closet pole on one side with enough room to hang three or four outfits. The first violinist just needed space for a lady's tux. Charlene's sartorial requirements were greater, more specific and far less formal.

She said, "So Riley, what's up? Need tickets for tonight?"

"Very funny, dear. I'll get right to it, I know you're busy. I tried emailing you and texting, left messages. Two days ago, I met with a man who said he represented a group he called the Troika. Ever hear of them?"

"No. Was he selling insurance?" She wasn't taking me seriously yet.

"In a way. Sorry I don't know of any other way to put it. He confessed to killing Johnny."

She was expecting a fastball and I had thrown her a slow curve. It took a lot to shock this girl, but I had. She tried to keep a poker face, but a stricken look passed her gorgeousness for a millisecond.

"And you believe him?"

"I do. I was willing to buy that the Russians did it. You were, too. But this guy made a pretty strong case."

She sat stone faced for a minute. "You know why we never talked much about it, Riley? We both thought that Johnny got what was coming to him. Maybe our lust made us look past all that jazz, I don't know."

"Was that all it was? Lust?"

"Come on, sugar. don't go there. That don't do either one of us any good, does it? You have a girlfriend living with you now, or so I've heard. I'm concentrating on my music. Let's let it go, all right?"

"Sure, if that's what you want. But here's our problem. Apparently this Troika considered the matter closed after they got rid of Johnny. They screwed you out of money by changing the will, but you never fought it. And Randee was willing to let it go when she found out about leaving all that money to Habitat. But now Randee has another bug up her ass that the buck didn't stop with Johnny. And somehow, the Troika knows and means to nip it in the bud."

Charlene had an open bottle of spring water on the counter and took a swig. "You know, I never really liked that old busybody, always sticking her nose in everybody's affairs. Did you know how she kept nagging me about you? *When's he going to give you a ring?* Shit like that.

She was your friend so I didn't say anything at the time, but she can be a real pain in the ass."

There is that side of Randee. Always has advice, mostly unsolicited. Never flinches when you tell her point blank it's none of her business. But her intrusions are well intended and her guidance is generally on target.

"Again, Charl, it's water under the bridge. The problem is that this Troika had Johnny killed. And now that Randee's poked the hornet's nest again, they think that you and I might be helping her."

"How? Johnny's in my rear view mirror, nine miles down a dirt road. And you said you weren't interested anymore."

"I wasn't. But if they move against Randee and you, I can't just let it be. They think you can identify them."

"How the hell can I identify them? What does this have to do with me?"

This constituted a direct threat to her just as her album was climbing the charts and sold out venues awaited her tour. She was about to cash in all the promissory notes her hard life had issued.

I said, "You lived with the man for years. You must know who his friends are. People he hung out with. The man who told me all this was the Troika's enforcer. He says he doesn't want to hurt anyone else and I think that's true. He threw out your name as a threat. I thought you should know."

She was cool again. "So can't you just tell the old lady to back off? Don't she listen to you?"

"I did tell her. But even if she does back off, what guarantee do we have that they won't just bide their time and then kill us at their leisure? They don't like loose ends and you and I are loose ends."

"What if something happens to Randee and you swear to this man that you've been scared into dropping the whole thing? That could be the end of it, no?"

I said, "And what if they pull a Corleone baptism and get us all at once? And even if I was willing to sacrifice Randee, which I'm not, we'd never be sure they'd just take our word for it and stop there. You willing to spend the rest of your life looking over your shoulder?"

Charlene cared about Charlene. That's how she had survived this long, given all the obstacles she had overcome. And now that her dreams were coming true, she was loath to sacrifice them for an old lady she didn't even like.

She said, "So what do we do, King?"

"I need to find out who these men are. That's our only chance of putting an end to this."

"And kill them?"

I said, "I need to bust this Troika somehow, or else we'll always feel like we're under siege, whether it's real or not."

"So what do you want from me now?"

"First off, you need to beef up your security. I didn't plan it this way, but if Rick Stone can put your guy down in ten seconds, trust me, their guy wouldn't take that long. Hire two more guys at least, armed."

"I'll get my tour manager right on it. Done."

She rose, assuming our conversation was over.

"Wait, Charl. You're not getting off that easy."

"What?"

"I have a short list of possible Troika members. I need you to look at it, maybe you can eliminate a couple or point me toward the ones you think are the bad guys. If I can get to even one of them, the others might cave."

She gave a quick look to the list Throat had provided and shook her head. None of the names were familiar to her as friends of Serpente's.

I said, "Can you think of anyone not on the list that he spoke of frequently? Or someone who called him often. Maybe left messages, that kind of thing?"

"He never really talked about friends. I kinda figured he didn't have any. And like I said, he kept his business dealings away from me. If we were to go out with another couple, it was always my friends. And to be honest sugar, he hated that. We always tussled if I set a dinner up without checking with him. After a while, I actually started to like it. Had more fun with my girls and their beaus without him around, sucking all the joy outta it."

"Think hard. No one comes to mind?"

"Give me a minute. I'm all sweaty and hot from the lights and I need to change."

In old movies, there always is a tall folding screen that the leading lady demurely stands behind to change outfits. Backlit and translucent, it reveals only a shapely silhouette. Frilly undergarments are tossed over the partition as she disrobes. The protagonist can only imagine what the ingénue looks like naked. He generally finds out by the third act. There was no such spot for privacy in this tiny room.

"You want me to wait outside?"

"Come on Riley, we're adults here. Nothing you haven't seen before."

Before I could protest, and I admit I didn't exactly leap to my feet to object, she pulled her tee shirt over her head. A quick shrug and her bra was off. Why was she doing this? She had made it clear that it was over between us. Was this exhibition a small *thank you* for caring enough to warn her? Or a cruel little tease, just to show me what I had been missing?

Charlene had pulled this stunt before. She had flashed Derek Davis while he was working on her master bath. She had given me a glimpse of the goodies way before we had become intimate. I'd like to say that I wasn't affected in the least by the display, but involuntary reflexes are just that.

There is always more going on with her than what meets the eye, although my eyes were met very nicely at the moment. I had to re-focus on the task at hand, however pleasant her attempts at distraction were.

I couldn't buy the fact that in all their time together, she couldn't give me even one name of her husband's associates. Pressing her further, she swore she couldn't think of anyone. As I left, she promised to be in touch if someone came to mind.

She must have known more than she was telling me. But what was her game? I hadn't a clue.

27

Stone and I were walking down Tryon Street in uptown Charlotte. The Audi was parked a couple blocks down on Church. The late summer day had turned cool and breezy, a preview of what we could expect on a daily basis a month from now. The streets weren't exactly bustling but there were plenty of pedestrians on this early Saturday evening, many of whom were nicely turned out young women, which kept Stone's head on a swivel.

"So what happened with Charlene, dog?" he asked.

"Not a lot, Ricky. I can fill you in over an early dinner at that Italian place just the other side of Fourth Street."

"No, that doesn't work for me. I need to get back to your place and pick up the Mustang. I'm coming back in for the concert. That babe I told you about in Charlene's band? She got me a house seat."

"A house *seat*? Did you ever think that I might want to catch the show, too?" I didn't, but this was a clear case of Rick's need to score overriding his sense of etiquette.

"Sorry, pal. I'll need some freedom to maneuver after the show, if you take my meaning. So let's head home so I can get duded up for tonight."

The man's libido never failed to astonish me. He had picked up a waitress the night before, and less than twelve hours later was on the make again. I dreaded the quotes from Ricky Nelson's *Travelling Man* that would be forthcoming if I pointed that out.

"If that's the way you want to play it. There's always pennant race baseball for me, I guess."

"*Oh, poor, poor pitiful you.*"

"Enough with the lyrics. You know what, Rick. I'll take you back to get your car. Just do me a favor. Whatever happens tonight, I don't want to hear about it."

"Fine."

We headed home in silence. I love Rick dearly but he just hasn't learned from his mistakes. As we drove off the inner beltway to 16 North, I reminded myself that Rick had been fired from a job that he'd held for twenty five years and had his second career as a golf pro shattered by the realization that his talent wasn't up to the task. He was now working at a low wattage station in a small market for wages, and wasn't thrilled about it. That was the excuse I accorded him for beating up the security guard. His outburst had actually worked in convincing Charlene that she needed extra protection.

I broke the stalemate first.

"Look Ricky, do what you want tonight but be careful. That security guy could have friends who might want to jump you in retaliation."

"I can handle it. And besides, I can keep an eye on Charlene tonight, too. Just in case your new best friend Ginn tries to pull something."

Funny how male jealousy works. Was I pissed at Stone for picking a cute backup singer over me tonight? A little. I figured we'd have a few drinks and watch some baseball. And now, if I read his tone correctly, he didn't appreciate that I may have found a kindred spirit in Moses Ginn. Someone who might supplant him.

I said, "I think she'll be okay. She always is."

"What about Randee? You want me to talk to her tomorrow, maybe reinforce what you told her about backing off?"

"Couldn't hurt. She's looking into auction laws for me. But you know Randee, she might start digging in bad places again. She can't sit still."

"I'll see if she'll do brunch tomorrow. I'm pretty good at reading the ladies, you know."

"Just don't make a move on Randee, horn dog. Although she's closer to your age than your little friend tonight."

"No way I'd do that, even with yours. Though I'll bet she was something in her day."

28

Sunday morning was one of those days when you love the fact that you are alive. Mornings like this are scarce as I've grown older. As a result, I appreciate them all the more. The sky was a bright Carolina blue; overnight rain had washed everything clean and taken the humidity away with it. It was pleasantly cool as I sat on my deck, the sun low on the eastern skyline over the lake. There was virtually no breeze off the water, which added to the serendipity of the day --- nothing to ruffle the Sunday Times. The coffee was good, Bosco was lying underfoot and all was right with the universe.

I had spoken with Jaime last night. Her business on the coast was going well and she thought she might be able to wrap it up in a few days. I said that it might be best for her to return to New Jersey for a bit and I would let her know when it was safe to come back here. She understood, but her disappointment was palpable.

I'd slept soundly after that. Fell off during the sixth inning of the Mets game, Bosco snoring quietly in Jaime's spot. I heard a sound around midnight, Stone coming back from the concert. No giggling or shushing, so it seemed he was alone.

I whipped up some buttermilk pancake batter which got Bosco excited. I told him I wasn't going to heat the griddle until Uncle Rick came out. He didn't seem to understand why I couldn't just make his pancake now and worry about Uncle Rick later. I was thinking the same thing.

Around nine, Rick stumbled out of the guest room, clearly hung over.

"You look like shit, Stone."

"Top of the morning to you, too." His voice was an octave lower than normal.

"You okay? Coffee's on, pancakes and bacon ready in ten minutes."

"Don't think I can eat right now. Coffee's enough."

At fifty six, Rick could pass for forty most days. This morning, every year showed and then some. His dark blonde hair had been thinning for years, and he had tried every potion and treatment available to slow its recession. Between the various regimes and some artful styling, he always looked well coiffed. But today, absent the normal attention, areas of scalp peeked through. The corners of his eyes were a delta of deepening lines, angry dark crescents underlining the bloodshot whites.

"So how was the concert?"

"I spent a lot of it wondering who you'd be better off with. Jaime is making big bucks as an agent, but damn, Charlene has got to be raking it in. And movies and television can't be far behind. She's got the tits and ass of a twenty year old. Not that Jaime isn't fine looking and I know Charlene's a bad lady, but she is a goddess, man."

"You know Rick, on this fine morning, I look at it this way: I've been privileged to have been intimately involved with both of them."

"You know King, if I wasn't already nauseous, hearing you say that would have me praying to the porcelain god."

"Sorry. Dare I ask, how did it go after the show?"

"Not so good."

He looked sullen, as he usually did when dealing with rejection. Although I wasn't interested in the gory details, maybe relating it aloud would help.

I said, "What happened? I thought that backup singer was hot for you."

"You're about the only person in the world I'd tell this to."

He took a deep drag on the steaming mug. "She left a ticket and backstage pass for me. After the show, we go for drinks at Wooden Vine. First thing she tells me is that she's originally from Jersey and that her dad and granddad are big fans of mine. Asks me to take a selfie with her, and then she sends it to them. That was bad enough, but after a couple of drinks, I suggested we head back to her hotel and well, you know, get it on."

"I hope you put it a bit more delicately than that."

"Whatever. You know what she said? She made that noise that these young chicks make. Like *Ewwww*. Said it would be like sleeping with her grandfather. Came right out and said it. Then her boyfriend shows up. Charlene's drummer. Skinny little wimpy shit, all tatted up. They split for a night of frolic, leaving me with the tab and a case of blue balls."

"Well, if it makes you feel better, Charlene's doing the bass player."

"This shit sounds like Fleetwood Mac in the seventies, man. God damn Riles, I looked in the mirror this morning and I saw an old man. I saw my dad. What happened?"

"*Time Waits for No One*. What Stones album was that on? At least, you look better than Keith and Mick these days."

"You know, I'm fucking lost. Lousy job, no woman. Remember that chick I was seeing in Jersey, Cindy?"

"The college student? Going to Ocean Community?"

"Yeah. I called her the other night. I thought I might fly her down for a few nights of frolic, for old times sake. Thanked me for the invite but declined. She's got a boyfriend now, getting married next spring."

"Look Rick, maybe it's time you stopped trying to nail everything that walks and start looking for something a little more permanent."

"I had that with Lisa. Didn't work out so well."

"I get it, she broke your heart. But that was years ago. You just got to stop looking at twenty-somethings and aim a little higher."

"You giving me advice? That's a laugh. Charlene dumped you for her career. Same as Lisa. And you respond by shacking up with a babe over ten years younger than you. Some role model you are."

On another morning, the nerve he touched would have spawned a harsh reaction. But given my function as shrink for him now, I couldn't let what he said get to me.

He gave me a rueful smile. "Sorry man, I know you've had your share of rough rides, too."

I said, "What's the old saying? Careful what you wish for? A few days ago, I was just counting the days until I could sell this place and move down to Hilton Head to enjoy a quiet life. Work only when I feel like it. Semi-retired. Now this Serpente thing comes along and it makes me feel young again, not old and in the way. It may kill me, but at least I feel alive."

"Shit man, if that works for you, great. But *it ain't me, babe*. I don't care what they say about sixty being the new forty, no big radio station is going to hire me at my age. My demos skew too old, is what they'll tell me. No one wants to hear stories of Mays and Mantle or Jim Brown or even Joe Montana. All they want are these punks playing the game now."

"Come on, it can't be that bad. You've got a job that at least keeps you busy and you love working for Ted. He leaves you alone and you can do whatever you want on the air."

"Yeah, there's that. But when I'm with a new woman, especially a young one, I feel like I can live forever. Like I still matter."

"Warren Beatty said that in *Shampoo*. Can't you come up with anything original?"

He sighed. "Taking a bullet for you and Jaime, man. That's all most people will remember about me. Rick Stone, he almost died saving a friend. Nothing else. But even that has a shelf life. Last night, that girl laughed at me. She laughed, Riles."

Even though we know better, all of us think that we are as attractive to the opposite sex as we were in our heyday. We're aware of our crow's feet, the gray hairs, soft bellies but the decline is gradual, like the slow erosion of a shoreline. Then one day we see a new photograph and wonder who the old man is. A bad angle, we tell ourselves.

Then we learn to avoid the camera entirely, because it seems they're all bad angles. The ads for hearing amplifiers, wrinkle serums and plastic surgeons that we once scoffed at --- now we wonder if they really work. We take it out on our mates. We blame them for allowing us to deteriorate before their eyes. We can't understand why they are still with us when they remain as beautiful as they were the day we first met.

I left Rick to his contemplation while I made breakfast. He attacked the food with his usual vigor, even though he had told me he wasn't hungry. Resistance is futile when it comes to my pancakes.

Changing the subject to keep from diving further into mortality issues, I said, "Hey, did you ever speak with Randee? You were going to try to meet her for brunch."

"Jeez, I almost forgot. I called her twice, left messages. Emailed. No reply."

"That's not like her. Let's try her again."

I went back to the kitchen to fetch my phone. Bosco was sitting at attention, staring intently at the island where I had placed his pancake to cool. I broke off a few pieces and put them in his dish. They vanished faster than a line of coke at a Hollywood party.

Randee was on my speed dial. It rang several times and then someone answered. Someone who was not Randee.

"Hello. I'm sorry if I misdialed. I'm calling for Randee Blankenship."

The female voice on the other end sounded Southern. Older. "Who's calling?"

"My name is Riley King. I'm a friend. Who am I speaking with?"

"Mr. King. I'm sorry I didn't call you last night. I'm at Carolinas Medical Center. I'm afraid there's been a ghastly accident."

29

Randee had no next of kin listed. No mention of any children or other blood relatives. The woman on the phone, a close friend of Randee's, told me that there had been an accident involving a firearm. The police had been notified. Randee was in critical but stable condition and wouldn't be able to speak for several days. I relayed all of this to Stone and he was enraged.

He said, "All right, let's go after the bastards now. I'm locked and loaded and ready."

"Go after who exactly?"

"How about we start with your pal Ginn?"

"How about you stop and breathe for a minute? First off, what if whatever happened really was an accident? Second, I have no idea where Ginn lives and I'm guessing a full frontal assault on the Nat might be overkill."

Stone shot me an incredulous look. "I can't believe you. Your friend, *an old lady* gets shot and you want to do nothing? You're reacting like someone told you your pedicure appointment will be ten minutes late. What the hell?"

I let him fume for a second. I *was* plenty shaken. But blindly striking out at the first thing that gets in the way is a losing strategy. Ask George Bush.

"Rick, all we know was that it was a gunshot injury. By law, it had to be reported to the cops. Let me call Shabielski, see what he can find out."

"You do that. Meanwhile, I'll get in touch with my friends Mr. Smith and Mr. Wesson."

I dialed Shabielski. As I told him about Randee, I heard the click of keystrokes.

"Got it, mate. Here it is, I was flagged on this one. I put in a global request to be notified of any activity involving you or Blankenship."

"There's a report already?"

"Yeppur. Incident was called in at 6:50 last night. Gun club in Cornelius. Subject was taking a concealed weapons class. Gun exploded in her face. Jesus."

"Wait a minute. Her gun exploded? She wasn't shot?"

"That's what the report says. They're taught care and cleaning of the weapons at this facility. I know it well, it's a legit operation. The instructor says she worked on it herself. She must have fucked up."

"They don't check the gun after the students work on it?"

"Sure they do. Liability must be through the roof so they can't afford accidents like this. Yeah, says here that she cleaned and oiled it yesterday, instructor inspected and approved the work. Was stored overnight in her locker. She arrived at 6:30 last night. Geared up, took the gun to the range and that's when it happened. Severe wounds to head and face. My God, she might lose an eye. I'm sorry, Riles."

The anger was welling up now and like Stone, I wanted to lash out at someone. Ginn *was* the most likely candidate. Maybe the night of drinking was intended to put me at ease, to let my guard down. I should have arranged protection for Randee, whether she wanted it or not. Although what could a bodyguard have done about an exploding handgun?

I said, "This was no accident. I told you I was warned the other day, and now they've followed through."

"Whoa there, buckaroo. I admit this looks bad, but I know the officer who wrote this. He knows a lot about guns. He bagged what was left of the weapon and sent it to our forensic guys, but said in his notes that he's seen things like this happen."

He paraphrased the report for me as he read it. "The owner of the place told him that Randee asked for a cheap gun, nothing fancy. He pointed her toward a pawn shop in Mooresville. She bought an old gun he didn't think was so good, but she insisted on using it. He told his guys to take extra care before clearing it for use each time. Lots of cops go up there to shoot. The owner is an ex-cop himself, runs a clean operation."

"So what are you saying? You think this *could* be an accident?"

"Only that it's possible. You were kind of sly the other day about this guy who warned you about Randee. Are you ready to give me a name so I can follow up or are you determined to go off half assed on your own?"

"I don't know. Let me think about it."

"Okay pal, but I'm warning you, no vigilante shit. Folks tend to get killed around you, case you hadn't noticed. I know you still have friends in the bureau but this happened on my turf. Chief would be thinking about nailing you for obstruction already since you told me something like this might be coming. You withheld information. I'm just sayin'."

"Peter, I can't say anything for sure yet. Like you say, this could just be a horrible coincidence."

"Riley, I know you well enough to know when you're shitting me. You help me, I'll help you, that's how it works."

"I know. I need to check out a few things on my own first, then I promise, I'll bring you in."

"You'd better. I don't want the next report they flag me on to be about a dead PI. Take care of yourself, King. Sounds like you're playing in the big leagues."

30

Call me an idiot, but I still had a hard time believing that Moses Ginn was deceiving me. The way he played with Bosco, the evening of drinks, ribs, and stories had me liking the guy. The other side was that he had admitted to killing Serpente. I needed to be convinced that Ginn was a malevolent force before taking him on.

Rick was still itching for action but I convinced him to take Bosco out for me while I made a couple of calls to determine our next move. He reluctantly agreed and said he'd be back in ten minutes.

It was only one call. Moses Ginn.

"Hello there, you son of a bitch," was my opening.

"King? How'd you get this number?"

"Maybe you'll think twice about leaving your phone on the table when you get up to take a piss."

"Number be changed 'fore I hang up, which I'm fixing to do now."

"My my, aren't we touchy this morning. Just wanted to let you know I'll be coming for you after what you did to Blankenship. Fair warning."

"Hold on. What the fuck you talking about?"

I expected no less. Ginn was old school. His credo would be if his wife found him in bed with another woman, he'd say he had no idea how she got there, must have snuck in while he was asleep.

"You know what I'm talking about. Blankenship's accident. Don't tell me you don't know what happened, since you orchestrated it."

"Listen, motherfucker, I wanted something to happen to the old bat, it would. I'm sure you ain't stupid enough to think I couldn't have blown you away if I wanted to the other night. You wasn't exactly in any condition to defend yourself. Now tell me what you talking about."

If he was lying, he was doing a good job of it.

"Randee had an accident at a shooting range in Cornelius. Gun blew up in her face. How did you manage that?"

"I didn't. First I'm hearing of it. Thought you told me you had her under control."

"I thought we had a truce, you and me. Guess I'm just a fool, aren't I, Moses?"

Silence on the other end.

"You still there?"

"I'm here. Listen to me, King. Whatever happened, I ain't got nothing to do with it. I told you there was new blood in the group. Not saying he was behind this, but it's possible, maybe even probable. If that's so, you let me handle it."

"Fool me once, shame on you."

"I know the rest. Shut your mouth. I got no truck with killing old ladies. You believe that or not. Up to you."

"There's one thing you can do to convince me. And only one thing."

"What's that?"

"You keep saying *new blood*. Give me a name."

Quiet again for a beat. "I do that, I be signing my own death warrant. You take a swing and miss, he be after me next. I told you, let me handle it."

"Not good enough."

"All I got. She dead, the old lady?"

"Nice of you to ask. No. But she's out of commission. Isn't that your M.O.? Stop short of killing when you can?"

"Some things be worse than killing. You say gun blew up in her face. Old lady playing with gun, don't know what the fuck she doing. Could be an accident."

"Reasonable doubt. Good job, Ginn. Exactly what the cops will say. I'm sure you think you didn't leave a trail they can follow up on. But I have friends. My previous employer in Washington. They have ways to find evidence that local cops can't even conceive of. You deny all you want. They can get you. Problem for you is, I'll get you first."

"Ain't scared of you, man. I just saying for your own good, even if you do get lucky and ace me, that don't eliminate your problem. You just be taking out somebody who can help you. But you do what you have to do and I'll do the same."

I wasn't going to come right out and tell him, but I was buying his rap. He could have just said that Randee's accident was a shot across the bow and I was next. He could have eliminated me two nights ago if he had a mind to. Maybe he was caught up in this web and was looking for a way out. Or maybe he was so smart that by proclaiming his innocence, he could lure me into another false sense of security and then strike.

"Ginn, I'd like to believe you, really I would. But I need more than just *trust me* here. Give me something solid and I'll think about it. No promises, but failing that, it's mano a mano."

"Give me the day. I go to work on this. Find out what I can. Then you and me meet up this evening. Come up with a plan then. Or if not, shake hands and come out fighting."

"This gets settled tonight, one way or the other. You keep this number active. I'll call you with a time and place."

I clicked off before he could answer. By agreeing to meet with him at all, it was highly possible I'd be walking into a trap. But if I could pick the time and place, I'd hold the upper hand. I'd bring Stone to cover me, maybe even Shabielski, off book.

Ginn would be showing good faith if he came alone. He'd be trusting that I wouldn't be setting him up. But if he brings reinforcements, tonight might turn into *The Gunfight at the OK Corral.*

31

MOSES GINN

Ginn drove a Mercedes Benz. Not a new one, although he could afford to. In keeping with his masquerade as a lowly clubhouse attendant, he opted for a 1983 380 SL Roadster. He'd always wanted one but didn't have the means back when they were new. The '80s versions of the two-seater were not in demand by collectors --- they preferred the sleeker models from a decade or two earlier. His could be had for under ten grand. But Ginn had always been entranced by the squared off look of the convertible he now drove. Although its original configuration did not offer modern conveniences like navigation, backup camera and Bluetooth, he'd made friends at a custom shop that incorporated aftermarket technology seamlessly into the classic dash. It gave him the best of both worlds --- the traditional look he prized with all the modern accoutrements.

With the Motown channel playing softly on his satellite radio, he rehearsed his lines aloud. Driving alone, he often talked to himself while trying to put words to his feelings, which didn't always come naturally to him. He was about to plead his case and he wouldn't be accorded another attempt if he failed to be convincing.

The city councilman was expecting him. The gates of the estate swung open as he pulled up. He left the Merc on the circular drive at the front entry. The grand residence was a mini-version of the Nat's clubhouse, although it is hard to describe an 8,000 square foot mansion as mini. Nothing about it was small.

For just a man and his wife in their late seventies, the sheer size was overpowering. They had justified it by telling themselves they needed its splendor for the lavish parties they threw to hail each upcoming season. In realty, the parties were seen as obligatory by their guests and were less well attended as the years passed. But it gave them something to spend their money on and look forward to planning, on a quarterly basis.

Most of the time it was just the two of them in residence with their housekeeper, and they rarely saw each other except for meals. They had separate bedchambers and hardly ever intruded on each others' space. She did charity work, much of which was spent in luncheon meetings with her peers.

But despite their disparate ways, when she died a year ago after a short bout with lymphoma, he was devastated and hadn't recovered. He expected he never would.

He was still on the city council, up for re-election every two years. But since participation in these off year contests was slight, just rallying his friends and cronies was more than enough to ensure another term. The council met infrequently and attendance was not considered mandatory unless there was a critical vote. Most issues had already been settled before they reached the floor.

So he spent much more time at the Nat, working his influence behind the scenes rather than in council meetings. He'd made a tentative tee time for a late afternoon nine with some political friends who eagerly accepted his invitation to play the pristine layout. It was just short of noon when Ginn arrived, but the man was already decked out for the links --- blood red pants, navy sweater vest over a long sleeve crimson polo. A plaid snap brim newsboy cap completed the ensemble.

"Welcome, Mo," he said, upon opening the splendid front door. No one else called him Mo, but Ginn didn't take offense at what the older man viewed as a term of endearment. Since no one was around to overhear, they could speak on equal terms. "I'm headed for the club in a couple of hours. What's so urgent that you had to drive out here?"

Ginn accepted the offered hand for a perfunctory shake. He never would have been so presumptuous as to offer his first.

"I didn't want to meet at the club, sir. Some things best be discussed in private."

"Of course. I had Mimosas with brunch and still have the fixings. May I interest you in one?"

"Sure." Ginn had never seen the man sloppy drunk, but since his wife had passed, he always seemed to have a drink in his hand. The councilman led him into the study, a generously proportioned room with floor to ceiling bookcases on two sides, straining to accommodate an immense collection of classic literature and conservative political philosophy. The old man was a Civil War buff --- swords, hats and other relics of the conflict were framed and mounted under glass on the remaining walls. Unlike many, Ginn took no offense at this Confederate symbolism. He rationalized that his host admired the bravery and devotion of the gray army, not the cause they fought for.

A tea cart was stationed next to a substantial oak desk, a champagne bottle protruding from a silver ice bucket. A clear decanter of fresh orange juice, elegant stemware at the ready. The ingredients were mixed and poured, glasses raised.

The councilman said, "Your call, Mo. What shall we toast?"

"To honor and clarity."

"Well said."

Ginn wasn't much for champagne but he could discern quality and this was a superior vintage. He never quite understood why anyone would mix expensive alcohol with a lesser beverage. He drank his single malt neat or on the rocks, so as not to dilute its essence.

"I'm sorry to bust in on your weekend sir, but I had to find out about last night. I wasn't in the loop and I'm not understanding why?"

The councilman cupped a palm to his ear. "Exactly what are you referring to?"

On the drive over, Moses had decided to feed it to him piecemeal to see what the man might volunteer.

"I'm talking what happened to Randee Blankenship," Ginn said.

"Moses, you have the advantage of me. What happened to the lady?"

"You don't know?"

The man's eyes flitted from their customary heavy-lidded glaze to the closest he could come to showing annoyance. "Damn it man, I asked you a question. What happened?"

He had never heard the councilman's voice raised, even when debating a contentious topic with his colleagues or constituents. This minor outburst was not staged.

"She had an accident at a shooting range. She's in a coma."

The man turned pale and backed away, body language revealing more than words. He retreated to his desk and folded himself awkwardly into the chair. For a moment, Ginn feared he was suffering a stroke.

"Oh my god, the bastard did it. He really did it".

Ginn let it sit for a moment. "The woman's not dead, at least not yet. But she could be. I always been consulted on these things and I wasn't this time. Where's that coming from?"

The councilman might have been a wax figure for all the expression he displayed. He arose from behind the desk, advanced toward Ginn and placed a paternal hand on his shoulder.

"Moses, if you'll be so kind. Please wait in the foyer. I need to make a call."

Ginn did as he was told, and the man closed the heavy doors to his sanctuary behind him. The councilman was calling another member of the Troika.

But which one? The cop or the lawyer? Depending on who it was, Ginn had just set events into motion that could either be game-changing or make him a dead man. The odds were fifty fifty.

32

Dan Logan is my best friend at the FBI and I couldn't have hitched my wagon to a greater star. We were rookies together a lifetime ago. Logan has always been extremely deft at bureaucratic politics, an area at which I was an abject failure. I washed out after ten years, but Logan patiently put up with all the crap I couldn't stomach and advanced up the ladder. Then he broke a complicated terrorist case on the Jersey docks and as a result, became the bureau's much lauded golden boy. I helped him on that one, and he never forgot.

His interventions from on high have saved my bacon more than once. For my part, I repay him with small errands and favors. I've used Jaime's media influence to score him tickets to Broadway opening nights and the occasional must-see sporting event. But since he has risen to agent-in-charge of the New York office, he rarely needs my help obtaining anything he desires.

It rubs me the wrong way to ask for aid when I can't reciprocate in kind, and Logan holds that over my head at every opportunity when our balance sheet is leaning too far in his direction. His jibes are friendly and he never denies me when it's important, but I still don't like being in arrears.

He was at home, watching the Giants play the Eagles in Philly when I called. I was fortunate that the game wasn't being played in New Jersey, or he'd be amongst the noisy throng rooting for the locals. As it was, it was difficult to command his full attention with the game blaring in the background.

He said, "Hey, King. Long time no speak, amigo. Giants have it on the Eagles' twenty two, third and four. Eli back to throw. Incomplete. Shit."

"Bob Costas has nothing to worry about from you. Hello, Daniel."

"I wasn't auditioning. Just thought you'd like to know how a real team is doing, not that horseshit Charlotte team that doesn't even take the name of the city."

"That's too bad because the Giants are here to play the Panthers in December and I was going to offer you tickets but obviously you've already put that in the win column so I won't bother. And speaking of names, don't the New York Giants play in New Jersey?"

"Wow. Fake field goal. Lateral to Beckham. First down. Great call. What did you say about December tickets?"

"Just that if you play your cards right and stop insulting my adopted city, you might get to see your beloved Giants lose to our squad in person."

"Okay, end of the first quarter. Giants seven, Cheese steaks nothing. I'm listening. What's up?"

This is the first time in recorded history that I was actually happy that the NFL has what seems like five minute commercial breaks between quarters. And if I really get lucky, the Giants will score on the next play and I'll have Logan's attention for another five.

"Dan, remember that Serpente case back a couple years? Russian guy, builder scamming low income housing? You guys looked into it. Said it was a mob hit and left it there?"

"Remember it well. And then you shacked up with the guy's ex. The ever so lovely Charlene Jones. Until she got wise and dumped your young ass. How's Jaime, by the way? She onto you yet?"

"You're a laugh riot today. Seriously, you told me that these Russian hit men are almost impossible to trace. How strong was your evidence at the time or did you just shunt it off to the locals?"

"We had a decent circumstantial case. Airline tickets, car rental receipts. We big-footed the locals and got the slugs. Matched the weapon of choice for the guy we liked for it although we didn't have the actual piece used in the shooting. Back then anyway."

"What do you mean *back then anyway*?"

"That's right. You and I haven't talked in a few months."

"You have my number too, pal. Phone works in both directions. But what did you mean by *back then*?"

"We busted a Ruskie bastard on another hit. Creep got sloppy and we nailed him. He was old school. Liked to use the same gun. Didn't chuck it into the East River like the younger generation does."

He held his hand over the phone and barked out something to his wife about refilling his bowl of Doritos.

"Actually Riles, I should have called and let you know. Thought you'd be curious. Once we had him dead to rights, he copped to the Charlotte killing as well. We went back and tested the ballistics and the slugs matched."

Well, knock me over with a feather. How had the Troika managed that?

"King, you there? What's the matter?"

"Nothing. It's just that I saw Charlene yesterday and it brought back some memories. You know, right after the shooting, I guess our hormones were working overtime and we didn't really worry about who shot Serpente, just happy that he was gone. Seemed at the time, you guys had the same attitude. One less bad guy to worry about."

"Wasn't my call but it did probably have low priority. Anyway, it's *case closed* now. Of course, the hitter isn't going to be charged with that one. He's a lifer without parole so no need to waste money piling on. And truth be told, I'd lay odds that the Russkies will silence him in the pokey before he spills any more of their secrets."

"And you're satisfied with the chain of evidence on the slugs?"

"Yeah, local guy with the lead on the case was very cooperative, was totally convinced it was the Russian mafiya. What the hell was his name? Oh yeah, Tucker. Richard Tucker. I remember because my Giants had two Tuckers, a tight end Bob Tucker and Tucker Frederickson. You know, I really should call him and let him know we got the guy. I'm sure he'd appreciate it."

"Hey, do me a favor and hold off on that."

An idea was forming and I didn't like where it was leading me.

Logan said, "No problem. May I ask why, Sherlock?"

"I'm working on something. Can't say what it is yet but when I have something stronger, I'll read you in."

"Ah, Riley King, International Man of Mystery. Well sport, Giants are on the five, first and goal. If there's nothing urgent you need to discuss now, I'll be in the office tomorrow."

"Plan on being in Charlotte second week of December, Logan. Bring the wife. You'll need consolation after Cam Newton whips your ass."

33

"You're serious? You're not going to go to the hospital?"

Stone was angry again, disagreeing with everything I proposed. He couldn't fathom why I wasn't at least willing to keep vigil at Randee's bedside at Carolinas Medical Center.

"Rick, she can't talk. She's heavily sedated. The best thing for her now is rest. And the best thing I can do is to find out who did this to her. But you're right. Someone should be there for her. You go to the hospital. You'll be a great comfort. And if whoever did this decides to finish the job, there's no one I'd rather have looking out for her than you."

"That's all well and good but where are you going to be? And what about this Ginn character?"

"I spoke to him. He denied it of course, and this doesn't fit his M.O. He volunteered to help, matter of fact. I'd rather have him on our side than not, so I'm going to believe him for now, until it proves otherwise. Maybe I'll go up to that shooting range and see what I can find out there. I'm not sure exactly where I'll be but I'll keep you posted. Now, off with you."

Stone said, "I hope he hasn't suckered you in. You might be underestimating that old black dude. Like I did on the golf course and he dusted me but good. All right, keep me posted. I'll call you when I know more about Randee."

He left and I dialed Shabielski again. Got his voicemail. He's normally good about getting back to me so I just told him to call back ASAP, it was important.

Rick had been gone for less than a minute when he came storming back into the kitchen.

"Damn it, Riles, the Mustang has a flat. That cheap piece of shit donut they give you is worthless. You have some kind of inflator so I can get to the nearest tire place?"

I said, "They might not be open on Sunday and even if they are, it'll take time. Here, take the Audi. I've got the MDX in the garage. I can use that today if I need transport. Haven't driven it in a while and it could use a little exercise."

I detached the Audi fob from my house keys and handed it to him. "And just because Charlotte is the home of NASCAR, don't think you're Dale Earnhardt Jr. and start racing with my baby. Take care of her."

"I will. And I'll take care of Randee."

I looked out my front window and watched in horror as he patched out of the driveway. I couldn't see his expression, but I could picture him laughing his ass off at the unsightly tread marks. His shiny red Mustang would pay the price for his frivolity.

I fired up the laptop. The shooting range had a website and I wanted to find out as much as I could about the owner before charging in.

My cell buzzed. Stone. He'd been gone less than five minutes. I hoped it wasn't car trouble on top of everything else. But he probably was just calling to taunt me about the driveway. *Boys will be boys.* I contemplated letting it go to voice mail but on the slightest chance that he had something important to tell me, I picked up.

"Riles..."

His voice sounded distant and weak.

"I'm sorry. I had an accident."
"Rick. Rick? Are you okay? Can you hear me?"
I was talking to myself. The line was dead.

34

I was worried that the battery on the MDX might have run down from disuse but it roared to life with a throaty growl. My phone instantly synced and I voice-dialed 911 as I sped down my driveway only a slight bit slower than Stone had mere minutes before.

Since there is only one two lane country road for a couple of miles outside my cul-de-sac, the accident had to have occurred on it. If he was still acting like a newly licensed teenager, there was one particularly sharp curve that even a NASCAR driver would have trouble negotiating faster than forty five. I told the 911 operator to send EMS there.

Two miles from my front porch, the Audi lay a smoking rubble, its front end crushed against a large maple. The airbags had deployed and Stone was slumped over on the driver's side. There was blood on his face.

I pulled a tire iron from the Acura's toolkit and forced open the door, which was jammed tight from the impact. Stone's body was limp as I detached his seatbelt and pulled him from the wreckage as delicately as I could. The blood was coming from a cut above his left eyebrow, but other than that, there was no visible damage. The angry gash must have been caused by something loose in the cockpit that had become a projectile. Or maybe the recalled but still unrepaired Takata airbags.

I redialed 911 and gave the exact location. I laid Rick down in the tall grass a hundred feet or so from the wreck. I didn't expect the car to explode like the ones you see in the movies but I wasn't about to take any chances.

I was going about all of this robotically, not thinking, merely reacting to the specific task before me. The accident had occurred nowhere near the sharp curve and unless he was texting or doing something equally distracting, there was no reason he should have veered off the macadam at the particular spot. The front tires were damaged beyond recognition so I couldn't tell if one of them had blown out and caused the vehicle to swerve.

Stone began to stir and his eyes opened slowly. "Chicken," he said in a furry voice.

"What? Are you okay? You have a cut on your forehead, but far as I can tell, you're not bleeding anywhere else. Does it feel like anything's broken?"

"Playing chicken with a truck. You always lose."

I couldn't expect him to make sense after what had happened, but this was crazy. On the way to the hospital, he was playing chicken with a truck?

"Talk to me, Stone. Tell me what hurts."

"Everything. Damned airbag knocked the shit out of me. Might've busted a rib. Can't tell."

"Looks like you hit that tree pretty hard. What happened?"

"Told you. A pickup truck. Big white one. Veered right in front of me. Like on purpose."

The EMS vehicle came careening around the bend, spotted us and screeched to a halt. Two men in white uniforms rushed out, medical bags in hand. They pushed me aside and tended to Stone, who was becoming more alert by the second.

There were lots of benign explanations. A truck lost control due to a mechanical glitch. The driver was distracted --- texting, tuning the radio, on the receiving end of oral sex. But anyone with half a conscience would have stopped and offered help, unless they were afraid that they'd be blamed for what had happened.

Maybe it was a kid who had "borrowed" the truck from a parent. Or someone with a history of vehicular infractions, scared that one more might be the tipping point. Someone driving impaired who might be facing vehicular manslaughter charges if Stone's injuries were serious.

Why was I coming up with excuses and tortured explanations for what was clearly an attack from the Troika? I was not eager to take on an organization that had no scruples about eliminating an old lady out to do good. As Ginn had suggested, this was likely the work of a rogue actor within the group. But why go after Stone?

One of the EMS guys stood up, looked around and approached me. "You know this man?"

"Yes, he's a friend. He borrowed my car to visit someone in the hospital. How is he?"

"Shaken up, obviously. We bandaged up the forehead, bled like the dickens but it's not deep. Not to scare you sir, but in these situations there's a chance of internal bleeding or a concussion. We're going to load him up and run him over to Lake Norman Medical. That's the closest ER. You want to follow us?"

"Yes."

As they prepared him for the trip, I could hear Stone protesting that he was all right and didn't need any hospital. He allowed the medics to strap him onto a stretcher, a wheeled gurney being impractical over the uneven terrain. I told him I'd be right behind.

I had to face up to the inconvenient truth. What happened to Rick was no accident. Someone had planned this. Was my heads-up to Moses Ginn in any way responsible? Had he accelerated his own timetable of attack or had someone in the Troika betrayed him? It seemed that such a well timed attack could not have been spur of the moment, there had to be some malice aforethought.

The other thought was something I knew all along. The assault had been directed toward my car, not Rick's. He just happened to be driving the Audi instead of me.

This act of naked aggression was aimed at Riley King as surely as if it had been a bullet. If there was still any ambivalence regarding Randee's misfortune, there was no mistaking this message.

It was a formal declaration of war.

35

THE TROIKA

The hastily called meeting took place in a quiet corner of the men's locker room. Moses Ginn was not invited. The city councilman spoke first, using formal language he might employ in a speech to his constituents.

"It's been brought to my attention that Randee Blankenship suffered an unfortunate accident last night. And my law enforcement sources inform me that a vehicle registered to Riley King was involved in a serious traffic mishap earlier this afternoon."

The cop knew that he was the one on the hot seat and attempted to reverse the energy. "I was at home on my only day off. This couldn't have waited?"

The politician said, "No, it couldn't. We've always had a code of ethics. There was to be no activity of this nature unless it was approved by a unanimous vote. I never agreed to any of this."

He let that sit, expecting a justification. Instead the cop held up his palms in a gesture of helplessness.

"What makes you think that either of us had anything to do with this? Far as I know from my law enforcement sources, which trump yours because I *am* law enforcement, the old lady met with an unfortunate accident with a handgun she obviously wasn't qualified to be using."

"And King's car?"

"Lincoln County isn't in my jurisdiction. I can reach out to my colleagues there and find out exactly what happened. I don't see why that can't wait until tomorrow."

"So you're denying any involvement? Just so you know, I called our esteemed counselor and made him aware of our conversation at breakfast yesterday. He was the one who suggested we meet."

The policeman showed no reaction. "I don't know what you want me to say. Either of you. It seems that fate has intervened in our favor. Do we know if the old crone is dead? And you said that King's car was involved. What about King himself? Dead, injured?"

The attorney had been staying on the sidelines, as if he was the arbiter, still deciding whose side to take. He finally spoke. "All right Dick, to be clear, you're saying that you had nothing to do with this. It's just good fortune as far as you're concerned."

The councilman was too incensed to hold his tongue. "Excuse me, but it strains credibility that you would have told me yesterday that we need to act and then voila! --- these two related *accidents*."

The cop said, "As Jeb Bush once said, shit happens."

"I'm glad you're taking this so casually because I can assure you I'm not." His voice rose unmindful of being overheard. The attorney shot him a quick frown, which caused him to back off slightly. "I do want to be fair though, if you can provide an alternative explanation."

The police captain said, "Matter of fact, I can. I'm no babe in the woods, gentlemen. I knew that after our little chat yesterday, you'd suspect that I engineered these events. You really think I'd be stupid enough to follow through on my own when you so clearly disapproved? I'll tell you what I think. I think that Moses Ginn is behind this."

"That doesn't make sense," the councilman said. "Ginn came to me and told me about Blankenship. Otherwise, I mightn't have been aware of it unless I saw it in the paper tomorrow, if indeed it even made the press."

"Exactly. Let's face it, gents, Ginn doesn't like me. He sees me as a threat. I see it from his angle. He's worried you're losing faith in him so he did this to prove he's still willing to take care of business. And he made sure that you knew about it, but didn't take credit in case you weren't on board. That old black boy is one sly fox, I'll give him that."

The councilman wasn't swayed. "That black *boy*, as you put it, is over twenty years your senior. Show some respect. Moses came to me out of concern. I've known the man a long time. He's never gone off the reservation before and I very much doubt he would now."

"Be that as it may. Before you interrupted I was going to say that more likely, he wants to pin it on me. He knew at our last meeting, I was pushing for some action. So he makes it look like I went rogue so you'd lose faith in me. And by the tone of your accusations, I'd say he succeeded."

With that he abruptly turned and strode off. The move reeked of theatricality as he played the aggrieved party. The other two were left alone to decide what came next.

The lawyer said, "What do you think?"

"We've known Moses for a lot longer than we've known Dick. We knew Dick's late dad forever, but that doesn't mean the son's as temperate as his father was."

"True enough. In all the years we worked together, Richard senior was never uncivil. When we accepted his son into our ranks, we both agreed that if we were to survive, we needed some fresh ideas and a more proactive approach."

The councilman splayed his hands outward. "He was quite explicit in telling us that he didn't want to be joining a group of old farts playing gin rummy. We went along with the idea that we needed to be more aggressive if we were to survive. But this is going too far. There's no doubt in my mind that he was behind both incidents."

"How can you be so sure?"

The politician was as upset as his friend had ever seen him. "I never said that the accident happened in Lincoln County. How could he know that?"

The attorney tried to mask his feelings, but his regret shone through. "I thought you and I would still be in control when it came to taking this kind of strong action. We let this thing get out of hand. I reluctantly agreed to the sanction on Serpente and I still think that was the only way to handle his situation. But once we took that step, there was no turning back."

"I've been thinking a lot about who we are and what we stand for. Moses even said we were violating our principles. Maybe it's time we think about disbanding."

"My father founded this group, Van. We've done a lot of good for this city. All right, we've hit a bit of a rough patch now. But does that mean we give up? We need some time to consider it and what it means going forward."

The councilman wanted a drink, and there was Gentleman Jack awaiting him in the taproom. "I *am* sure that your father didn't envision us becoming criminals. We could have gone to prison because we trusted that little builder who betrayed us and everything we stand for. But now, if we're at the point where we have to start killing anyone who we suspect is aware of our existence, we'll be more consumed with covering our collective butts than doing good. It's a step I'm not willing to take."

The attorney was nodding his agreement during most of the speech. "I wouldn't want you to violate your conscience. Let's sleep on it, my friend. Maybe there's a third way. "

The councilman agreed. "I hope there is. We crossed a line with Johnny Serpente, but the man not only betrayed our trust, he endangered thousands of innocent people out of sheer greed. As you said, I stand by that decision, although it gives me no joy to say so."

"You'll get no argument from me on that score. I understand your concerns. Before we consider tearing apart something that took decades to build, let's see if we can find an honorable way out."

They shook hands and parted. Their newest member had acted rashly and had undermined all that they stood for. But although the attorney seemed less troubled by the idea than his associate, he had actually feared that this day was coming and had made plans well in advance. He had been reluctant to let go of the power the Troika afforded him. In some ways, the cabal kept his father's spirit burning within his heart. But he saw that things were spiraling out of control and he was determined not to be the one left standing when the music stopped.

On the other side of the building, Moses Ginn folded his headphones and put them into the secret compartment in his desk. He hadn't known about King's accident until he heard their conversation, and it cast quite a different light on his plan. He had hoped that this rogue element could be exorcised without bloodshed but he could no longer afford to be magnanimous. His very survival was at stake.

36

Shabielski called back as I trailed the EMS vehicle. I told him what had happened to Rick. Although he knew and liked Stone, mostly as a friend of a friend, he maintained his cool and presence of mind as he digested the news.

"Lincoln County's not my beat. Let me make a call and I'll be right back at you."

I didn't expect words of solace from Pete. His businesslike manner put me slightly off before I decided that I needed to put aside the personal stuff. I had to treat this objectively, as if it had happened to a stranger. I needed to concentrate on a counterattack. In addition to Ginn, I now had another name.

Richard Tucker.

I hoped Shabielski might be able to furnish some background on him. Was he a lazy cop who sought to close a case by palming it off to the feds, or did he have a special interest in deflecting their efforts away from Ginn and the Troika?

All I could come up with was that they had sent Ginn's gun up to someone in the Russian Mafiya, knowing that the slugs would match. I still couldn't figure out how they had gotten the mob to go along with the plan to allow one of their soldiers to take the rap for Ginn. And how did the feds tie in?

The Troika had to have ties with the Char/Meck police to operate effectively, and Tucker might be the point man. Maybe he was the new blood Ginn had alluded to.

Peter called back in less than five minutes, by which time I had arrived at the hospital. Rick was chattering away, sounding perfectly normal, but internal bleeding and the possibility of a concussion were areas of concern to the medics and I wasn't about to help Stone overrule them. I backed off and took Shabielski's call outside the ER as they wheeled him in.

"Hey, Riles. Where are you?"

"Lake Norman Medical. They just took Rick in."

"Hope he's okay. Look, you and I need to get down to cases here. I need to know everything, and I do mean everything. We've worked together in the past. You know me. You know that if you need to do something that I can't, I try to look the other way. But connecting dots here, someone tried to kill you and wound up running your pal into a tree. When they find out they failed, they ain't quitting there."

He was right. I was taking on forces much larger than my one man crew. Rick and Randee had already been casualties and I wasn't about to put them in the line of fire again. I told Peter to meet me at the hospital coffee shop and said I'd read him in then. After a perfunctory grumble about deserting his family on a Sunday afternoon, he agreed.

Moses Ginn was next. I dialed the number I'd taken off his cell.

"Ginn. It's King."

"King! You all right? I heard you was in a wreck."

"Where'd you hear that? One of your hired killers report back to you?"

"Seriously man, you think I did this? No way. I don't know nothing about it, where it happened, how, whatever. You hurt?"

"No. I wasn't driving. I lent the car to a friend."

"Well, praise God for that. He okay?"

"None of your business. You asked me to give you the day. I did. You got anything to tell me?"

"You ain't gonna let me handle this on my own, are you?"

"Damn it, Ginn. How the hell can I trust you to handle it? Randee's in one hospital with half her face blown off and my friend is in another. Sorry, but I'm not impressed with the way you're handling it, unless of course, this is all your handiwork."

He had no immediate response and when he did answer, he sounded more humbled than I expected this war-tough vet to ever be. "You made your point. I fucked up. I trusted some folks I thought had some integrity and now I see they're just trying to cover up their own ass. You just tell me where you want to meet up, and I tell you everything. I be done with this lone wolf shit."

I told him I'd call him back with a time and place. I didn't tell him I'd have back up. Armed to the teeth.

37

I hate hospitals. People die there.

I hate the way they look, the way they smell. The people who work there must either develop calluses around their hearts or go home and self medicate with booze, drugs, or worse. They have to, given all the death they see. It may not be sudden and violent, like wartime, but it is death nonetheless.

My own mortality comes into sharp focus, whenever I visit a friend or client. As I walk down the corridors, it's hard to not gaze into the rooms containing terminal patients and their grieving families. I peer into my future and imagine myself in their place.

My morose musings about hospitals made me dread seeing Randee later. Even as I sat in the pleasantly outfitted Starbucks at Lake Norman Medical, sipping strong brew and indulging in an apricot scone, negativity overwhelmed my thoughts. I was trying to concentrate on a strategy to break this Troika, but my mind was constantly interrupting the flow with depressing distractions.

Before they wheeled Stone into a private area for tests, I told him that I'd wait for him in the coffee shop. The young physician said that he'd call me when Rick was finished and ready to be released. Also, not to worry, my friend appeared all right, they just were going to run routine tests to be sure.

As I sat waiting for Shabielski, Stone sauntered in, looking as fresh as if he'd just stepped out of the shower. I was jolted out of my contemplation, happily.

I said, "You son of a bitch, you must be made of steel. You look great."

"Yeah, turns out that heap of yours has five star safety ratings. I'm not sure the Mustang would have fared as well." He sat next to me, not even a hint of stiffness betrayed the act. "I'm sorry about the Audi. Can they save it?"

"I doubt it. I don't think it'll respond to treatment like you did. It looked totaled to me."

"Whatever the insurance doesn't cover is on me."

"Forget about it. It's obvious they were after me. If anyone owes anybody anything, I owe you. That's twice now. I'm not gonna let you step into the line of fire again if I can help it."

"Reminds me, where's my piece? You know, *happiness is a warm gun.* Is it still in the car?"

Back to quoting songs, a sure sign he was all right. "No, I got it out. Look, I'm meeting Shabielski here in a few minutes. If you're sure you're okay, stay with us and then I'll drive you home."

"No frigging way, Riles. The docs said I have bruised ribs, no concussion. Gave me Advil and sent me on my way."

"It's not your fight, Rick. You just got in the way."

"Hell it isn't. The bastards may have been after you, but I was the one those fuckers ran into a tree. They'll learn you don't mess with a Marine."

No talking him out of it. I wasn't about to try.

All I could say was, "Oorah!"

38

Shabielski arrived a few minutes later, sporting a black Carolina Panther hoodie and looking every bit the Sunday afternoon barbeque dad he is. His resemblance to a slightly younger Bruce Willis always tickles me, especially seeing him in casual dress as opposed to the bland suits he wears on duty.

"Stone, you're never going to scam the insurance company if you look so goddam robust," was his opening salvo. "Get a neck brace. Claim whiplash."

He nodded at me. "And poor King's little baby is totaled. You know how long he's had that German piece of shit? Maybe now he'll buy American. Help out our workers instead of the Krauts."

"Is the monologue over and can we bring on your guests now, Mr. Rickles?" Stone shot back.

"Just trying to lighten the mood, men. You guys are lucky the Panthers were blowing the Saints out or I would've been here later or maybe not at all. That coffee smells good, King. You drinking this?"

Without waiting for an answer, he scooped up my cup and took a long draught. Too bad I never get colds, or I'd be happy to pass one on to him.

"So boys, you finally decide to do this the right way. Very public spirited of you. I just wish you'd done this on a work day."

"*Crime waits for no one*", Stone sang, doing a nasal Mick Jagger impression that went over Shabielski's head.

I said, "Sit down, Peter. Would you like a cup of Joe of your own? Strong, black, no sugar."

"Like you like your women. Ah, I gotta retire that one. You grow up in Central Jersey, that shit just comes out naturally. Sure, if you're buying."

"Okay. Rick, keep this Neanderthal occupied while I get his coffee. You want anything?"

"A single malt would be nice but I'll settle for a latte."

There was no one I'd rather be in a foxhole with than these two clowns, but the opening badinage was getting old. As I headed for the counter, Shabielski started bragging on the Panthers, knowing that Stone is a Jet fan. Rick doesn't enjoy talking smack about sports off the clock, but maybe now that there isn't a clock, he'll be more indulgent. As I returned, they were debating whether Cam Newton or Luke Kuechly was more valuable to the team.

When the sports talk subsided, we got down to business and as promised, I spelled it all out for Pete, including my interplay with Ginn and my plans to meet him later.

"And I suppose you'll want me along for backup. Wanna wear a wire?"

"Don't think so. He went along with me naming the time and place, but he may pat me down, and I wouldn't blame him. On the chance that he's been straight with me all along, I don't want to risk him walking away if he thinks I'm setting him up."

"Well, aren't you?" Rick said.

"I don't know. Call me simple, but I'm still not sure that he's not trying to do the right thing here."

Shabielski scratched the top of his head. He still had thick hair, but it was shaved so close that he appeared bald. The naked pate worked well enough with his angular features, although he'd told me that his wife nagged him to grow out a luxuriant hairstyle while he was still able to pull it off.

Peter said, "You know Riles, this whole story is pretty out-there. Especially this Russkie hit man. Logan is no fool. And you know the feds' ballistics guys. There's no way they match the slugs unless they're sure."

He shook his head and sipped his coffee. "So how did this Troika pull that off? You're telling me they have enough juice to convince the Russian mafiya to give up one of their own for something he didn't do? That really strains credibility."

I said, "That sounded off to me as well. Only thing I can think of is that since their guy was going down anyway, somehow they got his bosses to set him up for this one in exchange for the Troika's role in knocking off Serpente. Hey, the Snake stole from them. If they knew where he was, they would have taken care of it themselves. Ginn spared them the trouble. And since they still took credit for it, it sends the same message --- don't mess with them because they'll get you, no matter how much time goes by."

Shabielski wasn't buying it. "So you're telling me a couple of seventy five year old country clubbers have enough leverage to reach out and make a deal with the Brighton Beach boys? How exactly would they do that?"

"*They* wouldn't. They'd send Ginn. Or since it's pretty obvious they have some influence in your department, maybe a little cross pollinating and one of your guys helped. What do you know about this Richard

Tucker? He's the one who was selling the feds on the Russian tie-in."

"Dick Tucker is the most tight ass dude in the department. I mean, I've actually never met the guy but his dad was a heartbeat away from being commissioner. The old man died last year but he was well respected. Fact is, most of the regulars thought he should be head of the department but he was passed over because he wasn't the right color. I hate to say it but it's true. The pols didn't want a repeat of Ferguson in their fair city and they hoped having a commissioner of color would immunize them."

Stone said, "Doesn't seem fair but it paid off once, Peter."

"You mean with the cop who shot that black kid, the Florida football player? There was one day of protests and no violence so maybe they had a point. But then after that druggie was capped going for his gun, the city was in lock down for days. Uptown was a war zone. It's a different ball game now. That racial stuff is back. Maybe it never went away."

I said, "Politics aside. Do you think there's any way Tucker's part of the Troika? He sure seemed to be carrying their water to the feds."

"Could I concoct a scenario where he resented his dad not getting his due, so he joins a group that engages in a little off the books activity? Makes sure justice gets done when the system fails? Gee, that kind of describes us, doesn't it?"

39

I called Ginn and gave him the time and place for the meet. I went with Shabielski's suggestion --- the Four Mile Creek parking area at dusk, which was less than an hour away. Peter had met CIs there and had scouted all the potential hiding places.

The plan was for Stone and Shabielski to camp out on opposite sides of the small paved lot, which accommodated about fifty cars. At Shabielski's insistence, I donned a light duty Kevlar vest and tucked the Beretta into my pants. Both of my friends had come with assorted armaments, prepared for a shooting war if one erupted.

But I was armed with something more powerful than anything they could muster.

Information.

Throat called me and what he had uncovered gave me a whole new perspective on one Moses Ginn. I couldn't wait to use it. Even though I hadn't pushed Throat on researching Ginn lately, the man's persistence paid off. Maybe he couldn't tolerate the idea that another computer geek could out maneuver him.

I reached Four Mile Creek fifteen minutes early. Ginn was already there. Illuminated by a mercury vapor street light designed to look old, he was standing alone, like some urban doo-wop singer fronting a fifties group. There were no other cars in the lot, other than Ginn's old Mercedes. Stone and Shabielski trailed my MDX by ninety seconds in Pete's Honda. They parked a half a football field away on the far side.

I saw Peter, dressed in jogging clothes, get out and casually walk toward the bank of shops across the median. He'd be circling back to cover my other flank after checking for signs of Ginn's posse. Stone would stay hunkered down in the car on the opposite side, ready to assist if the situation dictated.

"Hey, King." Ginn looked tired.

"Hey, yourself. Full disclosure. I come armed, I assume you do, too. So can we skip the pat down?"

He appeared disappointed. "Oh, ye of little faith. I come naked to the world. No gun. I be armed with just my good intentions."

"Spare me, pal. I'm onto you."

"What the fuck you talking about? You onto me."

My intent was to sucker punch him with what Throat had discovered. I wasn't sure if anyone else knew his secret, or if someone in his circle had found out recently and that was the cause of his current struggle.

"I'm onto the fact you never served. Never were special forces. You and I have something in common. Knee injury kept me out of the NBA, yours kept you out of the Army."

"I don't know where you came by that piece of misinformation but it ain't true."

"Ginn, I agreed to meet with you because you said you were going to tell me the whole truth. Now you start out by lying. So you just keep on living in your fantasy world and I'll deal with reality. Have a nice life, what's left of it."

I started to walk away.

"Hold on, King. Let's be smart here. I guess we got to trust each other. But you got to promise, you can't be spreading this around or I'm finished and I do mean finished."

If the Troika was as ruthless as I feared, he was right. If it came out that he'd been conning them for forty years, they might dispatch him without consideration for his loyal service.

I said, "Okay. But you lie to me, all bets are off."

He gave me an appraising look. Was I bluffing?

"All right, King. I just hope I picked the right pony with you. You fuck up and we both be dead. Where you want me to start?"

I felt like a priest in a confessional. Ginn had been holding these secrets in for forty years and was grateful for the opportunity to unburden himself. But if Throat hadn't uncovered a few key items from his past, he never would have been forthcoming. As it was, after some initial hesitancy, it poured out of him like muddy water over a flooded spillway.

"'Course you know, things was segregated here when I grew up. My mom worked, hotel chambermaid, my dad said he was a traveling salesman. He wasn't around much. But whether it was his or my mama's work, we always had food on the table and decent clothes."

"Brothers and sisters?"

"No, just me. I expect there was beginnings of one or two but they never got born. Don't know if by accident or the cut wife took care of it. Anyway, I was never much for book learning in high school, but damn, I could run the football. Had moves, too. Summers I caddied at the Nat and worked in the clubhouse fixing spikes, fetching drinks and such. Saved every dime 'cept what I gave to my mom to help us get by. Never touched drugs or even drink back then. Lived clean."

"Your knee give out in high school?"

"No, college. Carolina Central. Black college gave me a full ride. They was looking to be like Grambling, big colored football power. Had some good squads. They set me up with an old beater car. A little cash on the sly. Again man, I saved all of it. Local black shopkeepers more than happy to give a player a break, a meal, some clothes and such. We played a couple big schools. Didn't know it at the time but we were scheduled early so's they could beat up on us and build up their record. I had to play both ways, linebacker and scat back."

There was a little smile creasing the corners of his mouth as he recounted his football career. "Last game of the season was when it happened. We was winning big, but I was still in the game. Coach was looking to pad his résumé, see. Run up the score so's he could move on to a bigger school. Team we was playing wasn't happy about us piling it on so they was taking cheap shots whenever they could. I was already on the ground when one of them went after my knee with his helmet. Busted it up good."

"The knee. We have that in common."

"One reason I liked you from the get-go. I knew about that. Don't know as you'd a been a big pro player but that pretty much sealed it, didn't it? But you was white, had grades, and FBI came knocking. Me, after spring practices, they saw I lost a step and coach cut me loose. Couldn't afford dead wood on the team. I went back home, my dad beat the tar outta me. Blamed me for getting hurt, blowing the scholarship. Said I should join up in the army, make a man out of me. I didn't cotton much to that idea, being 'Nam was raging and such, but I figured if I enlisted, I might be able to finish college afterwards."

"But the knee made you 4-F."

"Yes, sir. I couldn't go home. My dad would have killed me, and I do mean literally. So I took that old whip before the school could take it back and pointed my compass North. Didn't know where I was headed exactly, just needed to get away.

"Car finally gave out in Syracuse, New York. I gravitated to a golf club up there called Drumlins. Did lot of the same stuff I did at the Nat. That's where I met Frank Tartaglia."

I knew the name. Tartaglia headed a crime family in upstate New York. Typical stuff --- numbers, drugs, sanitation, etc. I told Ginn I was familiar with the operation.

He just nodded and continued his story.

"Some reason, he liked me. Gave me a job in his organization. Selling weed to college kids at first. Nothing heavy, but I s'pose with my size, he saw some potential. Hooked me up with a man called Luigi Laporta. I guess you'd call him an enforcer. Somebody late with their payment, old Louie got called on to take care of it. Luigi *was* special ops in 'Nam. Righteous dude. Taught me a lot. He was more a dad to me than my own flesh and blood."

"So a mafia goon was your inspiration?"

"He wasn't like that. Louie was educated, smart as the day is long. Even though he was white, I got to callin' him Brother Louie, after that song came out. He'd seen horrible shit overseas. You see, he was opposite of Teddy Roosevelt. Used big talk but not the big stick. He'd huff and puff. He had a nasty rep as someone who'd cut off your balls soon as look at you. He taught me his act. How to dress, look dangerous. Word got around that you didn't fuck with Louie or me. Yeah, once in a while, he used the things he learned to kick the shit out of somebody. But never did permanent damage. Got by for years, mostly on legend alone."

"Interesting. But I think I know how this ends. Some young shooter wants to make his bones by knocking off the top gun."

Ginn went from sweet reminiscence to sorrow. "Got that right. Punk he trusted suckered him. I was there. He blew Louie away so fast there was nothing I could do. But as he was going down, ole Luigi got off one shot. To this day, I couldn't tell you who died first."

"So Tartaglia made you his chief enforcer."

"Nope. Equal opportunity as he was, didn't want no nigger being his main man. He imported muscle from New York. Besides, I never watched no one die before, much less someone I loved like a father. I was lucky that Tartaglia was getting on in years and when I told him I wanted to go back home, he let me. Younger days, I would have been a loose end that he would have had to deal with."

"You're talking mid-seventies now. Old Frankie T. bought it in 1977. Same day as Elvis, matter of fact. Natural causes."

"So I heard. Yeah, well. I went back to the Nat. Spreading the word that I'd been in 'Nam. Special Forces. Basically stole Louie's whole story. Wasn't like now with the internet where's you can find out anything about anybody. Nobody really checked out my pedigree, just accepted it face value. Anybody did ask, I told them I did work that the government didn't want civilians to know about and that shut 'em up."

"You told me the rest when we first met. How you volunteered to help the Troika."

"Pretty much. They didn't think I had the necessities to understand so they talked loose around me. Heard them talking 'bout a problem they had. Said my training might be able to help and it did. Worked with skells up North. Worked a whole lot easier down here with some of these redneck assholes. They was scared as hell of me, and I barely had to raise my voice."

40

Ginn was a pro. He took satisfaction in a job well done, an able journeyman. He expected no praise. The only credit he sought was from within his small circle of powerful men who didn't want to get their hands dirty. So he performed their janitorial services for a price. In return, he had a nice condo, a vintage car that he loved. A comfortable lifestyle.

And ironically, until now he was the real power behind the Troika. He was their risk manager. He guided their best intentions along the smoothest path. He gave them good value.

But now, his accommodating ways were being undermined by the new member, a man who saw compromise as defeat. Someone used to getting his own way and was unwilling to bend. A dangerous addition to a small circle who seemed to have outsize influence.

At least that was how Ginn was spinning it. His story made sense so far, but the final piece was yet to fall into place before I could accept it as fact.

I said, "So that brings us to Serpente. The original reason you and I crossed paths. You said you killed him. You're telling me that your negotiating skills had eroded by then and you had no choice?"

Again he hesitated. I was directly involved in the Serpente business and prone to act on any information he divulged. The truth might turn out to be his enemy, or as they say, it might set him free.

He said, "You and me did some business before, not like I knew you real well. I figured you was a reasonable man that would leave well enough alone. Maybe you could scare Blankenship into leaving it be, too. I told you that I did Serpente because I thought that might convince you to back off. You know, before things got out of hand."

"So you didn't kill Serpente, did you? Yes or no?"

"I was gonna tell him the truth that his partners had decided he had to go and they sent me to do it. So he had to get his shit together and leave town. Go to some island somewhere with that hot gash of his and his millions and just vanish."

"How would you have explained that to your friends at the club? If he disappeared before you could kill him?"

"They never wanted no details, they just wanted him gone. I told them upfront we can't just blow him away, we needed to set it up right so's we get no blow back. I woulda said he split town before I got to him. That's if he went with my idea to save his ass."

"So what did happen?"

"When I got to his place, he was already dead. Pro hit, I could see that. Don't know who, maybe the mob or maybe even you."

"Weren't you afraid that if I had, I'd have called your bluff when you told me you did it?"

"Talking to you at the diner, I could tell you had no clue who killed Johnny. So I confessed. Made me look tough, like I'd be taking no shit if you wouldn't be getting with the program. I told the Troika I done it. Enhanced my rep with them, too. Publicly, we pushed the Russian mob thing. Feds bought it."

"Well, for your information, they bought it because it was true. They got a confession and matched the slugs with an SVR vet from Brighton Beach."

"Didn't know that for sure, but figured that's what mighta happened."

Shabielski and Stone were doing a good job. I was so engrossed in Ginn's story that I had forgotten they were watching. They had a parabolic microphone aimed at us, so they heard everything Ginn told me. If I was being gullible in believing him, one or both would call me on it.

I wasn't sure what to think. Everything I had just heard was plausible. Could a smart young man like Ginn forty years ago deceive a bunch of old Southern gents bent on advancing utopian dreams for their city? Men who weren't all that interested in process, just results. And Moses had given them the desired outcomes, but without the minor violence they imagined he had committed.

Still, he had lied to me initially and now swore that he was telling the truth. Although just maybe he was a man cut from the same cloth as me. Willing to use the sword only as the last resort after all else has failed.

I said, "Ginn, one thing I still don't get. If he was making them money doing their bidding, why did the Troika want Serpente dead?"

"I told you a bunch of times and you still ain't getting it. He betrayed them. They weren't worried much about cheating on some uptight building codes to get things done on the cheap, but when they found out those folks was in danger --- asbestos and bad wiring and shit? He was putting all them folks at risk to line his own pockets, man. Scamming more than his cut. Money that was due them."

"Honor among thieves."

"Call it that if you be inclined. But see, they even tricked up his will to make amends. Gave money to Habitat, out of the wife's share. Tried to clean up the mess. If they was evil, they wouldn't be doing that."

"So why come after Randee and me? If these are such good men, why start killing people who might discover that they exist?"

"They weren't into that. They was talking about disbanding, instead of killing you and the old bat. It was the new blood, acting on his own."

"And the new guy's name?"

"Dick Tucker. A real son of a bitch."

41

Ginn refused to give me the other two names. He said that they weren't the problem and that once Tucker was dealt with, the others would fall in line and disband the Troika. He had no interest in punishing them for the past. He was convinced that they had been a force for good. They bore no responsibility for Randee or Stone, in fact had been angry at Tucker when they found out.

I said, "Ginn, I need their names. They might give us some help nailing Tucker, if they truly are as bothered by this as you are. All you're doing by holding out is burning daylight and putting others in danger. Give me something solid on Tucker --- proof that he set up this thing with Randee or he was behind what happened to Stone today."

"You don't think I would if I could? Got nothing for ya, man. I got no doubts it was him but they had a meet a few hours back and they asked him point blank if he did this on his own. He denied it. Matter of fact, the motherfucker tried to blame me. Said I was setting him up."

I tried persuading him to give me the other two names with every ploy in my repertoire. Nothing worked. As I was about to give up after several minutes of fruitless effort, I caught some movement out of the corner of my eye. Had Ginn been followed by one of Tucker's cronies? Or had he brought reinforcements, as I had? I tried not to look too suspicious as the figure slowly approached, but the Beretta was cold reassurance if anything nasty was about to go down.

As the figure drew closer, I realized through the darkness that it was Shabielski. I couldn't begin to guess why he was walking toward us, nonchalantly. Ginn picked up on my eye movement, shot a casual glance over his shoulder, then turned back towards me. That proved to be a mistake.

Ginn stopped speaking as Peter came within earshot, waiting for him to pass. But my detective friend didn't pass. Something metallic flashed in his left hand.

Slicker than Houdini, Shabielski sprang from behind Ginn, brandishing a set of handcuffs. Pete is compact and strong, but six inches shorter than Ginn. Grabbing the larger man's left arm, he slapped the cuffs on one wrist and spun him around in one motion to complete the job. Executed in less than a second, it was an impressive move --- subduing his prey before the surprised Ginn knew what hit him. This wasn't Peter's first rodeo either.

"Moses Ginn, you are under arrest for attempted murder and conspiracy to commit murder," he said, proceeding to recite the Miranda warning from memory.

I'll never forget the look in Ginn's eyes as Pete read him his rights. There was hurt and disappointment at what seemed like betrayal from someone he had wanted to trust. I *had* invited a Char/Meck cop along knowing that he had the capability to eavesdrop on our conversation.

"You sure this is how you want to play this, King?" Ginn asked, in a calm voice. If he was scared or nervous, it didn't show. He knew that he hadn't said anything really incriminating and that he had access to top notch legal representation through his Troika contacts.

I couldn't imagine what Peter's game was, unless he thought the threat of jail would intimidate Ginn. I knew better. The time for recrimination would come later, but for now, I had to play along with Shabielski.

I said, "Randee was hurt bad and Stone could have been. Come on Moses, why the hell are you protecting the men who ordered it?"

"Shut up, King." Shabielski's tone was commanding. He might have been playacting for Ginn's benefit. Bad cop/ bad cop?

"King asked me to come along in case you tried something. Lucky for you that you didn't or else we'd be scraping pieces of you off the pavement. You just confessed to withholding material information regarding two serious crimes over the last forty eight hours. Now we'll see what some time in the slammer does to your resolve, *Mister Moses Ginn.*"

42

Shabielski winked at me as he shoved Ginn into the back seat of his Accord. He tossed Stone the keys to Ginn's Mercedes, and commanded us both to follow him, me trailing the others in the MDX. Our little motorcade eased out of the parking lot, headed for parts unknown.

What had I missed about Moses Ginn that had caused Peter to cuff him on the spot? This was totally out of character for Shabielski. On numerous occasions, he had looked the other way as I pursued justice my own way. As long as the outcome worked, he was willing to stretch the envelope when it came to procedure.

Now he was confounding me even more as his driving became erratic, as if he was trying to lose us, after ordering us to follow him. I was more skilled when it came to tailing suspects, but Stone was holding his own through Peter's evasive tactics --- signaling in one direction and abruptly turning the other. Or rushing through yellow, just-turning-red, lights.

My worst fear was that somehow Tucker had recruited my friend to join a *Magnum Force* group of conspirators. In that Dirty Harry film, Clint Eastwood was pitted against a group of rogue cops, headed by a dirty captain played by Hal Holbrook. I recalled talking about the film with Shabielski years ago, and he had expressed sympathy for the faction who took matters into their own hands. He even speculated that such forces exist, mostly in rural Southern areas. He always took the side of his fellow officers whenever there was a gray area regarding the use of deadly force. But like most sane twenty first century Americans, he condemned the concept of cops doing extracurricular work with vigilante groups.

But that was a late night beer fueled conversation years ago, and the tide has definitely turned in the opposite direction. Now with dash-cams and body-cams recording an officer's every move, extra-legal tactics, even for righteous reasons, can result in losing your job and pension or in extreme cases --- incarceration.

These fears were coursing through my brain. I was hoping that Peter hadn't fallen victim to the 'Us vs. Them' mentality that had torn the country apart in recent years. I'd never really engaged him on the *Black Lives Matter* movement, but I knew that Peter wasn't a bigot. He just hated bad guys, regardless of color.

Would Peter take Tucker's word over Ginn's? A decorated police captain over a fake enforcer for a shadow group? The possibility existed.

Although I'm not familiar with the location of all the station houses and precincts in the county, it seemed that he had no intention of heading for the nearest lockup. We were pointed northwest, beyond the Charlotte city limits. After a few minutes, his zigzag approach led us into familiar territory.

My house on Lake Norman. Its seclusion offers many options, most of which would be unappetizing to Moses Ginn. We parked as far down my winding driveway as we could, out of sight from the road. I hoped Peter's rash actions didn't lead us all into a quagmire.

To my surprise, Ginn emerged from the back seat of the Pete's Honda under his own power, un-cuffed and in good spirits. Shabielski came around from the driver's side and placed a hand gently on Ginn's back, as if guiding an elderly lady over uneven terrain.

Stone was astonished. "What the fuck is going on, Peter?"

Shabielski turned on the high beams, flashing us his best shit-eating grin. He shushed us with a gesture and pointed to the front door, which I unlocked and opened. Bosco bounded out, sniffed everybody's cuffs, and then urinated for a full thirty seconds on Shabielski's front left tire. I couldn't have instructed him better.

When the five of us got inside, Peter instructed us all to sit, like he was addressing my dog. It might have been a Thursday night meeting of the senior bridge club for all the drama in his manner.

I said, "Okay Peter, cut the crap. What the hell are you doing? Are you oblivious to what's going on in this country? A white cop kidnapping a black man? A real arrest doesn't wind up at my place at midnight. You see how this looks?"

Drinks would wait, although we all could use one.

"Had you all going, didn't I?"

"This isn't funny. You're lucky you're a cop or I would've blown your tires out or worse. You couldn't trust us to tell us what you think you're doing?"

"Calm down, boys. Let's have a jolt or two. When I explain, you'll see I've had things under control all along. I got this, pal."

43

We gave Peter our undivided attention. He said, "I laid this all out to Mr. Ginn on the ride over. Stone, would you go over to King's liquor cabinet and bring some ice and glasses and a bottle of Jack for me and whatever single malt your other friends are addicted to. Thanks."

Stone put his hand up. "All right, I'll get the booze. Start talking Peter, I can hear you from the wet bar."

Bosco snuggled in under the coffee table underneath me after checking everyone else out, pronouncing them friendly one by one by resting his snout in their respective crotches.

Peter waited until we were all comfortable with a healthy measure of our beverage of choice. He took a long swig of aged bourbon and began, "When we got to Four Mile Creek, I did a little recon on the perimeter. I spotted a guy near the trailhead, trying too obviously to look casual. There weren't a lot of cars parked on the street there this late on a Sunday so I ran all the plates. One of them came back registered to one of my brothers in blue. So, any-hoo, since this guy was already there when we arrived, I figured he must be tailing Ginn. Possibly sent by Tucker. That's why I drove the way I did, trying to shake a tail."

I said, "You almost shook us. So why didn't you just go up to him and start a conversation. You could have found out for sure who sent him."

"Thought about that. But I was monitoring your little chat with Moses and I wasn't sure if you might need me and Stone to jump in. When I heard Ginn say that Tucker was setting him up, an idea came to me. Let the cop see me arrest Ginn. Then he reports back that Moses is taking the fall for Blankenship and Stone."

He drank again, this time draining the glass. "By the way, if I had lost you, I would have called your cell and told you to rendezvous back here."

I said, "Peter, you didn't think this through. Tucker will want to see an arrest report. He'll want to know what lock up Ginn is in."

"Who said we need to lock him up? He just disappears. The guy watching him doesn't know me from Adam. So when Ginn doesn't turn up with an arrest report, Tucker figures that you guys took the law into your own hands and blew Moses away."

Stone said, "Great, so you lay a murder rap on us."

"No murder rap when Ginn shows up later and says he just took a few days off to visit a sick friend."

Ginn spoke for the first time. "See, what he's getting at is buying us some time. Tucker thinks I be the scapegoat, he lays offa you for the time being. The message is sent, I get blamed and nobody be the wiser. Give us a few days space to do what we got to do."

Stone said, "Which is?"

Ginn deferred to Shabielski. "First step is to sweat the cop tailing Moses. There might be layers between him and Tucker. And by the way gentlemen, Mr. Ginn has agreed to give us the names of the two other Troika members."

That pissed me off. "God damn it Moses, you and I had a rapport going and you stonewalled me on the names.

You know Shabielski here for two seconds and you sing like Marvin Gaye."

Peter said, "Calm down, Riles. I convinced him on the way over that we're not out to hurt these guys, just eliminate Tucker."

"They been good to me over the years," Ginn said. "Only since Tucker came aboard that they disrespect me and even then they don't do it outright. I think they'll fade away nice and quiet like once Tucker be put in his place. I don't want this to come back on the others. You play your cards right, they back off. Tucker's the only one you got to fret over."

44

THE TROIKA

Scott Coleman was reading a book about how Detroit was once a great city. He rarely received phone calls this late on a Sunday evening, but tonight was special and he answered Richard Tucker's call immediately. He was expecting someone else, but the news he was being given confirmed that his plan was sound and that he was doing the right thing.

He kept his own time. No set appointments. No obligations. Accountants paid his bills. His personal aid arranged for his apartment and automobiles to be maintained. Every Wednesday evening, a different lady would arrive to accommodate his other needs. He was free, unencumbered by financial or societal restraints. The partners and associates at the law firm regarded him like Denny Crain on *Boston Legal* --- a demented figurehead whose name was on the door but was around mainly for entertainment.

He was aware of their disdain and actually encouraged it. The fewer who knew of his still formidable intellect, the better. That way he could operate surreptitiously while playing the eccentric fool. He relished the non sequiturs he tossed out like so much confetti when they tried to bait him with an uncomplicated challenge. He delighted in using obscure references they would never comprehend unless they took the time to research his seemingly meaningless parables. He came out from the clouds and showed his true self rarely these days at the office. He only intervened when he needed to save the firm from a critical misstep and even then he played the idiot savant.

Tucker harbored no such illusions about Coleman. He did think that the third member of their group, Van Jackson, was showing signs of slippage. The old councilman seemed ready to fade away. And since both his colleagues were in their late seventies anyway, neither was very long for the world.

"Thought you'd like to know, counselor," Richard Tucker said. "Looks like Moses Ginn has been arrested for those little incidents our esteemed colleague accused me of."

Coleman took the news of the arrest with aplomb. "Has he been formally charged?"

"Not yet. The man I had tailing him just reported in that he was picked up by an undercover cop and arrested."

"One of your men arrested him?"

"No. And I don't know where they took him to be booked yet. My tail lost him but got the tag number of the car they drove away in. Belongs to a Peter Shabielski. Detective First Grade."

Coleman took a sip of the Cointreau he had poured earlier and listened. "That's why I called you as soon as I found out. Sorry for the lateness of the hour, but I need to make sure he doesn't tell them anything."

The lawyer said, "I've known Moses for decades, and he is the most loyal man on the face of the earth. He's not about to give us up. But we need details of the arrest as soon as possible. What evidence could this Shabielski have on him? This can't have been part of any long term investigation. The only thing I can imagine is that you left evidence implicating him with Blankenship or the accident with King's car."

"What do you mean, *I* left evidence?"

"Richard, Richard, I may play the fool but I'm surprised that you of all people, take me for one. We both know that Ginn had nothing to do with what happened to Blankenship and King. This reeks of your work."

"All right, counselor, I won't deny what you just said. But I did nothing to set Ginn up with this cop, swear to God. I'm no fool either. I need to see what this Shabielski guy's game is. Since I outrank him, it shouldn't be hard."

Coleman took another sip of brandy. "Tell me about the details of this arrest. Exactly how did it occur?"

"My guy tailed Ginn to a parking area. It was obvious he was meeting somebody. Turns out it was Riley King. He and King talked for a few minutes, then this Shabielski character comes out of the shadows and slaps the cuffs on Ginn. My guy was too far away to hear *everything*, but he did hear the Miranda stuff. I ran a quick check on this Shabielski. He got run out of New Jersey because he was bent. He knows King from there. My guess is that King thinks Ginn's behind the mishaps his friends suffered. Shabielski's dirty so if he's in on it, he'll look the other way while King deals with Ginn. My guess is that old Moses is dead meat. That *could* be the end of it but we can't leave it at that."

"Sounds like King may have been wearing a wire. But Ginn had nothing to do with Blankenship or the car. If his life was on the line, he might tell them *you* were responsible."

Tucker said, "You just told me that Ginn is completely loyal. You think he'd talk?"

"If he thought the buck would stop with you. What do you think?"

"I know he thinks I'm some kind of interloper out to take his job."

"Well, aren't you? He's an old man now. He may have regrets. For your own sake Richard, you need to haul this Shabielski in and find out what he knows."

"I can do that. But sir, you do realize if Ginn talked to King, I may have to take extreme measures. I can't let this go any further."

"You mean kill them. Say it. Rather than risk the consequences of your actions, you may need to kill King and maybe this detective Shabanski or whatever. I don't think you'd ever convince Jackson to go along with it. Especially if you decide that this policeman knows too much."

"I hate the idea of killing a cop, even if it's a dirty one. There might be a way I can convince this Shabielski to hook up with us and keep his trap shut."

"Keep me posted."

With that, he hung up. Tucker was responsible for this mess and would be left holding the bag along with the esteemed councilman if things went awry. Scott Coleman, Esq. had other plans.

45

Shabielski had gone home. I left Stone at my house to babysit Ginn and Bosco, while I headed for the hospital to see Randee. Before I left, I contacted Throat and told him to dig up everything he could on Van Jackson, Scott Coleman and Richard Tucker. I warned him to be careful; he dismissed my cautions as redundant.

I had no doubts that his research would come up with vulnerabilities, and all I really needed was a breach into one of them. The lawyer and city councilman in their seventies should be easy to leverage, since they were worried about their legacy.

The city's biggest hospital has expanded in the last decade as the city had, adding wings and outbuildings, linked by high tech, glassed-in second story tunnels. The older parts have been updated to the point where it is impossible to distinguish them from their more recent counterparts. Randee's room had been constructed thirty years ago, but its contemporary design and technology blended in with the newly opened sections.

When I arrived at her second floor quarters, she wasn't alone.

Sitting bedside was a slightly built woman, perhaps a few years younger than Blankenship. She had close cropped grey hair, a strong, lived-in face, more handsome than pretty. When she spoke, her voice was gentle and full of the Deep South. She was the woman I had spoken to on the phone who informed me of the incident.

As I had feared, one side of Randee's body was swathed in bandages. She was connected to a breathing apparatus and intravenous devices. She seemed to be sleeping peacefully. I almost cried when I saw her; a resolute woman laid low by a cowardly attack simply because she stood up against corruption.

I said, "I'm Riley King. The friend of Randee's who called earlier. Any news?"

"She's spoken of you often, Mr. King. I'm Ida May Wright."

Randee had never introduced me to any of her friends. I thought about that on the drive over. It wasn't like she and I were bosom buddies. We had been through an ordeal together. She knew she could count on me when she needed support, and I knew I could count on her to do whatever she believed served humanity at any given time.

I said, "It's very late. Have you been here long, Ms. Wright?"

"Call me Ida. Since late morning, just before you called. Randee and I were supposed to meet for breakfast and she never showed. Very unlike her. I made some calls and found out about her accident. I've been here ever since."

A lesser friend might have been angry and would not have followed up, clinging to aggrieved-party status. But this lady must know Randee well and figured that something significant had caused her to miss the engagement.

"Have the doctors told you anything recently?"

"Just that she's in an induced coma. There's too much swelling to get an accurate MRI or X-ray, but they think it's unlikely there's any brain damage. Her right eye may not be salvageable and her right hand and arm are severely damaged. They believe she'll survive this and knowing Randee, she'll do whatever it takes to get back to a normal life."

"No doubt about that. How do you know her?"

"We're very close friends. We've talked about moving in together."

This was new information. It emphasized how little I really knew about Randee Blankenship. She had never spoken of a husband. She had flirted casually with Derek and me, knowing that we were spoken for and would never act on her suggestions. Stone barely knew her but was a fan. Almost all of what we talked about were her various causes. We shared very little of our personal lives, although she knew about my relationship with Charlene and now Jaime. I never had a clue about her past or present loves. That was all right with me, detailed narratives of the sex life of a seventy year old were not a major curiosity. Not yet.

I said, "Do you know anything about her day yesterday, Ida? Leading up to the accident."

"I stayed over Friday night. Saturday morning we parted after breakfast and I went back to my place. Around mid afternoon, she called and we made plans to meet early Sunday."

"Did she say anything about going to the shooting range Saturday?"

"No, because she knew I didn't approve of her taking these shooting lessons. I told her that I was behind her all the way on her good deeds, but that if one of them was so dangerous that she needed to arm herself that she should concentrate on something else. There are plenty of wrongs to right in the world without painting a target on your back."

THE PUNCH LIST

"I've had the same conversations. But you know Randee, asking her to divert her attention when she has her sights set on something only makes her more determined."

Ida May was holding up well when many would be on the verge of breaking down. "It's what I loved and hated about her. She's so god damned stubborn. She wouldn't tell me exactly what she was into this time, only that it was big and could shake up the whole city. I begged her to turn it over to someone else, but she insisted on going forward. But what are you thinking? That this wasn't an accident?"

I wasn't sure how to answer. Ida seemed like a more common sense version of Randee, somebody more like me actually. Someone with an internal ledger of pros and cons who understand that some battles are too big for one person to take on. But throughout history, those who achieve greatness are probably more like Randee --- they have a singular vision and the courage to follow wherever it leads.

I said, "It's a possibility, Ida. She was stirring up trouble with some powerful people who don't fight by conventional rules. I tried to tell her that last week and get her to slow down, but maybe the die had already been cast."

"I even told her I'd call my brother for help, even though he and I aren't very close. We haven't spoken for months, but if it would help protect Randee, I'd make the call."

"Your brother?"

"Daniel Wright. You've probably heard of him. We come from old money but he made a fortune of his own in real estate. My brother knows everybody who is anybody in Charlotte and most of them owe him favors. But Randee wouldn't let me try to enlist his help. I mean, I love Daniel but she had a problem with him. She knows he doesn't approve of what he calls my *lifestyle*."

Daniel Wright. Yes, I've heard of him. The man who owns the Nat.

46

When I got home from the hospital after midnight, Stone and Ginn were deep in their cups, arguing sports like longtime friends. Stone was challenging Ginn's assertions and recollections of gridiron heroics and Moses was dishing it right back.

My display bottle of single malt was empty. Even Stone doesn't know where I keep my secret back-up, *gran reserve Glenfiddich*, and I had to go through some sleight of hand to pour myself a taste from its hidey hole without them seeing. They had moved on to brandy, which convinced me that neither one of them would be of any use tomorrow.

Both men felt that their discussion of the relative merits of Peyton Manning and Tom Brady versus Joe Montana was more important than pursuing my diagnosis on Randee for very long. I excused myself and retreated to the quiet of my bedroom so I could talk to someone who might still be sober enough to grasp the complexity of our situation.

Jaime. On the West Coast Waiting.

I gave her a quick rundown of my day. She had attended a football party at Leo's house and was about to pack for her flight back to New Jersey. She didn't seem to notice that I had no idea who Leo was (or care for that matter), until I picked up in context that she was referencing young Jack Dawson of *Titanic* fame. From there, my mind downshifted to Rose's nude pencil drawing before I snapped back to the present.

"So this guy Ginn and Rick are whooping it up in the other room," she said. "Just yesterday, you weren't sure that he wasn't out to kill you and poison Bosco. Now you trust him in our guest room?"

"Yeah, funny how that works, Jaime. He's had numerous chances to kill me and so far he hasn't. If he's playing a long game, he's light years ahead of me. Although apparently, he's fooled his comrades at the club for decades and they still aren't onto him."

"Sausage making."

"What?"

"It's like sausage making. H and I were talking about it yesterday. We were talking about the process of movie making, how it can get ugly, but in the end, all the public cares about is the finished product."

"It's late and you've lost me. And I do wish you'd stop dropping names. Or should I say abbreviations."

"I'm sorry, force of habit. You know that H is Harrison Ford. Anyway, the men you're after care only about results and it seems this man Ginn delivers. They don't want to know how he does it, just that it works. This new fellow apparently has them questioning that philosophy. Made them think that because Ginn is getting old, his techniques aren't effective anymore."

A peal of laughter erupted from the other room. Stone was a Marine and I couldn't imagine he approved of Ginn's faking a service record. But that didn't stop them from bonding.

I said, "That's the root of it. Tucker wants the power that he thinks Moses has over these guys."

I heard a couple of beeps indicating an incoming call. Shabielski.

"Jaime, I have to take this. It's Peter. How long do you think you'll need to be in Jersey?"

"I might really only need a day or so. Can I come back to Charlotte then?"

"I'll let you know. I think this phony arrest may buy us time, but I don't want to risk putting you in any danger until I'm sure this is over for good. Let's see where we are tomorrow. Maybe we can meet in Hilton Head instead. Love you."

"You, too. Bye."

How I longed to get back to my boring normal life. Wine dinners with Jaime, long walks with her and Bosco. But I was vegging out living like that and as tense as things were now, I feel alive and of some value.

I answered Peter's call.

He got straight to the point. "Riles. What are you doing this morning around eight a.m.?"

"Sounds like I'm meeting with you. I can't believe you're up this late. Isn't it past your bedtime, dad?"

"I don't sleep much these days. Just checked messages at work and got one from my ballistics guy. Says he's got it figured out about what happened to Blankenship. Wants to meet with me in his lab early, before the brass filters in."

"Just me, I'd assume. Ginn and Stone are drinking up a storm tonight, they wouldn't be much use anyway."

"Yeah, just you. Weird how those two gravitated to each other. I could tell they'd hit it off. Although, I've got to say, just talking to him in the car driving to your place, I took a liking to Ginn right away. He's a cool dude, you know sorta like a cross between Morgan Freeman and Cassius Clay."

"You mean Muhammad Ali?"

"He'll always be draft dodging Clay to me, may he rest in peace. But old Moses, maybe it's that laid back way he talks. That deep voice. He might be full of shit, but whatever he says sounds good. He's a foxhole guy if there ever was one."

He was using one of his Jersey hero Bill Parcells' ways of affirming a player's worth. He's the kind of guy you want in a foxhole with you, a man who's always got your back. Or your six as Tom Cruise would say in the movies. I wonder if Jaime has encountered *him* in her Hollywood travels. Could Scientology be far behind?

I said, "We have to be careful trusting him, Peter. The man's military career is a myth."

"Damn good one, though. I'll email you where to meet up in the morning. Hey, save some of that hideaway Scotch for me, eh pal? The 21 year old good stuff."

How the hell did he know about that?

47

I slept fitfully, finally getting out of bed and into the shower before seven. I figured after taking Bosco out and feeding him, I'd grab a quick coffee and a couple of donuts at Dunkin' on the way to meet Shabielski at the ballistics lab. I should be there within a quarter hour this time of the morning.

I was unprepared for what I saw in my kitchen. I had expected Ginn and Stone to sleep late after their night of drinking, but I was only half right. Stone was nowhere to be seen; Ginn was not only up-and-at-em, but in the process of preparing breakfast.

"Mornin', King. Sleep all right?"

"Not really. Where's Bosco? I need to take him out."

"Taken care of. He's had his breakfast too. Wasn't sure how much you give him and I did mix some bacon with that god-awful shit you be feeding him. Seemed to like it better."

Judging by the way my dog was lying at Ginn's feet, watching his every move as he bustled around the stove, I'd say he was only temporarily sated as far as food goes. I think he lives perpetually in that condition.

"Don't go spoiling him now," I said, echoing Jaime's scolds, which cause me to be more cunning about sneaking him treats.

Ginn said, "I rummaged round in your fridge and put together an omelet with what I scared up. Not a bad pantry for bachelor digs. No buttermilk though for hotcakes, which is my specialty."

"Look, Ginn, I appreciate the thought but I need to get going."

"Breakfast is the most important meal. I can't have you going out fighting crime on an empty stomach. Dog's taken care of, use that time to have yourself some sustenance."

I had to admit whatever he was improvising smelled great and was more nutritious than a couple of Dunkins'. The food and the coffee were first-rate, the best morning spread I'd had in some time. If I could just combine Ginn's culinary skills with Jaime's feminine assets, I'll have the perfect mate. I began to ruminate on Ginn's future employment after we busted the Troika. Visions of Carson on *Downton Abbey* floated in my brain before I snapped back into the real world.

He sat opposite me, coffee in hand.

"So what's our plan for today?" Ginn asked, as I devoured his handiwork.

"Nothing for you," I said, ignoring my childhood instructions not to speak with a mouthful of food. "You sit tight with Stone until you hear from me. Did he say anything about doing his radio show from here?"

"Man called his boss last night and said he needed a few days off. Personal matter. Must be a great boss to do that, no questions asked."

"They go way back. I'm sure he'll tell you about it sometime. I'm just worried that since you disappeared, I wouldn't put it past Tucker to have someone watching this place. They might have already seen you when you took Bosco out."

"I didn't come down with last night's rain, my man. It was dark and I took him out back. After I reconnoitered a bit to make sure no one was out there."

"Good job. You need to stay out of sight. I'm meeting Shabielski to see what they found out about Randee's gun, and then I might check out that cop who tailed us yesterday."

"I can't be cooling my heels forever, you know. This is my fight too. Mainly my fight, way I see it."

"Moses, don't be pig-headed. I got your laptop out of your car, you can use my wi-fi. Why don't you and Stone do some research on the cop who tailed us and come up with something that I can use on him?"

"I can do that."

"Let's leave your car in the garage for the time being so if Tucker does send someone here, they won't see it. You'll have your chance to get involved. Just be patient."

Even as the words were coming out, I realized how many times I had ignored the very advice I was dispensing. Once engaged, I seldom let the battle come to me --- I've always been the aggressor. Ginn and I are similar creatures in that respect. We want to control the time and place of our skirmishes, not wait for our opponent to make those calls.

Ginn said, "No promises, man. I see an opening, I take it."

"Just stay put. Don't go messing up the plan."

"And what exactly is the plan?"

"I'll let you know when I come up with it. Thanks for breakfast."

48

"You look like shit, King. What did you guys do after I left last night? Polish off half your liquor cabinet?"

Damn Shabielski. Whatever he had done after returning home had taken no toll on his appearance. He looked fresh as a spring morning --- shaved meticulously, smelling of barber shop cologne. No dark circles, eyes bright and clear.

"Actually, I had one drink then tried to sleep, unsuccessfully. Part of the reason was your call. You couldn't just tell me what this guy found out without me traipsing down here at oh-dark-thirty?"

"Oh-dark-thirty? What do you keep, bankers' hours? It's mid morning in my world and I've already gotten a lot accomplished."

We were in the bowels of the Char/Meck police headquarters, two stories under the main level. It housed the forensic labs, including ballistics, and the morgue. Some nimrod must have figured that the occasional test firings next door wouldn't disturb the occupants of the aluminum drawers. Smart urban planning.

We walked through heavy metal doors using Shabielski's key card and were greeted by a rangy young man in a white lab coat. He had a long pale scar down the left side of his face. It gave him a rather dashing Pirate look, which was accented by dark shoulder length hair and colorful neck tattoo.

"Thanks for coming in early, sir," he nodded to Shabielski, his deferential manner at odds with his puckish appearance.

"I owe you one, Jim. Jim Hawkins, this is Riley King. He's a PI. A friend of the victim. You can trust him to keep his mouth shut."

"No worries," the techie said. "You've got a rep around here, sir, for doing the right thing. I'm happy to help."

"Thanks. Call me Pete. So what've you got, Jim?"

"I was going to prepare a demonstration but I couldn't put it together in time. I'll issue a formal report, of course."

I was fine with letting Peter take the lead. After all, this is his turf. I'd give him a nudge if he failed to ask the right questions, although I was sure he'd have everything covered.

Peter said, "Let's hold on to that report for a few days, Jim. It might be easier for me to track this down if that info isn't out there."

"It would only circulate in the department but whatever you say. I've got a lot of other stuff to process, so as long as nobody upstairs starts pressuring me for answers, I'm cool with holding on."

The lab was well equipped, but still minor league compared to what they have at the FBI. For budgetary reasons, the locals still lag behind the bureau and defer to their expertise if a given bit of evidence becomes proves elusive. Of course, nothing can rival the fictional lab of Abby on NCIS, but the layout here serves its purpose. If a jury has misgivings, a realistic CGI video can be compiled to assuage any doubts.

We didn't need show-and-tell, just a summary, which Hawkins delivered without emotion.

"Most blowups are caused by using improper ammo, not structurally deficient weaponry. Quality control is very good regarding casings and such, and has been for well over a century. Only high grade alloys are used. During the Civil War, there were lots of casualties due to misfires and exploding weapons. Especially the South. They had to make do with what they had or could manufacture hastily. It's interesting, despite the bad rap the NRA gets, they historically had a hand in making sure that ammo is safe before it hits the market."

The irony of "safe" bullets amused me.

Peter said, "Fascinating, Jim. Let's forego the history lesson. I just need your best guess."

"Oh, it's more than a guess, sir. You see, despite what I just told you, it's still possible to load a weapon with improper ammo. What happened here was the lady's gun was loaded with .357 magnum cartridges. Her gun was a snub nosed .38 Special. Could be concealed in a lady's handbag. Now you might not think that .357s would fit and in most cases they wouldn't, but this was a cheap gun obtained at a pawn shop. The heavier load in the magnum carts blew up the magazine and sent shrapnel flying."

"How could you be sure that's what happened?" I asked.

"Two ways. We confiscated the ammo box in the lady's locker. Along with a couple of proper .38 calibers, we found .357 bullets. Now an experienced marksman would notice the difference immediately, but a beginner would see the coloring and shape were roughly the same and think nothing of it. And second, some of the fragments I found were consistent with the heavier gauge. I took the liberty of sending the box and remaining slugs to the fingerprint folks, and nothing came back other than the lady's prints. It's likely whoever switched the ammo wore gloves."

Pete and I let that sink in for a moment. He asked, "Is it possible that this was a mistake on the manufacturer's part? That somehow they screwed up at the factory?"

"Highly unlikely. Like I said, quality control is excellent these days. You rarely see blowups like this anymore, even in our uneducated hinterlands. As much as I hate to say it, human hands on site made this happen. Carelessness or deliberate, that I can't say."

Shabielski and I had suspected this from the beginning. We knew there was enough information on the dark web that an angry teenager could create this catastrophe, given enough motive and a modicum of cunning. Since there were no prints, it would be hard to prove who substituted the bullets at the range, but we had to follow that lead.

We had all we needed from Hawkins. Peter thanked the gunny and re-emphasized that he should withhold his written report until we'd had an opportunity to dig further. We took the elevator to the main floor and exited the building through the lobby. There were surveillance cameras at every turn. Was I being paranoid to think that Tucker or those allied with him might be monitoring our movements and might lip read if no audio was available?

Regardless, we stayed silent until we were out on the street, away from prying eyes and ears.

I said, "I guess the question is, who goes up to Cornelius to check out the shooting range? You do it in your official capacity and it might cause you some heat with the department. Lines of authority and all."

"I need to find out who has lead on this now and if I can trust him."

His cell buzzed. He quickly glanced at the number and took the call. He listened, nodded a couple of times, mumbled "yes sir" and "Okay, right away" and clicked off.

"Everything okay?" I asked.

"Guess who? Oh fuck it, don't guess. I've got a two minute elevator ride to come up with a new plan, thank you very much. That was Captain Richard Tucker. Wants to see me upstairs. Now."

49

PETER SHABIELSKI

Shabielski rarely visited the top floor where the higher-ups in the department were ensconced. He had no ambitions to rise to a supervisory level, preferring the hands-on grind of the street where he could see tangible results instead of a column of favorable numbers. Even when he was called upstairs for praise, he dreaded the experience and couldn't wait to get back to his peers.

The area the brass occupied was distinctly more elegant than Shabielski's confederates' on the lower floors. Tucker's accommodations weren't quite corner office, but it bore the imprint of a designer. The walls were tinted a dark gray, barely visible for all the commendations and awards that covered them. Many of the citations had been awarded to Tucker's father which were purposely segregated from his own by a wide strip of fluted molding. Floor to ceiling curtains covered the window wall.

Scandinavian furniture of light maple and ash contrasted fluently with the darker walls. Its design presented a streamlined, uncluttered statement that was all business. Stainless steel office chairs upholstered in black leather provided seating, both behind and in front of the sleek chrome desk, which was topped with inch thick translucent glass.

After introducing himself to Tucker's male secretary, Shabielski was ushered into an empty office. "The Captain will be with you momentarily," he was told. Peter killed the waiting time by perusing the citations that father and son had garnered over the years, noting that the first ones were issued years before he was born.

Within minutes, Tucker entered, all good cheer and welcoming. After a perfunctory offer of coffee which Peter turned down, he was directed to a seating area in the corner of the space. Tucker touched a hidden button and the curtains slowly opened, revealing a commanding view of the city. The act was intended to intimidate and impress, but Shabielski didn't acknowledge the exhibit of power, barely giving it a glance.

"I know you're a busy fellow so I won't waste your time, detective," Tucker began. "I was informed you made an arrest yesterday but I can't find any record of it. I'm not here to scold you. After all, it happened on a Sunday evening and you might have had family priorities to deal with. You may have figured you'd file the paperwork this morning. But it involved a person of color and well, I'm sure you are aware of the sensitivities in that community."

Shabielski had a ready response. It was simply a blank look and a helpless gesture. "Arrest? Yesterday? There must be some mistake."

Tucker frowned. "We're talking Sunday evening."

"I understand. But I didn't arrest anyone last night. Or all weekend for that matter. Where did you hear that I did?"

"You're denying that you arrested a man named Moses Ginn?"

"The only Ginn I know of is Ted Ginn, Jr. The ex-wideout for the Panthers. Some game they played, wasn't it?"

Tucker was forced to improvise, something he wasn't used to doing. "Detective, I don't know why you're denying it, but you were observed with Mr. Ginn at approximately 8:20 yesterday evening."

"Not me. Where are you hearing this, sir?"

Tucker had already divulged more than he had planned to but was forced into showing his cards in hopes of getting the information he sought. "What I'm about to tell you can't leave this room. We have been following this Moses Ginn for a few days now. We suspect him of embezzling funds and perhaps much more serious offenses. Our man observed you arresting him last night. He clearly heard you reading him his rights."

Shabielski could stonewall with the best of them. If he had worked for Nixon in the seventies, the man would have served both terms. "Wasn't me. Can't say who it might have been, but you have me at a loss."

"Stay there, detective. I'll be right back."

Tucker left the room. Peter hoped that it wasn't to retrieve some sort of evidence that supported his contention. It was a nervous few minutes until he returned.

Tucker said, "Mr. Ginn did not report for work this morning. He didn't call in either. Quite unlike him. He seems to be missing. I think you know where he is."

"As I said, I'm sure whoever you had assigned to this is very capable, but this must be a case of mistaken identity."

"My man noted your tag number. You drive a 2014 Honda Accord, no?"

"I do, at times. I have two daughters who use that car as well. Wait a minute, you said 8:20? It's already pretty dark by then. Easy to misread a tag number by a digit or two and there are lots of Hondas on the road."

"Detective Shabielski," Tucker's voice rose, using the surname for the first time, mispronouncing it.

"Excuse me sir, it's pronounced Sha-bowl-ski."

Tucker was getting flustered. "Whatever. Do you deny you know a man named Riley King?"

"Not denying it at all. You never asked me about King."

"What's the extent of your relationship with him?"

"Are you implying some kind of homosexual liaison, sir? I'm happily married, have been for twenty five years."

Tucker's face was beginning to color, and he flashed angry eyes. "Come off it, detective. How well do you know him?"

Shabielski couldn't lie about this. It would be too easy to check. "I've known Riley King for years. We originally met in New Jersey. I was a cop there. I worked a couple of cases he was involved with. He moved down here a few years after I did. We keep in touch. Talk on the phone once in a while. Don't socialize much. He's a bachelor, and as I said, I'm a married man with kids."

"Did you know he's been seen with Ginn? In fact, he was present last night at the arrest."

"Riley King told you that I arrested this Ginn character? I'm confused. He's working with the department?"

"No, he isn't." Tucker took an exasperated deep breath and continued. "Let me ask you this, hypothetically. King is a friend of yours. If you were presented evidence that he was guilty of a serious crime, would you act on it or would you protect your friend?"

"Captain, I've been a cop all my life. It's my sworn duty to uphold the law," Shabielski said, paraphrasing the oath of office. "I'd do what's required of me. If that means taking down someone I know, so be it."

Tucker shifted in his chair and leaned in. He lowered his voice to a conspiratorial undertone. "Let's say your friend is a very clever man. A man who has committed many crimes but leaves no trail. Would you consider acting outside of channels to prevent him from doing more damage?"

"I'm not sure what you mean, sir."

"Why did you leave New Jersey?"

Tucker was being cautious, feeling him out so that he could retreat and have deniability if Peter wasn't simpatico with his plan.

"The weather got to me."

"Don't take me for a fool. I've asked around about you." His eyes were lasered on Peter's, unblinking. "Don't bullshit me, detective."

"I'm not at liberty to discuss this. I have a non-disclosure agreement. And in actuality, I'm not even 100 per cent sure what happened. All I can say is that I had a dispute with the department up there and we agreed to disagree."

"Then let me tell *you* what happened. You were doing undercover work. You were offered a bribe. You reported it. You were unaware that your boss was in bed with these people and that the gratuity you were offered was with his full knowledge and consent. When you tried to take the matter over his head, he came down on you like a ton of bricks. You hired a lawyer. He worked out a settlement to be disbursed over a number of years. You weren't allowed to go public or the payments would stop and you'd be busted for some extracurricular activity you'd participated in. Something about use of excessive force to bring some minority gang members to justice. That about it?"

"Interesting story."

"Let me tell you another one. There's another man from New Jersey, a little older than you. A woman he was involved with was killed. The man who the authorities suspected was shot, execution style. The DA was aware of who this executioner was, but didn't press charges. A year later, another woman is killed. This same man was involved with her. Again, her alleged killer died violently. Evidence was produced which pointed toward this man but there was no trial. But meanwhile, this executioner took up with the woman's daughter. Who, by the way, inherited her mother's lucrative business. A couple years later, the scene shifts to the south. A builder named Serpente is killed. The man was a crook with mob connections, no one mourned his death. But the same man who executed the two perps up north is in Charlotte now, and lo and behold, he shacks up with the builder's ex-wife. Now you're a good cop. You detect a pattern here?"

"Are you finished?"

"Oh no, there's more. Just within the past year, this same man is hired to locate a woman for a wealthy client. And how about this for coincidence? The lady is murdered, a girl by the name of Stephanie Perry. An old man confessed, but he died in jail before he could be tried. Our executioner friend was paid high six figures for his troubles. Seems like a lot to find someone a Google search would have turned up in milliseconds."

"So your point is...."

"My point is that your buddy Riley King is one of two things. A hit man or a serial killer. Take your pick. Now what are we going to do about it?"

50

PETER SHABIELSKI

Going in, Shabielski expected Tucker to pump him for information about Ginn. But the indictment of King was something he hadn't figured on. The chief had done his homework and it became clear that Tucker was a lot more savvy than he'd been letting on. Down to the mispronunciation of his surname, the chief was encouraging Peter to underestimate him.

Shabielski hadn't done anything to hide his friendship with King within the department, but he hadn't advertised it either. Letting his final question linger in the air, Tucker strode over to a single serving coffee maker and the push of a button yielded a steaming cup of strong espresso. He glanced back at Shabielski and gestured toward the cup. Peter shook his head.

Tucker was not a tall man, but he was solidly built, iron-pumping strong. His suits were altered to accommodate his oversized biceps and thick thighs. The desk job was taking its toll on his midsection, but it was still years away from being soft.

"So, detective, can I count on your help?" Tucker asked, as if closing the sale on a used car.

"I'm still chewing on what you just told me," Peter replied. "I'm familiar with all the cases you mentioned. King definitely killed that lawyer responsible for the death of his girlfriend. He's admitted as much --- said it was self defense and the DA agreed. He was initially a suspect in the Paige White murder. But it didn't stick and they found who really did it, a man called Peter Geist."

"Think about it, detective. I've seen the police reports from Vermont. King's story was backed up by his friend Rick Stone and his lover, this Johansen woman who inherited Paige White's business. Convenient, wouldn't you say? All three had something to gain by framing Geist."

Shabielski was sliding into character. He knew he had to accept Tucker's scenario to gain his trust, but if he did this without a degree of protest, the veteran chief would suspect that he was being played.

"But Jaime was Paige's daughter and would have gotten the business anyway. King wasn't under any heat from Ocean County on the murder, they had nothing. So why go to all the trouble to set up Geist? And his friend Stone was almost killed in that exchange."

Tucker smiled and cautiously brought the espresso to his lips. "Damn coffeemaker makes this shit too hot. Had them in to fix it but it still burns your tongue if you don't let it cool a bit. Okay, I hear what you're saying but that's the genius of this guy. Maybe he set up Stone to be a sacrificial lamb. Or maybe this Geist got the drop on him unexpectedly. Bottom line is, it all ended there, nobody asking more questions. It was all wrapped up in a neat bundle."

He sipped the hot beverage. "Ah, that's good. Sorry you won't try it. But anyway, King moves down here. Serpente is killed, ba-da-bing as you Joisey boys say, and your pal shacks up with the lovely Mrs. a couple months later. Convenient timing, right after the feds fingered the Russian mob."

"Okay, Chief Tucker. I'll admit you might have something there. I knew that King considered Serpente a threat at the time and I could see how he *might* have taken him out, pre-emptively. But I wouldn't lose any sleep over it."

"Aha. Exactly. If King did this, he saved the county a lot of money and embarrassment. But that next case he shows up on troubles me even more. He locates a woman for a man named Ted McCarver. Then she winds up dead. King has a scapegoat all set up, an old man who was dying of cancer --- a widower who was willing to take the rap in exchange for McCarver leaving his adopted daughter a sum of money. A huge sum of money winds up in King's account plus a share in a beach house in Hilton Head. All that for locating someone I could have found in the phone book."

Tucker was playing the role of prosecutor effectively. As an opening argument, it passed muster and without knowing King as well as he did, Shabielski could buy into it. After all, he had no direct knowledge of these events; he only knew what King had told him. Deep in character now, it was easy to roll along with the tide.

He still needed to show resistance, so he peppered his response with signs of doubt. "I met McCarver when I was in New Jersey. The man could have had any woman he wanted. He was rich, great looking, and very smart. I can't believe he'd hire King to knock off some girl."

Tucker looked at Shabielski with amusement. "With a man like McCarver who seemingly has everything, the one woman he couldn't get might haunt him. Hey, now. I'm no shrink. I just see what's in front of me."

"So if you have a case against King, why not arrest him?"

"Because as you say, I can't prove any of this beyond a reasonable doubt. He's too good. I want to stop him before he hurts anyone else. Especially after what he did this weekend."

Tucker might be about to overplay his hand, Shabielski thought.

"What are you talking about, sir?"

"A woman named Randee Blankenship. Recently, she started digging into Serpente's death. Her cell indicates that King called her late last week after they hadn't spoken for a while. She met with an unfortunate accident Saturday evening. She was taking a concealed weapons course and someone rigged her gun with an oversize load. Exploded in the poor lady's face."

There was no way Tucker could know exactly how the gun was tampered with unless he had done it himself or commissioned one of his lackeys to do it.

"That's horrible, Captain. You think he did this. Why?"

"Blankenship might have uncovered something that proves King killed Serpente. From what I understand, this lady was a crusader for the truth. She wouldn't think twice of turning in a friend she suspected of a cold blooded murder, no matter who the victim was. Can I say the same for you?"

51

I expected Peter to be subjected to a five minute dressing down by his superior, followed by a ten minute Q and A session aimed at locating Moses Ginn. I waited for Shabielski at an uptown coffee house, which was sparsely populated in the nether region between the morning rush and the lunch crowd. Mindful of Throat's warnings, I avoided the public Wi-Fi they provided and read only the cached newspapers that were automatically delivered to my tablet each morning. I tried to stick to the sports section to avoid over-thinking what was going on in the halls of justice overhead and the predicament I'd gotten my friend into.

I called Throat's burner and left a quick message with instructions to find out everything he could about Tucker and the young cop he had dispatched to follow Ginn. I also dialed Stone's cell, aware he would still be comatose after trying to keep up with Ginn's alcohol consumption. I left a message telling him to keep close tabs on Ginn, since our newly enlisted ally liked to act without informing his partners. Sort of like Peter was doing.

Shabielski wandered into our pre-arranged meeting spot just over an hour after he'd been called away. He wore a sheepish grin, as if harboring a bit of scandalous gossip he couldn't wait to share.

I said, "Another five minutes and I was going to round up a SWAT team to storm the Bastille and free you."

"Time well spent, my friend, time well spent. Grab me a dark roast, will you. I've got to use the little boys' room."

I did and he did. After we completed our respective duties, we hunkered down at a corner table.

My opening question is one I'm particularly proud of and use often. It is brief and precisely on point.

"So?" I said.

"My new job is to kill you."

"Funny. What did you really talk about? Or did you just listen while he reamed you a new one?"

"No. It was a constructive session."

He proceeded to lay out Tucker's bogus case against me. When we were finished with the list of my supposed crimes, I asked, "Do you need me to refute them one by one, or will you stipulate to the fact that it's all bullshit, officer?"

"The latter. What happened next was more revealing. You see, he started by sounding me out about Ginn and the arrest. Which I denied, of course."

"As we thought he would. Did you think he was setting you up?"

"I can't know for sure, but I assumed everything said in his office was being recorded. He was careful. He stopped short of actually ordering me to shoot you, but we agreed to meet later and get into specifics."

"You're serious. He wants you to shoot me?"

"Like I said, no specifics yet. Could be stabbing, drowning, poison, nuclear isotope. I got the sense the methodology wasn't the point, just that he needs one less Riley King in the world."

"I'm glad you think this is funny. You're telling me that a police captain in Charlotte is ordering a hit on me. I mean, we knew that someone was sending a message with the car accident, but this guy seriously wants me dead."

"Relax. Look who he's recruiting to do it."

Shabielski's bemused look was out of sync with the news he was delivering. I had to separate myself from hearing that someone in a powerful position had declared open season on Riley King, and assess what we could do about it.

I said, "I'm sorry I got you in the middle of this, Peter."

"Don't be sorry. Be thankful. Dig it. The fact that he's asking me means that he doesn't have anyone else. Anyone with half a brain would assume I'd be loyal to you after knowing you for more than twenty years. Why else would he take the chance to sell me on it unless he had no better alternative?"

"There's that."

"Well, *that* is a big fucking deal. My guess is that he has some cops under him that he can assign to surveillance duty on Ginn or you or Randee or whoever. I'm betting he doesn't have anyone he can trust to do the real dirty work, like run Stone off the road or overloading Randee's gun, which he had to have done. I checked with Hawkins on the way out and he swore he told no one exactly how her gun misfired. Only the man behind it would know that and Tucker sure as shit did."

I said, "But what I don't get is he must have been the one in the truck who ran Stone off the road and now you're saying he doesn't have the stones to kill me himself."

"He did show some guts there. He would have veered off at the last second had Stone not run off the road first but it would have sent the message, like you said. One thing he didn't do was finish the job. He could have gone over to the Audi after the crash to make sure Stone was dead. And help him along in case he wasn't. I think the guy's chickenshit. I've seen his type in the department before. Big talker, but no action when it comes to wet work."

"But why would he think he could trust you? A man who's been my friend for over twenty years?"

"Because he's sure I arrested Ginn last night. Come on, he had a watcher who copied my tag number. He saw you and Ginn together before I came on the scene. I never admitted it but he had to know it was me."

Again my sharp interrogation methods shone forth. "So?"

"So ... he knew I'd be willing to circumvent procedure to achieve a result. Don't you see? He couldn't get me to admit I picked up Ginn. He admires that and thinks he can count on my silence if he can bend me into doing this for him. If he thinks he's convinced me that you're a serial killer or a hit man who can't be stopped legally, then he and I can come up with a way to get rid of you that serves the greater good. That's what I bet he'll try to sell me on. Of course, we know his motives aren't so pure."

"So he thinks you arrested Ginn and that we killed him and disposed of the body?"

"Or are water boarding him in your secret basement dungeon. If that's the case, he's got to befriend me in case Moses talks and spills the beans on the Troika. My guess is that he thinks we believe that Ginn was behind the Randee incident and the car wreck and we decided to take vengeance into our own hands."

"So why go after me? Why wouldn't he just be grateful that we eliminated his competition with the Troika for him? Then all loose ends are settled and he can solidify his position with them."

"You're still a threat. And maybe Randee is, too. Moses said this guy doesn't like to leave anything to chance. We're meeting late this afternoon. At the Nat, actually. In the meantime, we need to confirm that I'm right and he doesn't have a squad of killers at his disposal. Starting with the cop who was watching us last night. We have his name and I found out where he has lunch every day. You need to pay him a visit."

"What about the gun range?" I said.

"I already checked. Gunny told us no prints on the bullets or the locker. When I asked him on the way out about whether he told Tucker, he also told me that the place has no surveillance cameras, given it's always crawling with cops. And even if someone saw Tucker there and is willing to testify to that, what does it prove? I'm convinced he's behind it, aren't you? No, you concentrate on the cop who saw the arrest."

"Will do. I already have Moses and somebody else working background on the guy to come up with a pressure point. I hope you're wrong about Tucker. Maybe he just wants you to scare me off and he'll trust you if you say you did."

"Don't hold out much hope for that, King. Make no mistake. He wants you dead."

52

Shabielski and I parted, caffeinated to the gills and prepared for the battles that lay ahead. I walked over to the garage where the MDX was parked. The sight of the chunky black SUV brought to mind the fate of my sleek Audi A5. Its final resting place was a rundown gas station in Denver where the Lincoln County authorities had it towed. It was depressing as hell to think that my constant motoring companion for the last six years had met its maker. I'd formed an emotional attachment to that lifeless ton and a half chunk of metal --- a bond that would be hard to duplicate. Hopefully, something could be salvaged out of the wreck and incorporated in memoriam into whatever ride I chose next.

With these depressing thoughts occupying my brain, I had to force myself to put matters into perspective, that the junkyard destiny of my vehicle was a minor worry compared to the threat that faced its owner. My buzzing phone was welcome relief.

It turned out to be Throat, communicating sans electronic modification.

"I have the information you sought on Hector Lopez."

Why the hell would he be calling me about a former Yankee who dated back to the dark ages, an obscure participant from one of their infrequent losing eras? Then I remembered.

Lopez was the cop Tucker had enlisted to tail Ginn.

I said, "I'm in the car. Send the file to my tablet and I'll download it when I get to a secure spot. Meanwhile, just give me a quick summary of what you think I can use to pressure him."

"This man is an accredited law enforcement officer. I need your solemn word that the tactics you employ will serve the cause of justice and not visit undue harm on a public servant sworn to protect and serve his community."

Hearing him again brought forth the same reaction I had before: This man had to be an android from the future, sent back to torture me at times while providing invaluable assistance at others. Even without electronic masking, his voice and syntax were still so unnatural that they seemed computer generated. Had I not met him in person, I would hypothesize that he was a digital artifact, not flesh and blood.

"All I can tell you is that there's corruption in the local constabulary," I said. *My god, I'm starting to sound like him.* "Although I don't know that this Lopez himself is crooked, he could point me to someone who is. That's the best I can do for you."

"It will suffice. Please understand that if you do use anything I give you for nefarious purposes, I am fully insulated and you will bear the brunt of whatever consequence befalls you."

This guy should write those warnings for prescription medicines that comprise those densely printed magazine pages. Nobody ever reads them but I guess they serve to cover the drug companies' collective asses. "I'm fine with that."

"Officer Lopez is twenty four years of age. He is married, no children but one is on the way, a male due in three months."

He already had information about a child who wasn't scheduled to leave the womb for ninety days. In the big picture, this is more troubling than anything he has ever revealed to me. We need to close these digital portals before they do us serious harm, if they haven't already. But for now, I had to focus on a more pressing issue: staying alive.

He went on. "You asked for vulnerabilities. Officer Hector Lopez is in arrears to his creditors to a much greater extent than his regular salary can sustain. The principle reason for this unbalance is an apparent addiction to gambling on sporting events. This time of year, that addiction is cosseted by those insidious websites promoting what is colloquially termed 'fantasy football'."

"You said his *regular* salary."

"His wages from the police department are transferred directly into his checking account on a bi-weekly basis. However, within the last thirty days, a supplemental amount exceeding his base salary has been electronically deposited."

"Can you trace its source?"

"Do ursine creatures defecate in forested regions?"

This was as close to humor as I could expect from Throat. I forced an appreciative grunt.

He said, "The answer is yes, I can and I did. The source disguised the routing but the attempts were somewhat clumsy. The funds came from an account I tracked to the other individual you asked me to investigate. A Richard Tucker. I assume you would have me forward my findings regarding Mr. Tucker, or should I say Chief Tucker, to your email as well?"

This was too much information for me to digest. My head was overloaded like the .357 magnum cartridge

Tucker had jammed into Randee's .38 special, and the explosion could have analogous repercussions.

"Throat, as always, you've done great work. Send that file to my regular account along with your invoice."

"It is being processed as we speak. There is one more thing I would ask of you, Riley King, if I may be so bold."

He'd earned the right. "Sure, go ahead."

"I have become increasingly uncomfortable with the designation *Throat,* considering its pornographic genesis. Please refer to me as Crain in the future. It is my actual middle name, fallen into disuse. I have confidence in your discretion."

For someone as obviously paranoid as I knew Throat/Crain to be, this represented a large step. A call to Logan at my former job, detailing the man's age, location and unusual middle name, could point to Crain's true identity. I felt privileged that he would trust me and my work enough to take that risk. In an odd way it was bracing, reaffirming that I was on the side of the angels, something that my twisted history had frequently caused me to doubt.

I thanked him for his faith and rang off.

53

Rick Stone had once told me that the colorful Don Henley song *Sunset Grill* was about a hot dog stand in Los Angeles. It was during one of his many digressions into the history of rock and roll which seemed to crop up whenever there is a rare lull in our conversations. Most of the time his little music trivia items went in and out of my head faster than yesterday's soccer scores, (a tedious sport that the TV networks are trying to inflict on America. I guess the greedy bastards aren't making enough money on football).

The reason the Henley song resonated with me today was that Hector Lopez always took lunch at the same food truck every day he was on normal duty. It was parked under one of the inner beltway's overpasses in Charlotte, a few blocks northwest of center city. I wasn't sure how legal the whole setup is, given that there were a few cheap aluminum tables scattered about on public property. There wasn't enough seating for all the patrons. Most of them dined in their cars or standing in the sun if the weather was nice, sheltered under the bridge if it wasn't.

Being the ace detective that my website purports me to be, I soon figured out why the proprietors hadn't been busted. Although I'm not really a big fan of Mexican food, the smell was intoxicating to the point where I was tempted to order lunch and catch up with Lopez later. The second and most important reason was that the few tables that existed were occupied solely by cops. There was a healthy mix of white, black and Latin officers bunched together, even a couple of women. There was not wait service as such, but I did notice a quick nod or gesture from one of the tables brought someone out of the truck with a refill of whatever beverage the coppers were drinking.

I was thankful that Throat/Crain had sent me a picture of Lopez because it would have been hard to pick him out without staring at each cop's nameplate. Hector was sporting his regulation blues, standing in the cool shadows and munching on something that was messy but looked delicious. A twenty ounce soda rested next to him on a concrete abutment of the structure that supported thirty thousand motorists a day.

"Is this corner taken?" I said, flashing my friendliest smile, as if Lopez really *was* the old Yankee outfielder/second sacker.

"Help yourself," he said, clearly not recognizing me from last evening. "No reservations here, amigo."

"Could have fooled me. Seems like our brothers in blue have all the tables. Strange how that happens."

He gave me a closer look, still not knowing who I was. "Brothers in blue? You on the job?" he asked.

He had just made my life a lot easier. I still had an ID from my days as a fed, but the faded photo and date wouldn't withstand scrutiny of more than a cursory glance. I should also add that I am wary of impersonating law enforcement. It comes with pretty harsh penalties, although I could probably skirt them given my connections. Logan would be willing to vouch for me if it came down to it. So Lopez's question set me up perfectly for a quick wink and a "You might say that."

"Federal?"

"Um. How'd you do on the Panthers yesterday? Do you have Newton as your fantasy quarterback?"

A look of panic flashed over his features. Lopez was a bit on the chubby side. Baby fat, we used to call it; in his case, the two thousand calorie lunch he was devouring might be the culprit. And I noted that the word *diet* was nowhere to be found on his soda bottle.

He had short black hair combed straight down, wide set almond shaped eyes. Despite his weight, his uniform was pristine, neatly pressed and devoid of stains from sweat or lunch. He gave off the vibe of a good worker bee, a cop who would do what was asked of him but little more. Hardly a gung-ho candidate for *Magnum Force*.

"Don't worry, Hector, I'm not here to bust you on that." I needed to make this quick, lest he realize who I was. The more time he had to look at me, the likelier the possibility. It was dark last night and he had to be at least a hundred yards away, I told myself. I had been wearing a Mets cap, today I was bare headed.

"You have some ID?" he asked.

"Not any I need to show you. I just have a couple of questions. I'm aware that you've been following a man named Moses Ginn. Who ordered you to do that?"

He looked at me hard, but still no sign of recognition. "Do I need a PBA rep?"

"Again, Hector, I'm not interested in you, only who gave the order. It's no big deal. Just protocol. We want to make sure that your time on the books is being used properly and we have no record of any surveillance ordered on Mr. Ginn. As a minority yourself, you must be sensitive toward the issue of unwarranted harassment."

He said, "Now wait a minute, whoever you are. I never harassed nobody. My chief just told me that Mr. Ginn was under suspicion of embezzling from a club he was working at. It's strictly a favor for the boss, not on my regular beat. Look, I think I need to see some ID. Otherwise I got nothing more to say."

"I'm sure you can understand that we don't want a man like Captain Tucker to know we're looking into this matter. He's been known to use his influence with the politicians to obstruct. And we do have sources so if you mention this visit to him, we'll be aware of it. Just saying, that could make you an accessory. If we find anything, that is."

"Accessory to what?"

"Mr. Ginn is currently missing. Didn't show for work today. Could be he has the flu or could be someone kidnapped him or worse."

"I had nothing to do with this. I saw him being arrested last night. I turned in the tag number of the vehicle they put him in to Captain Tucker. That's it. The Captain said unless someone is in danger of bodily harm, I was just there to observe and report."

"That's all I wanted to hear. And you were paid separately for this?"

"Yes, sir. Odd weeks from my regular. Captain said that's the way they pay undercover work. Maybe so the bad guys can't trace it. I don't know exactly, but the money's always there on time."

"Excellent, Officer Lopez. My report will state that nothing you've said or done implicates you. But I caution you again, this meeting never took place. Officer, have a nice day."

He started to say something but thought better of it. *Accept the win.* He wrapped up the remainder of his lunch and tossed it into a large wire container he was standing near. I turned to walk away, but I couldn't resist a parting shot.

"Oh, by the way, Lopez. Just a friendly word of advice. Despite what you see on those commercials, the house always wins in those betting schemes. How do you think they afford that multi-million dollar advertising on television? You've got a baby boy coming. Don't blow it, officer."

54

Moses and Stone were not in the house when I returned. My dog was AWOL as well. If they had foolishly taken Bosco for a walk, they might risk being seen by someone in Tucker's camp and blow the whole ruse. They couldn't be that stupid, could they? Ginn was more savvy than that and Stone was generally rational too, except it comes to pursuing barely legal women.

On the off chance that they had been imprudent enough to go for a joyride, I checked the garage. As soon as I opened the door from the kitchen, Bosco leapt to his feet and sprang to greet his master. While attempting to curb his canine enthusiasm, I caught sight of two pairs of feet on the cement floor, toes pointed upward.

For a split second I feared we'd been breached, but as it turned out, both Stone and Ginn were on dollies under Ginn's Mercedes.

"Ah, boys, I'm home," I said, loud enough to rouse the dead.

"Just a minute, King," was the non-urgent reply from Rick.

One of Bosco's dog beds was in the corner, and my mechanic's tool box open next to the Merc.

I shouted, "Hell of a time for an oil change."

There was a bit of muttering and seconds later, both men emerged. Ginn was wearing one of my tee shirts, which hung loosely on his lanky frame. There was a dark spot of grease on one of the sleeves.

I said, "Help yourself to my wardrobe, Moses. What's mine is yours." He couldn't miss the sarcasm, could he? And did he keep a box of motor oil in the boot of his Mercedes for occasions such as this? Nope, as evidenced by my open case of expensive high grade synthetic on the shelf.

Moses said, "Didn't think you'd mind. Your Audi ain't gonna be needing a drink of this anytime soon. This shirt's seen better days. I didn't bring no change of clothes, improvised as all this shit is," he said, a broad smile revealing those perfect teeth of his.

"That shirt was given to me by Stone, matter of fact. He got it at a Springsteen concert. Told me it was a collector's item."

Ginn countered, "Ah, the Boss ain't been the same since the big man passed. Wouldn't you say, Rick?"

Stone disagreed. "Still one of my faves. Sorry Riley, Ginn and I were just *strapping our hands cross these engines*."

We were all in serious danger and he was still quoting lyrics. I said, "If you gentlemen could tear yourself away from being Click and Clack for a minute, we need to talk."

Ginn said, "Man, I loved them two dudes. I still listen Saturday mornings, even though one of them passed. They a hoot. Back at the 'Cuse, I worked in a garage for a while before I hooked up with Tartaglias. Restored this Benz from the ground up myself, 'cepting for the paint," Ginn said, his pride showing. The old car *was* sweet.

Led by Bosco, we marched into the breakfast area. Ginn had already commandeered the kitchen and the garage and was now acting like ruler of the roost. He asked, "Before we get down to business, anybody need anything? Rick and me was into your cold cuts for lunch. I do a mean club sandwich, King. Got the fixings ready, if you're hungry."

"Sure." I wasn't thinking of food at the moment, but I hadn't eaten since breakfast. I told them about Shabielski and Tucker's meeting and my conversation with Lopez.

The food was ready as I concluded. I had to admit, Ginn is a culinary wizard. I don't know how he seasons the common ingredients I keep in the fridge, but they taste much better than when I combine them.

"So they be meeting at the Nat," Ginn said. "Any particular time?"

"Four o'clock. You told me back when we first met that you have some kind of monitoring system there. How does it work?"

"You don't need to know exactly how it works, just that it do. Tucker's likely take your friend into the private dining room for his pitch. I got that bugged."

"That's why I wanted to know how it works. You record everything on a hard drive? A disk? The cloud?"

Moses said, "Why don't you just tell me what you need? You want to hear what Tucker's saying to Shabielski? Record it? That what you're looking to do?"

I wasn't sure why he was so reluctant to explain how his system worked but it didn't take a genius to figure out what I was after. I nodded.

Stone said, "So the plan is to get Pete to make Tucker think he'd go along with his scheme to kill you and record it. Then what? Give it to the police? Are you sure Tucker wouldn't use his juice to discredit it? Then we'd be giving away our ace."

I didn't have a well considered answer. "Let's take this one step at a time. See what we have first, then we can figure out what to do with it. Maybe I can funnel it to Logan. Or he can point me to a clean DA in Charlotte. We'll have choices but none of that matters until we know what we have."

Ginn wasn't on board with that. "Tucker be fair game. I want to nail that motherfucker's ass more than you do. But I don't want this blowing back on the other two."

Stone was incredulous. "Why, Moses? You said yourself they were ready to sell you out to save their own butts. Why are you concerned about protecting them?"

Ginn rose and walked to the bay window facing the lake. He stared out at the water for a moment, not answering. Then he turned and leaned against the sill. "I been with these men a long time now. Their fathers before them. They old men, do a lot of good for my people over the years. Treated me fine, gave me a lot. They just got swayed by Tucker. I can't believe they'd let him do dirty to me. I find otherwise, I'll take care of it my own way. Them's my terms."

His loyalty in the face of everything was an admirable quality. Tucker was the enemy who wanted Ginn out of the way; the other two were willing to listen. But he trusted that they would never sell him out.

I said, "All right, Ginn. Let's confine ourselves to Tucker. But the time has come for these men to step aside. I don't have chapter and verse of all the good you say they've done, but this shadow government stuff needs to stop. You figure out a way to do that and I won't stand in your way. Deal?"

The big man extended his hand, his grip crushing mine to the point of pain. Pain I wouldn't acknowledge, of course, macho man that I am.

"Now," he said. "You got Wi-Fi. I got a computer with a card slot and a few SDs. Let's listen from here and record everything they say. I got it covered."

55

Just a couple days ago, I was wishing that Shabielski would be a little less risk-averse. Now I was worried that he was sticking his neck out too far. He'd gone up against his boss in New Jersey and had been exiled as punishment. The fact that the banishment had turned into a reward was a happy accident. Peter had told me more than once that his quality of life was far superior now and that he wouldn't go back North for double the money.

I called him while he was on his way to the Nat and following Ginn's guidance, we worked out a text code for him to let us know specifically where the conversation with Tucker was to take place. We doubted that Shabielski would be able to coax the captain toward a particular spot but Moses said that the audio quality in the small private dining room was optimum.

A few minutes later, fortune favored us. Tucker had indeed picked the small room for the meeting. Moses fiddled with some keystrokes and we were quickly treated to the reassuring hum of the Nat's HVAC system, the ambient room noise of an unoccupied space. Then, we heard a door open, some muffled comments and shuffling about as the two men were seated. Ginn was spot on about the audio --- it sounded like we were camped around the table.

~~~~~

Tucker: I took the liberty of ordering you a bottle of Gentleman Jack.

Peter: Thank you. That's some fine sipping whiskey.

Tucker: You almost sound like a native the way you said that. You've acclimated well, but then again, you hardly had a choice about leaving New Jersey, did you?

Peter: Not exactly true, sir. I could have fought it. Gone public or taken it to court. But I had a young family and the best thing was to take the money and move. Charlotte seemed like a nice place and it's worked out well.

Tucker: I know some folks up in the Garden Sewer, er, State. I'm told that if you hadn't accepted the deal, they had quite a bit of dirt on you. There were some incidents that wouldn't pass muster today. You'd have trouble getting a job as a night watchman at a kennel if any of this went public.

Peter: As I told you before, I'm under strict non-disclosure terms. And besides, I'm not here to plead my New Jersey case to you, or am I?

Tucker: (laughing) No, you're not. My point is that you did some extracurricular things up there and it seems that you've continued to operate that way here.

Peter: (sighs deeply) I don't know what you're referring to.

Tucker: Well, detective, Moses Ginn for one. Let's not play games. You arrested him last night or should I say, pretended to. My guess is that you teamed with King to make Mr. Ginn go away permanently. Or you have him squirreled away somewhere awaiting his fate. Now before you protest and claim innocence again, let me make it perfectly clear --- I don't care.

~~~~~

Stone and I turned to Ginn, who raised an eyebrow with an "I told you so" look. It appeared we had nabbed old Moses just in time, before Tucker could get his hands on him.

~~~~~

Tucker: You see, Ginn was a stone in my shoe. I won't get too specific with you until we get to know each other a little better, but Ginn is a bad man. If his bones wash up on the shores of Lake Norman, there won't be any mourners.

Peter: Why are you telling me this?

Tucker: I've been looking for a while for someone who has some street in him. A realist who's seen the world for what it is and is willing to do what's needed, even if it doesn't conform to the rules the politicians make to pander to their simple-minded constituents. Look, I'm a hands-on guy. I don't like to delegate when I can do something myself. But I think you and I can be honest with each other and talk turkey, given your history.

Peter: Okay, since we're being honest. I'll admit you've hit some chords with me. But I can't agree to some vague bullshit without understanding exactly what's entailed.

Tucker: I'll explain it in simple terms so there'll be no misunderstanding. Today's negative environment against police work makes it hard to do my job. *Black lives matter* and other bullshit. We need to take stronger measures to get things done. Things that the public secretly craves, but doesn't want to know about. I need a soldier. Someone I can trust and reward in kind.

Peter: You mean an assassin. Luca Brasi to your Don Corleone.

Tucker: Nothing so crude. But yes, I need someone willing to do what it takes. Given the restrictions the left has saddled us with, we have no legal recourse but to leave these vermin on the streets to prey upon honest citizens. Call my methods what you will, but in the end, they'll save lives. I think I've identified one of these predators for you already.

Peter: You're talking about Riley King.

Tucker: I've had my eye on this man for quite some time now. I know that you're his friend and that you helped him with Ginn. I don't know what incentive he gave you to conspire with him on that, but it seems to me that he would scapegoat you if Mr. Ginn's disappearance attracts attention.

Peter: Which you told me it wouldn't.

Tucker: I said it *shouldn't* but, you need to understand, it could go either way. Ginn has worked at this place for decades. There might be some members who question why he's no longer here. I could design a cover story, lay a false trail. Or not. I could lead an investigation into his disappearance. Or not.

Peter: And if you did?

Tucker: If I did, it would start with you. I have a reliable eyewitness who'll swear under oath that the last time Ginn was seen alive was in your custody. King was also at the scene. So you see, if you become my friend, this whole Moses Ginn business goes away and we all live happily ever after. Riley King gets his just desserts. Win-win. But if you decide to obstruct the investigation, things could get quite messy and who knows how deep the repercussions will go. Your choice, detective. And I'll need your answer now.

56

I had to give Tucker credit. He recruited Shabielski on a number of levels. He first appealed to his sense of justice in acknowledgement of Peter's past adventures. I didn't think for a minute that my friend had outright murdered any suspects in New Jersey, but after a couple of stiff bourbons, his cavalier way of describing how he nailed a skell led me to believe that the Geneva Convention wouldn't approve of his techniques.

Just in case that argument didn't fully convince him, Tucker believed he had Shabielski over a barrel and could hold the threat of blackmail over him. Lopez could testify that he had witnessed Peter arresting Ginn and participating in his disappearance.

If Moses were then to surface and deny being arrested, the captain would be stalemated. Tucker was betting against the fact that Ginn was still alive.

Shabielski still had to play the reluctant quarry to maintain credibility.

~~~~~

Peter: If I agree to this, what's in it for me? Whatever you may have heard from up North, I've never been a gun for hire. (pause, a glass sliding, a sipping sound) However, you're right, I *have* seen how the world works. And I'm getting on a bit and I can hardly depend on the pittance the department considers pension to live on. So I'm open to persuasion in the right form.

Tucker: I'm on the verge of something big. I can't be a hundred per cent candid about my plans but let's just say I'll soon be one of the most powerful men in the area. I'm talking money, influence, you name it. All I'm asking is to help rid the world of a low rent PI who has killed for his clients, or even worse, does it just because he can and he enjoys it.

Peter: And how are we going to be different? The lines seem a little blurry from where I'm sitting.

Tucker: I'm a sworn officer of the law. I'm not asking you to do this on a whim or out of some sense of vengeance. I take this very seriously. But trust me, I've tried other ways and he's anticipated my every move.

Peter: How does killing King help achieve that power for you? That's what I don't get.

Tucker: Who said anything about killing? All right, I'll lay it all out. I was part of the Serpente investigation. Somehow he knows I'm not satisfied with the idea that the Russian mob did it, and he knows I'm trying to trace it back to him. He may just kill me before I can make it stick.

Peter: And you're telling me that if King isn't stopped now, he's got others aside from you on this list, too?

Tucker: I'm sure of it. My Lincoln County contacts tell me that his friend Stone was deliberately run off the road. Randee Blankenship met with a near fatal accident at a shooting range. And the mistress who walked out on him, that singer Charlene Jones. That has to burn his ego."

~~~~~

I smiled at my friends and shook my head. Tucker was attributing his own misdeeds to me. If only I was as devious and brilliant as he was describing me. Shabielski must be laughing inside. It must have taken all his willpower to keep it from showing.

~~~~~

Tucker: Think about it. His girlfriend in New Jersey, Elizabeth Huntington --- dead. Another woman he worked with, the agent Paige White ---- dead. Serpente, the man blocking him from Charlene Jones --- dead. Then most recently, a woman he located for a client, Stephanie Perry --- dead. You've heard of Black Widow killers. This guy doesn't marry them, but it's the same difference. They all wind up dead.

Peter: And you've tried to collect evidence on all of these and can't make a case?

Tucker: I told you, he found a scapegoat for every one of them. I wouldn't be surprised if he set up Ginn to take the fall and has trumped up some kind of suicide confession when his body is found. Or how about this --- he'll pin it all on you. If your files from Jersey leak out, a jury might buy it.

Peter: (heavy sigh) All right. You've made your case. I'm going to need a little show of faith. Maybe some earnest money to start? Like you said, he's really smart. He's had me bamboozled all these years if what you say is true. I have to be smarter. I can't leave anything to chance. Give me time, Captain, but I'm on board.

The meeting ended with the two exchanging private cell numbers.

57

From the road a few minutes later, Shabielski called to tell us he was headed toward my place to strategize. It was nearly dinnertime. He said that he'd alerted his family that he'd be home late and that they should eat without him.

"You still don't want me being out in public?" Ginn asked, while dismantling the surveillance gear.

"Uh, yeah, that could blow the whole deal. Why?"

"Well, I been rummaging through your freezer and you ain't got shit left to eat for dinner here. Seeing as we can't exactly go out, I figured I'd throw sometime together but I need to get to the Harris-Teeter."

We both turned to Stone. "Looks like you're nominated, Ricky. Moses, you put together a list of what you need. Rick, you know where the store is. Take your Mustang and try to stay on the pavement this time."

Stone didn't think that was funny.

He said, "All right, I'll go now. I want to be back when Peter gets here."

Ginn scribbled out a list of necessities and then reached into his wallet for cash. He was about to give Stone two fifties when I stopped him. "Use your card, Rick. I'll reimburse you out of expenses."

Normally I'd bill meal money to the client, but in this case, the client was me. Ginn had never hired me --- our diner encounter was a ruse to tell me about the trouble

Randee was starting with her digging. Now my agenda was saving my own hide, protecting Ginn from Tucker, and keeping Randee and Charlene safe from further attacks. I wasn't aware of any direct actions against Ms. Jones, and at this point, she was the least of my worries. I felt I'd discharged my duties with the warning I'd passed on before her concert.

After Rick left, Ginn went to my fridge and grabbed a couple of beers, the one essential I was not in short supply of. We sat in the breakfast area, the stereo tuned to Sirius/XM's *Soul Town*. His choice.

"You and Stone never married?" he said.

"Rick actually was married years ago. Divorced young while he was in the Marines overseas. I came close once a long time ago, and then with Charlene Jones not long ago, but never took the vows."

"Ya'll ain't gay or nothing? Not that it'd be a problem if you was, just need to know who I be dealing with."

"I'm not seeing any rings on your left hand either, big man. Something you trying to tell me?"

"Naw," he laughed, with gusto. "Get outta here. My line of work, I can't be getting hitched up. Got my stable of fine fillies, but they all know the ground rules."

"I got a great girl. I've mentioned her to you before. Jaime Johansen's her name. She lives here part time. Got an apartment in Jersey, stays with her dad on the West Coast. She's an agent and she travels a lot."

"Yeah, I recall I was gonna meet her in Hilton Head last year before things went sour. Where she be now?"

"Up north. I told her not to come back here until we get this under control. Don't want her exposed to this. That why you never hooked up with anyone full time?"

"More or less. Don't need no one close to my business and I got a bachelor's taste for freedom," he winked. "I was just joshing 'bout you boys being gay. I just wondering how you let that Charlene Jones get away. Man, that some fine 'tang going on there."

"Well, don't be a slave to the beauty," I said, quoting Mary Chapin Carpenter, hero of Charlene's. "She dumped me out of the blue. I thought things were going great. Thinking about a ring. Rich client of mine hooked her up with a recording deal and she was out of here. Right there, she showed me where her priorities were and it wasn't me."

"Feel kind of like you was used, I s'pose. Yeah, I had a few flings with women like that. Models. Actresses. None of them amounted to anything, but they was always trying."

Even though I have a doorbell, Shabielski always announces his presence with the "shave and a haircut" knock, as a tribute to Perry Mason's investigator, Paul Drake. It was his juvenile way of mocking my profession.

I opened the door and there stood Shabielski, holding up a nearly full bottle of Gentleman Jack.

"Compliments of Richard Tucker," he said as he barged in. "Insisted I take the remainder of the bottle. It'll partially make up for what your guests guzzled last night. Evening, Moses."

I said, "I'll stick with Scotch in case he had you poison the Jack. I heard what you agreed to with Tucker."

"I'd never do that to fine whiskey. So I even had you going, eh? That's good."

Ginn was at my wet bar, throwing ice into a glass. "Much as I appreciate the sentiment, I ain't drinking that man's hooch either. I'll stick with Red Stripe."

Peter said, "More for me then. Where's Stone. Out chasing college girls?"

"Went to the market. He'll be back soon."

Shabielski accepted the glass from Ginn and poured himself a short measure. "Got to keep a clear head. So you recorded everything? You got a way you can play it back for me?"

Ginn nodded but asked, "Why? You was there."

Shabielski savored his drink. "Nice. If we're going to try to use this tape or whatever you call it these days, I need to hear how it sounds. When you're actually in the room, you pick up on facial expressions, body language and shit that doesn't come across on audio. I just want to make sure it plays back the way I remember it."

Ginn produced an iPod and somehow blue-toothed it into my speaker system. It takes me a half hour to figure that out whenever I try it. He had it up and running in a flash. The three of us nursed our drinks while listening and I watched the expressions on Peter's face as it played. He didn't seem happy.

When it was finished, he refreshed his drink. He was shaking his head the whole time as he sat and said, "Nice try gentlemen, but we can't use any of this. We need a Plan B."

58

THE TROIKA

The massive iron gate to Vander Jackson's mansion creaked open, not fast enough for an impatient Tucker. Things were clicking along now, the plan coming to fruition. He was jazzed from his meeting with Shabielski, but frustrated that he hadn't been able to contact Scott Coleman, the third member of the group.

He would have preferred to address them both and resolve everything at once. As it was, after dispensing with Jackson, he planned to drive to Coleman's uptown apartment to complete his business. He couldn't be sure he'd find Coleman there. After his wife had passed five years prior, the man had downsized dramatically. He'd sold his home and his collection of classic cars, save one. He had relocated to a compact rental unit in a chic center city building. He'd already gifted his art and rare book collection to a spoiled daughter, his one remaining offspring. An only son had pre-deceased him --- an alcohol fueled automobile accident under circumstances that Tucker had helped keep under wraps.

Jackson was a widower as well but he'd remained in the family compound, living alone. He employed a personal aide who often worked from the mansion, a devoted assistant who had been with him for twenty years. Tucker knew that it was unlikely for anyone else to be present this hour of the evening.

His intuition was borne out when Jackson himself greeted him at the door. Although the councilman kept his tippling under control during business hours, he usually maintained a pleasant buzz afterwards. Tonight was no exception --- Tucker could smell the bourbon on his breathe and an overly enthusiastic handshake confirmed the suspicion.

"I'm sorry to intrude on your evening, sir," Tucker began.

"Your visits are never an intrusion, Dick. You know, I always told your dad he was welcome here any time and that extends to you as well. How's your mom? What a dear lady."

They walked through the foyer, passing through leaded glass doors which led to Jackson's inner sanctum. Tucker was a bit surprised that the man was so gracious after the accusations he leveled yesterday. What had changed?

"They're treating her well at the home. I don't get to see her too often. It's pretty uncomfortable. Most of the time she thinks I'm her husband, my dad. She's gotten pretty mean about it, always accusing him of cheating on her, slapping her around. She's attacked me physically a couple times. So I just visit on birthdays and such, not that she'd know and I don't stay long. Hard to take, especially her ravings about dad."

Richard Tucker had never opened up about his private life with his colleagues. Jackson was unsure how to process this information but why worry about it? Especially tonight.

He said, "I'm sorry to hear that. Sadly Dick, I've seen this happen a lot with friends. The best you can do for her is to make sure she's getting the best care. I've heard horror stories about how some of those places abuse the residents."

Since Tucker had shared some of his burden, Jackson felt obligated to reciprocate in sympathy. "My Betty was sharp as a tack, right to the end. I don't know what's worse, for the body to betray you as hers did with the cancer, or for your mind to go. Your mother may actually be lucky. She's living in a dream world, maybe not in any pain. Fantasizing about the past. Betty refused the drugs for a long time, but the pain became too much. At the end, she might have been living in the same state as your mom."

In reality, Tucker was unsentimental about his mother. She'd always been a mean spirited woman who treated him badly. He didn't approve of his father's rage and physical abuse, but he could see a Depression era man believing that she had it coming. In fact, if he thought he could get away with it, Tucker himself would have found a way to end her days as soon as the dementia began to overtake her.

Tucker shrugged. "In any case Councilman, the choice isn't ours, is it? Right now, I'm thinking if I get to that point, physically or mentally, I'll take matters into my own hands. I can't imagine there's a good ending to it. Just more years of suffering. Better to spare myself and others the pain."

If Tucker only knew how often he'd had the same thoughts. Jackson merely nodded in agreement, his face betraying nothing.

He asked, "Can I get you anything? I have quite a selection of fine liquors. You name it, I probably have it somewhere."

"No, just a club soda for me."

As Jackson prepared the drinks, he said, "Now, what did you want to talk about? You said there was an interesting development."

Tucker told Jackson how Moses Ginn had been arrested by a rogue officer and had disappeared.

"Dick, before you go further, let me stop you right here. Scottie and I talked yesterday and we came to the conclusion that it might be time to dissolve our little group."

Tucker began to protest but Jackson cut him off. "Please, let me finish. There was a time when our involvement was absolutely essential to the future of this city. But it's time for my generation to move on. I'm sorry you've only been officially with us a year. We agreed with you that a more pro-active approach was called for, but as things progressed, I realized we don't have the stomach for it. In theory, we accepted the need to act decisively on matters like this, but in practice, it's just not who we are. I'm sorry."

Tucker tried to look penitent. Inside, he felt like a coach who prepared his team to battle a longtime nemesis, only to find that the other side had forfeited and his men would be declared champions by default. He'd already exploited the Troika's contacts and had added some of his own. His need for the support and connections of these two old men was over.

"Van, it would be presumptuous of me to try to dissuade you. I *will* say that you both have my support and gratitude forever. Your good deeds will live on." He raised his glass, halfway meaning the salute.

The councilman said, "Legacies are for those who think they'll be able to look down from heaven and see how others regard their life. I hold no such illusions.

People will think what they will, true or untrue and I'll be in no place to care, one way or the other."

Jackson's voice had been modulated through the entire discussion, partly due to the level of intoxicants he'd ingested and partly because it was his nature.

But now, his voice took on an edge. "Dick, whatever you decide to do going forward is up to you. I'm just telling you now that any more violence is without my blessing. I would advise you against it. I think we've covered our tracks well over the years, and I'm not concerned that anything we've done on the margins will surface. That includes your recent involvement. The books are closed."

"I can respect that."

Jackson nodded and raised his own glass. "God bless, Dick. Best of luck."

Vander Jackson had always been a man of his word, but Tucker knew that age and remorse can do tricky things to otherwise trustworthy men. He hadn't planned any direct action this evening, just a feeling-out session. But after King was taken care of, Jackson might have to be dealt with.

It was getting late. Tucker made his goodbyes, got into his Lexus and maneuvered down the long drive to the steel gate.

From his window, Vander Jackson watched the car pull away. He dialed Scott Coleman and got his machine for the fourth time in the last twenty four hours. Each previous time, he had made a quick request to call him. This time, he left a message.

Jackson poured himself a nightcap, his rarest bourbon, an old Van Winkle. He turned on his stereo, an ancient two channel receiver connected to an outdated CD carousel. On a display shelf was his wedding picture, which he jimmied out of its frame. He wrote something on the back.

There was a small compartment under lock and key in his bottom desk drawer. He removed a small prescription bottle of Betty's pills, which were nearing their expiration date. There was a time during her final days when he had considered hastening the end, but she was a staunchly religious woman and would never have accepted his tender mercies.

He shared no such qualms. Leaving nothing to chance, he swallowed the dozen pills that remained, washing them down with his whiskey.

The CD player alighted on Vivaldi's *The Four Seasons*. By the allegro pastoral of La Primavera, he was gone.

59

Ginn was in the process of ladling out dinner and passing plates to us. He'd concocted something I'd never seen before --- a product of Stone's quick trip to the market and the meager contents of my pantry. It looked and smelled great and my questions as to its pedigree could wait.

After we brought him up to date, Stone was mystified as to why Shabielski had problems with the recording. "Peter, what do you mean, we can't use this? Tucker is telling you to kill King. That's not against the law in the Carolinas?"

I spared Peter the trouble of responding since he was busy attacking his meal. "All Tucker has to do is say that he's trying to entrap Peter, a dirty cop. He can say he came into information that Peter had mistreated suspects in New Jersey and was up to his old tricks here. No doubt he could get Lopez to say he'd witnessed Moses' false arrest, and since Peter denied it, he came up with a trick to see if he'd be agreeable into taking things even further. Pete could turn that around claiming he was the one doing the entrapping, so in the end, it's stalemate and Pete goes down with the ship. And he said very plainly toward the end, *who said anything about killing.*"

"Um, thas it," Shabielski mumbled, his mouth working far more efficiently on the food than his diction.

"What is this stuff, Moses? It's good. I need to give my wife the recipe."

"Just something I throw together. Ain't no recipe. My mama called it Slumgullion. Depression folks took leftovers, whatever scraps they come up with and season the hell out of them. I cheated using some of the stuff I had Ricky pick up at the store, but it's all made up on the fly. Just like your half-ass plan to get Tucker."

"Hey, I said nice things about your cooking," Peter replied. "Look, I'm not saying this recording doesn't have some value. Just that we need more than this if we want to put this guy away. All we got now is a vague conspiracy and he'll turn that back on me. A good defense attorney can blow that out in no time. Plus with my non-disclosure agreement, I could lose my buyout payments from Jersey and even risk them prosecuting me up there. God knows, what shit they'd make up to keep from paying me the rest. And if that stuff gets out, I can kiss any job prospects goodbye. Tucker was right about that."

I said, "We can't ask Peter to risk that. We could try to edit those parts out, but edit points can be detected these days and that would invalidate the whole recording. On Randee's accident we've got no prints or witnesses putting Tucker at the range. And you can't identify him driving the truck that forced you off the road, can you Rick?"

Stone said, "It would help if you backwards rebels had license plates in the front and not just in the rear. But wouldn't you bet that the truck couldn't be traced back to him anyway? Stolen plates or whatever?"

Peter said, "Seems that our best bet is for me to move this along with Tucker. See if I can't get him to trust me enough to make a mistake."

We finished our dinner and Moses then unveiled a store baked apple pie that Stone had picked up. He served it with a slice of cheddar, old school. We chatted about manly things through dessert, trying to avoid any further talk of our troubles. We said goodbye to Peter and I turned in early. Monday night football ended at halftime for me.

Ginn shook me awake at eight the next morning. His face was as ashen as a man of color could get.

He said, "King, you need to get up now. Something bad has happened. Real bad. Get your shit together and come on out. Don't worry 'bout your dog, I done took care of him."

I stumbled out to the kitchen. I felt groggy from the extra sleep my body told me I needed. Knowing Ginn, I half expected breakfast to be waiting but there was coffee, nothing else.

He spoke in a deep, sad monotone. "Breaking story on the local news. Longtime City Councilman Van Jackson. His man came in early this morning. Found him dead. O.D. Saying it be suicide."

Was Tucker erasing everything and everyone that might trace back to him? "My God. I'm sorry, Moses I know you worked with him a long time. Awfully quick to be calling it suicide though. How would the local news have that anyway?"

"He was a politician. His man probably called reporters right after he called the po-pos. They saying he wrote on the back of his wedding picture. *Without Betty, What's the point?*"

60

There is no all news radio station in Charlotte and no need for one. Although I sometimes miss the two 24/7 New York stations that come booming into New Jersey, mostly they consist of repeating headlines involving fires and sensationalized scandals bracketed by cloying commercials and celebrity gossip.

The one news/talk right wing propaganda machine here was full of speculation about Van Jackson's death with little factual information to support it. After listening to a few minutes of platitudes and self-promoting encomiums from the politicians he worked with, we switched off the radio.

Ginn had been stoic throughout, but beneath the tough exterior I had no doubt that he was shaken. Even though the tide had been turning against him with his colleagues, it was clear he still valued how they had taken care of him, grateful for his contributions to their agenda.

"I know you want to keep me under wraps, but we need to find Mister Coleman. If Tucker made this happen with Mr. Jackson, he'll be next in line," he said, while searching the internet for more news.

"I assume you have a bunch of numbers for him. Wouldn't you think Coleman would be at Jackson's place already, trying to keep the cops from prying into his personal files? Stuff that might expose the Troika?"

"You'd think. You buying that Mr. Jackson did this to himself? You not seeing Tucker's hand in this?"

I said, "All we know is they're calling it an overdose. That could mean a lot of things. I'd wager that the forensic guys down here aren't the sharpest knives in the drawer. If I could sell Dan Logan on some kind of Homeland threat, he might send one of his guys, but I can't think of an angle on that."

Ginn was adamant. "Mister Coleman is next. That you can make book on. We need to get to him."

He called the numbers he had for Coleman. The cell went directly to a message stating that the owner was out of range and to leave a number. The landline was linked to an old fashioned answering machine that was full. His law office said he wasn't expected in today and when he asked nicely, they said he hadn't been in yesterday either.

Moses said, "If Tucker killed Mr. Jackson, he might have already done Mr. Coleman too. We need to get to his apartment."

"Me, not us, Moses."

"Mr. Coleman wouldn't talk to you. I'm there, we can lay it out for him and I bet he sees things our way."

"And if he's in league with Tucker?"

Moses said, "Listen up, King. I've known these men since I was a boy. It's true that they brought Tucker into the fold, but they still was partial to me. When that stuff this weekend went down and Tucker tried to lay it on me, they listened, but they wasn't buying it. I'll even wear a disguise if you like, but I got to be there."

He did make sense. For me to approach Coleman on my own might convince him that Tucker was right and I was getting too close.

I said, "What kind of disguise? A man your size would have to go as a Wookie to fool people."

"Ain't no time for jokes. I wear a hat. Pick up a pair of clear glasses at the drug store. A little padding, little slouch. Won't look like me."

"Where does Coleman live?"

"That's another reason I got to go. His crib is in my building. He got a nice furnished place, used to be a model. Not that big. Was just him."

"So how do you get through the lobby in disguise?"

"Garage elevators go right to his floor. Just got to know the code."

I rounded up the Beretta and my set of picks. I had a pair of low magnification readers that wouldn't give Ginn a headache in the short time he'd need them. I even found a fake moustache and an Afro wig from a kit I hadn't used in decades since the Magnum/porn star look went out. Ginn said he'd rather Tucker shoot him than go with that look.

I shook Stone awake and told him our plan. He wanted to come along but I convinced him to stay with Randee, in case Tucker was bent on eliminating all his enemies in one fell swoop.

When Ginn emerged from the guest room, he did look like a different person. Knowing about the transformation, I could recognize him but he wouldn't elicit a second look from most people.

I told him to hunker down in the back seat as I pulled the MDX out, in case we were being watched by Lopez or another one of Tucker's cops. Once we were out on the highway and I was sure there was no one following us, I told him he could sit up front with me.

He said, "You not into *Driving Miss Daisy* in reverse, King?"

I still didn't know Ginn well enough to trash talk him like I do with Stone. I had a few wicked replies that he'd either find funny or cause him to knock me upside the head.

As we reached the stately building in the center city area, Ginn punched in the key code to gain us entry into the underground garage and I parked the Acura in his space. A minute later we were in the elevator headed for one of the upper floors.

"Nice digs you got here, Ginn. Maintenance fees must be a bitch though."

"Not so bad. This building wouldn't be here if not for the Troika. Had to jump through some hoops to get zoning variances to build this tall. They selling pretty good now that the economy's back humming. Almost full up."

I was curious as to where Ginn's apartment was and how he kept it, but we didn't have time for such curiosities. He didn't volunteer, I didn't ask. As it was, Coleman's place was one floor short of the penthouse. Facing southwest, I imagined the views would be incredible.

We knocked to no avail. I said, "Easy lock to pick. I suppose with the security guard in the lobby and the elevator in the garage, they don't feel the need."

"Ain't no New York City place, for sure."

"My friend, we are at a crossroads here. Now I know that B and E is a pretty minor offense, given what we've both done in our time. But if we find Coleman like you found Serpente on the bathroom floor with a couple slugs in him, we'll have some explaining to do. I'm thinking if we do go in, Tucker could make a case that either you or me or both of us are responsible. You think it's possible this is a set-up? Is he that smart?"

"Damn man, you ain't a fed no more. Stop thinking like one."

"We just need to be careful, is all. I brought latex gloves. No harm in putting them on."

"No harm. I been here before so my prints'd be no surprise. You, another story. You want a shower cap so they can't analyze your dandruff?"

I withheld a smartass remark. The door was open within seconds. My speculation about the view was correct. On this clear early autumn morning, you could see the Piedmont gradually give way to the mountains in the west, and the burgeoning housing and shopping development to the South. You could peak into the stadium where the Panthers played and you had a full frontal view of the ballpark that the Charlotte Knights Triple A baseball team called home.

Free baseball? I'm there.

The place had an antiseptic smell about it, as if it had been recently cleaned by professionals. Ginn had mentioned it was a model at one point, and it retained that sterile perfection, an elegantly staged residence designed to suggest how someone would actually live there. There were no dishes in the sink, no magazines or newspapers on the polished quartz counters. The entire living area was devoid of any personal items --- no books, houseplants; in short anything that indicated the presence of a human.

There were two bedrooms. The spacious master included a walk-in closet where no clothes were hung. The queen bed was tightly made, colorful pillows and bolsters arranged at its head. The bath had a long floating vanity, with two glass vessel sinks. No toiletries, cosmetics or medications to be found anywhere.

"Moses, when was the last time you were here?"

"Few weeks back. I didn't exactly inspect the place but it wasn't nothing like it is now. This look like someone getting ready to sell. No pictures on the wall of family, just fruit bowls and flowers and shit. No Mister Scott Coleman in a pool of blood anywhere either, so that's cool."

Back out in the living area, there was a large flat screen television. A compact sectional sofa surrounded the TV. I lifted the cushions, hoping to find some sign of life that had slipped from someone's pocket. No loose change. I looked underneath the coffee table and opened the built-ins. All empty.

The other bedroom was set up as an office with bookshelves on the far wall. The volumes they contained were generic, nothing anyone might actually read, just there for show. The desk was modern, tempered glass and stainless steel --- but no computer or anything other than a leather mat and a small bin containing gel pens and a note pad. A blinking red light caught my eye. Behind the desk was an answering machine, the kind they no longer make, that used cassettes for outgoing and incoming messages. I called for Ginn to join me before I hit the PLAY button.

The indicator said there were 12 messages. The incoming cassette looked like it held at least ten minutes. The first few were hang-ups, followed by the beeping of a phone no longer connected. Then a voice that Ginn identified as Jackson's, asking Coleman to call him. There was a call from a car service, confirming that Mr. Coleman would be picked up at his residence at noon. I used one of the pens to write down the name.

Three more calls from Jackson followed, each increasing in urgency. A couple of unidentified callers were next. Then Jackson again, this time calm and resigned.

As we spooled through the first eleven calls, they were brief enough not to tax the cassette's load. None really mattered except for the final one, that clocked almost five minutes.

It was Jackson, warning Coleman that Tucker might be headed his way. He then gave us his suicide proclamation, in full.

61

There was nothing in Jackson's final message that implicated Tucker as having anything to do with his death. The councilman admitted that they had made a mistake inviting him into their club but there was nothing specific about the police captain, other than whatever he did in the future was on him. He said that his little group had outlived its usefulness. He hoped that Coleman could find the peace of mind that had eluded him and that in sum, he had done more good in his time on earth than bad. He never mentioned the Troika by name.

Ginn listened to the speech without comment. He avoided eye contact, but his brain was churning. When the tape ran out, he simply said, "Damn, the man was righteous to the end. Never said nothing that helps us much with Tucker. I was hoping we could take this tape and nail that motherfucker."

"The warning that anything Tucker does from now on is off his conscience could be useful. That is, if we survive whatever he has in store for us. Our problem is explaining how we got the tape. We broke into Coleman's place so it's the fruit of a poison tree. Tucker gets the right judge and this gets thrown out."

There was righteous anger was burning in Ginn now. "Who said anything 'bout a judge? You still got a lot of fed in you, King. You want to run this through the system. Like I say first day we met. I seen the system fail more times than not. You got to take things into your own hands."

"Now you sound like Tucker. Look Moses, you knew Jackson, I didn't. But what I heard was a man with a lot of regrets for letting things get out of hand. Let's try to do this the right way. That doesn't work, then we think about what you're saying."

"And what is the right way, 5-0?"

"For starters, if we leave the cassette here, Tucker might break in here like we did and find it. So we need to make a copy. I have my digital recorder with me. It's a crude way of doing it, like I used to do when I recorded songs off the radio when I was a kid. Play it back, record it through the speakers."

"And you think some judge wouldn't throw that out?"

"That's our back up copy. After we record it, we hide the original cassette somewhere Tucker wouldn't look for it. Then in a day or so, someone anonymous calls Shabielski or someone he trusts and reports that Coleman is missing. He has probable cause to come here and look around. He finds the tape where we tell him we hid it."

"Fucking devious, King."

"Thank you, Moses. I'll take that as a compliment coming from you."

Ginn said, "Problem is, we do that and Coleman and Jackson could get exposed."

I knew all along that it would come to this. There was no way to surgically remove Tucker from the Troika without the others getting caught in the web. If we play this straight, the obvious defense for Tucker would be that he was acting on the others' orders. Jackson wasn't around to deny it, and now it seemed, neither was Coleman. Either way, the other two would get dragged into this and their reputations would be soiled. There was no way around it. I told Ginn as much.

He didn't like hearing it spelled out in those terms. "Man disfigured the old lady, almost killed your friend. You asking me if I be willing to let him skate on that to protect my friends? We gonna have a problem with that, you and me?"

"You were willing to give Serpente an out. Let him take off to parts unknown. Escape justice, even though his building practices might be responsible for killing a lot of folks in the long run."

"Made my peace with that, King. The men you so willing to throw under the bus made that right. Did a re-do of the buildings Serpente fucked up. Fixed the ones they could, demolished the others and relocated folks. And you didn't even know that, did you? That's how these men worked. Quiet-like. I ain't messing with that, my man, no way."

"So what's your answer? I'm listening."

Moses said, "Only thing I can think of is we find Mr. Coleman. He might have another way out. He was a great lawyer in his day. He might already have figured on something like this happening and had a plan for it."

"I think we're seeing his plan. He vamoosed without a trace. Seems like you're more worried about his reputation than he is, otherwise he might have stuck around to fight it."

Ginn was unconvinced. "How 'bout we do this? We do your thing, 5-0. Record the tape, hide it, hip your cop friend to where it's hid. Then you and me look for Mr. Coleman. I believe that the man panicked and took off. Let's find him and see what gives."

"I know you respect these men, Moses. But Coleman must have planned this well in advance. You just don't disappear and wipe all traces from your condo in one day. This has been in the works for a while. Push comes to shove, if it comes down to cold blooded murder of a cop, however dirty he might be, or exposing your pals, it's a no-brainer for me. You need to work with me on this, or we have a big problem."

62

The late afternoon shadows were lengthening as I sat with Peter Shabielski in my MDX, parked on Church Street, uptown. I had taken Ginn back to my place, trusting that he'd stay anchored to the phone and internet, searching for leads on Coleman. Stone was at the hospital. There was no change in Randee's condition and Ida May Wright was with him, keeping vigil.

Shabielski said, "So Coleman's on the lam and Jackson's dead. Whoop-de-damn-do. Now what, Sherlock?"

"I just got back from the car service office. I sweet-talked the lady there into telling me that Coleman was never picked up yesterday. He was supposed to be taken to Charlotte Douglas at noon. They went to his building and he wasn't there. Already had his card on record so they charged him anyway."

"Good to know they didn't get ripped off," he said, deadpanning the sarcasm. "Tucker wants to meet again."

"What do you think he wants now?"

"I suspect he knows Coleman is gone, maybe because he caused it. You know Riles, after all this, we got ugatz as my Italian brethren say. The good news is that this Troika is finished. But the bad news is we can't prove Tucker did anything to Randee or Stone. The word *impasse* come to mind?"

"I just had this conversation with Ginn. What are you saying? Just let him get away with it?"

"That's just it, with what? The Randee thing could have another explanation. Just because he knew about the wrong cartridges, it could have been a guess on his part. The man knows firearms. And without anything solid on the truck that wrecked your car, that could have been coincidence as well."

"Come on, Peter. All within 24 hours? Not bloody likely. And what about the small detail of enlisting you to kill me?"

"Like I said before, he'll claim I'm a dirty cop he's trying to set up. Do I believe he's guilty of all these things? Damn straight, I do. But he's smart. Didn't leave any tracks."

"Unless Coleman is dead, killed by Tucker. Might explain why the car service didn't pick him up. I had Crain check flight records. Nothing in the last forty eight hours out of Charlotte-Douglas in Coleman's name. Maybe he was planning to disappear but Tucker got to him first."

"Doesn't compute. If Coleman was planning to vanish on his own, why kill him? And if Tucker is such a natural born killer, why recruit me? Like you've been saying all along, why trust a man who's a longtime friend of yours? He'd just do it himself."

"Maybe he doesn't have the guts to do it with a knife or a gun, but what about poison? I know that's more a lady's choice but he could have drugged Jackson, pumped him full of booze and pills and made it look like an OD. That phone message could be interpreted as a farewell to the Troika, not necessarily a suicide note. Might have done the same to Coleman and they just haven't found the body yet."

"Why? These men were his path to glory. They let him in their little club with all their connections. Why eliminate that?"

The more I know, the less I understand. Did some great philosopher say that or was it Don Henley? Maybe they're one and the same.

I said, "I don't know, Pete. I was just thinking out loud. Maybe they're the only ones who can tie him to some bad stuff and if they're gone, he's clear. So, are you going to meet with him?"

"Yes, I kind of have to now. Ginn was his immediate problem and Tucker thinks we took care of that for him. Bottom line, maybe I can convince him that you're no threat to him now. If he promises to leave you alone, are you willing to let this whole thing drop?"

Something wasn't right. Less than a day ago, Pete rejected my idea that Tucker could be convinced that I was no longer a danger. He was gung-ho about stopping him before he got to us. Now he seemed content to let him walk away unscathed if he promised to be a good boy going forward. Something had happened to spook him. Macho guy that he is, Pete would never admit it. Had Tucker threatened his family?

No matter what, Tucker had to answer for Randee, through legal channels or otherwise. I couldn't live with myself if I let that go unspoken for

"Detente, eh?" I said. "What sticks in my craw is that I let things go with Serpente and now it's coming back to haunt me. I want this over. I'm tired of this shit. I want a normal life, none of this drama."

"You're in the wrong line of work for that, my friend. Just a few days ago, you were complaining about being bored. Feeling useless. Now you're back in the soup and you hate it. What's it going to be?"

I let that sit for a minute. "I'll have to go forward without you then. You've already stuck your neck out. If you've come to the conclusion that the price is too high now, I have to respect that."

He said, "You and I have been there before, haven't we? But there *are* times when shit happens and there ain't no easy solve. And even an honest man just has to turn the page. Know what I'm saying?"

"Be careful with Tucker, Peter. Do what you think is best. I'll work out my end."

My end might be letting Ginn kill Tucker.

He said, "I'll try to make Tucker see that the smart move is to quit while he's ahead. Like you say, he may not have the stones to do the dirty work himself and if I can convince him that you're not a threat any more, he may back off."

I gave him a quick grin, acknowledging that we both knew this whole affair was headed sideways. Shabielski squeezed my arm gently and got out of the car. There was something final about it that made me shiver.

63

PETER SHABIELSKI

The meeting was set for early evening and Tucker had selected a secluded spot in a small park bordering Lake Norman. Although there was frequently posted signage stating that the facility closed at dusk and violators would be prosecuted, there was no one charged with enforcing the dictum. As a partial consequence of this budget-driven negligence, many generations of high school girls had surrendered their maiden virtue for the first time on its grounds.

There was a green painted cinder block building shielded by small trees just off the parking area which served as a public restroom. The waxing moon cast enough light so that Peter could find his way to the building without using his phone for illumination. He saw a small red dot in the distance, which turned out to be the glow from the cigar that Tucker was puffing.

Shabielski tried to sound casual to mask his apprehension at the circumstances. "Hello, Chief. Nice evening. Pretty comfortable for this time of year."

"Care for a Cohiba? Making these easier to get might be the single most positive achievement that shithead who was in the White House did in all his eight years."

"I don't indulge, but thanks anyway. I'm curious as to why you wanted to meet here rather than at the club. A bit more civilized there, wouldn't you say?"

"We won't be meeting at the Nat anytime in the near future."

It was hard to read the man's face in the darkness, but his tone was brusque. "May I ask why, Captain?"

"Care to hazard a guess? Or do you already know?"

"I'm afraid you've lost me."

"Yeah, I'm afraid of that, too. You see, when the late Mr. Ginn didn't show up for work for the second consecutive day, we went through his desk. Without getting too technical, we found that his Ethernet connection had a splitter switch concealed in a drawer's false bottom connected to another network. Ginn had the place bugged. We located a couple of hidden mics, but there probably are more. Nothing was labeled. I've got a team coming in tomorrow to sweep the place."

"You're thinking Ginn had a recording of our conversation?"

"That's why you need to tell me the truth now. No bullshit. If Ginn is alive somewhere, he might have that recording and maybe some others that could be harmful to me personally and to us both. I need you to tell me where he is."

Shabielski was boxed in. He had already anticipated Tucker's defense if yesterday's session came to light. But now of more immediate concern, if he admitted that Ginn was alive, Tucker would undoubtedly press him to divulge his whereabouts to rectify that condition.

"Ginn won't be a problem any longer."

"Evasive answer, detective. That could mean a great many things."

Peter caught the glint of a cruel smile on the man's face in the dim moonlight. "Is he dead? Yes or no."

"Yes."

It's the only answer I can give. If Tucker was wearing a wire and was trying to set him up, his defense would be simple --- he could produce a living, breathing Moses Ginn.

Tucker reached behind his back as if to scratch a mosquito bite. But Tucker wasn't scratching. He was reaching for his 9mm Glock, which he then leveled at Peter.

"Prove it. Up against the wall, detective."

Shabielski was stunned but did as he was told. Tucker patted him down and removed his service revolver, tucking it into a jacket pocket.

Peter said, "Wait a minute, sir. I thought we were working together here. I don't understand."

"You think I'm an idiot? You and King have been friends for years. You think just because you told me yesterday that you were willing to consider killing him that I bought it, hook, line and sinker? You need to go a lot further than that to gain my trust."

"But Captain, you started this train rolling. You came to me and sold me on all that stuff about King. I was skeptical at first, but after thinking about it, what you said added up."

"So I'm to believe that my circumstantial case would cause you to turn on a friend and be on board to kill him? That kind of paper thin loyalty doesn't impress me for someone I'd consider as a partner. No, young feller, you didn't have me snookered for a minute. I want Ginn. If you can prove that he's dead, that'd be step one in convincing me you're for real. Then maybe, just maybe, we can talk about what to do with King."

Shabielski's brain was in overdrive. "What if we cut him up and threw him into the lake? How could I prove he's dead then?"

"I thought you might say that. I can keep you on ice for forty eight hours. You tell me where you hid the body, I'll have that area dragged. We find him or a piece of him, I cut you loose. If not, maybe something happens to you. You never know what kind of company a cop might find in a holding cell."

"How do I know you won't pin Ginn's murder on me?"

"The only one who saw you arrest him is a fellow I have under control. He won't talk if I tell him not to. Depending on how this plays out, we'll lay all the blame on King. Kill two birds with one stone. Now, what's it going to be, detective?"

Shabielski had to come up with a plan on the fly and those were usually fraught with holes. He had to somehow get reinforcements, and the only way he could think of on the spur of the moment was to lead Tucker to King's place.

He said, "Ginn's not in the lake. He's dead, but we haven't disposed of the body yet. It's in King's basement. We needed to get Stone away from there. He doesn't know we killed Ginn. He thought we just rousted him and let him go, like a practical joke, an initiation into our little circle."

"You're telling me this Stone fellow isn't part of this?"

"He's just a radio sports guy. Worthless piece of shit, but King likes him. The other thing is, King doesn't own a boat. We need to borrow one to dump the body in a deep part of the lake. King was working on that. It was going to happen soon, maybe even tonight."

"Perfect. Take me there. Is King at home now?"

"I don't know. What if he is?"

"You and I are law enforcement. We find a body in the basement. King tries to shoot his way out. I think you can fill in the rest. Now move. You drive. Trust me, you try to pull anything, I have a plan to explain your untimely demise as well. Let's roll."

64

Moses threw together another improvised meal that was every bit as tasty as the one he'd prepared the night before. He, Stone and I picked at our food, making small talk about sports, women, politics --- anything to take our minds off the impending doom we saw coming.

Stone asked if we could spare him tonight. He wanted to blow off some tension. So far, his boss had been understanding about his taking time off to deal with what he termed a "personal issue", but Ted McCarver wasn't stupid. A couple more days and the radio exec would insert himself into the situation, a complication none of us needed.

Stone said he had a convenient lady the next town over who would accommodate his needs on the spur of the moment. I couldn't see any reason to object other than my constant mantra about him and his dalliances with millennials. He took off in the Mustang, leaving Ginn and me to a quiet evening in front of the screen.

Ginn suggested a baseball game involving his favorite team, the Atlanta Braves. Being a Mets fan, I've always hated the Braves but I gave in to his wishes. Rockies 6 Braves 0, bottom 5. That gave me a momentary pang of pleasure.

I was waiting to hear from Shabielski about his meeting with Tucker, hoping he'd found an opening that could extract us from this morass. I wanted to go along as back up, but he refused. By nine thirty, I was tempted to call him, but if he was still involved with the chief, a friendly hello from me would not work to his advantage.

I said, "Hey Ginn, my Metsies are on the coast getting set to play the Dodgers. Mind if we switch over to that game in a few minutes?"

"It's your screen, 5-0. I'm thinking of turning in now anyway. My squad ain't coming back in this one. Knock on my door if you hear from Pete, okay?"

"Will do. But, do me a favor please. Stop with the 5-0. I'm not a fed anymore. 'Night, Moses."

Bosco followed him toward the guest bedroom that he shared temporarily with Stone. Moses stopped at the door and gestured at the dog.

I said, "Just leave the door open a crack. He'll sleep on the floor in front of the bed for a while, then he'll probably want to join his dad. He's fickle that way. Unless you mind, of course."

"Not hardly. Good to have the company. See you in the AM, King."

I waited until he was through the bedroom door before turning off the torture of the Braves game to switch over to Keith Hernandez and the Mets' pregame. I was getting a bit drowsy myself and doubted I'd make it to the middle innings or Stone's return, whichever came first.

Kershaw had just thrown the first pitch when I heard the doorbell ring. Rick usually just barged in after a quick tap. Peter always did his "shave and a haircut" routine. Jaime was in New Jersey. Who could this be?

"Yeah, hold on," I said, adjusting my belt and sliding into my New Balances in case it was Stone with female companionship.

"It's Peter. Open up, Riles."

No special knock this time. Whatever. I was too drowsy to take any precautions so I just opened the door.

Peter stumbled in, shoved violently from behind. Standing in my doorway was a short, muscle bound oaf, waving a gun at us both.

I said, "Richard Tucker, I presume. Welcome to my humble abode. Fix you a drink?"

65

"**I** will say you're better looking than your pictures, King. I'll pick a nice one for your obit, I promise," Tucker said.

With that bit of gloomy foreshadowing, it was obvious the cop had forced Peter to lead him to my place.

Shabielski said, "He knows, Riley. Don't try to waste his time bluffing. He knows we killed Ginn."

"Shut up, detective. I control the agenda here," Tucker said.

Peter had told Tucker we had killed Ginn in retaliation for his supposed attacks on Randee and me. Now I understood the play. But I had little power to direct the antagonist. I knew his motivation, but he might not choose to follow my script.

I tried to project a breezy tone. "So Captain Tucker, you're here to thank me for removing a thorn from your paw. You're welcome."

"You'll have my undying gratitude. Sorry the undying part won't apply to you. I'm a cop. I'm here to see that you pay for killing a valued employee of the Nat, even though we both know he was a no good, lying thug."

"Devilishly charming rascal, though, give him credit. All right, read me my rights. I'll go quietly."

Tucker smiled. "You know, King, you are just wrong on so many levels. If I really believed you'd let things rest, I'd be tempted to give you a pass. But I know your history. You'll keep picking at the scab. So let me save you the trouble. Ginn didn't do Blankenship or bruise up your pal Stone. Where is Stone, by the way?"

"He's out for the night with a lady friend. He won't be back till morning."

"Shame he'll miss all the fun. I'm afraid you two jerkoffs killed an impotent old coon. A pain in the ass but merely a minor obstacle. He was too much of a pussy to do what needed to be done, so I had to take things into my own hands. But I'm thorough, to a degree you can't even imagine. You would never have been able to prove I hot-loaded the old crone's gun or ran your radio friend off the road."

His gun was pointed at me. Peter was a few feet away, not close enough to disarm Tucker with a quick move if he saw an opening. The blatant admission of guilt meant that Shabielski was dead meat as well.

I tried to reason with him, knowing his low opinion of my ethics. "Ginn threatened me. I couldn't afford to risk that he'd follow through. I called his bluff and he paid the ultimate price. But think about it. The Troika is history. Jackson is dead. Coleman missing. You're on your own now. And far as I'm concerned, it's over. Stone is okay, and Randee'll recover. Nobody cares about Serpente. I'm satisfied. We can shake hands and call it a day."

"Can't do it. I told your pal on the way over, maybe the old men are gone but I was never one for committees anyway. Suffice to say, I've got their contacts under my influence now. I don't need those two old men, may they rest in peace."

"So Coleman's dead, too?"

"As good as. That gutless shyster bailed as soon as he saw things headed south. He called before he left and swore he'd never say anything about anything. I actually don't believe he'll talk, because if he does, he screws himself in the process. But I'm not one to leave anything to chance. I'll find him and he'll meet with an unfortunate accident. Pity."

Ginn was in the guest room. I glanced over and noticed the door was now completely closed. That explained why Bosco hadn't bolted out when he heard the door. I just hoped that Ginn was resourceful enough to figure a way out of this before Tucker shot us.

Stalling for time, I said, "You know Cap'n Dick, the one thing I can't figure about you is why you're doing all this. Your dad was assistant commissioner. That could have been your future, too. Power, decent bucks, a nice life. That wasn't enough?"

"Hey shit for brains, you think I don't know what you're doing? The longer we talk, you're hoping I'll slip up and you or your friend will get the drop on me. Well, I'll indulge you one last time to satisfy your curiosity. My dad should have been the top cop in this town, but he was the wrong color. So am I. The blacks have taken over Charlotte. Vote fucking Democrat like lemmings. But a few miles away, in South Carolina? The whites still rule and will for the foreseeable future."

"So, basically you're a racist. Is that it?"

"Nothing against the blacks, I work with them every day. Some of them are really good folks. Their politics just don't align with my interests, is all. I've already got big time tentacles down in Fort Mill. Virgin territory. I'll have power there I'd never have in Charlotte. Coleman and Jackson were short sighted. Looked at South Carolina as low rent and only had a few interests there. Well, I groomed those people and added some more, gave them respect. I just picked up a huge tract of land for twenty grand. That's where I'll build *my* empire. The Troika never cared about South Carolina, that was all me."

The few hours I spent with Bill Flores and his boss sealed my fate. How could I have known that?

Tucker said, "You poked your nose in there and that bit of snooping signed your death warrant. I have to convince my new partners that they're covered and there's no danger of exposure. I can't let you threaten my grand design on York County. It's too big."

I said, "*Poor man want to be rich, rich man want to be king and the king ain't satisfied 'til he rules everything.* Springsteen had it right". I couldn't reference as many tunes as Stone, but I knew the good ones.

"Whatever. Never did like those lefty rock stars. Gimme Blake Shelton any day. Now, let's get down to business. Detective Shabielski. Handcuff this man."

Peter did as he was instructed, but neglected to click the right cuff closed. Tucker didn't notice. That meant I'd have both hands free and might even be able to swing the loose manacle as a weapon.

"Now, last order of business. Show me the body. I need to be a hundred per cent sure that Ginn is dead and not sitting on some island in the Caribbean with Coleman, plotting revenge."

My thoughts exactly. Where was Ginn? How could he sleep through this?

Peter said, "It's pointless to try anything Riles. I told him where we hid Ginn's body in the basement."

Tucker was cautious but he was buying it. "You two lead me down there. You first, King."

The stairs to the basement were down a short hallway, that branched off toward the guest bedrooms. Peter was directly behind me. If I could stumble and trip him up, one of us might be able to go for Tucker's gun before he got off more than one shot. I couldn't think of any way out without blood. One of us would likely be hit, but the other might be able to subdue Tucker.

Just as I was ready to dive, the guest room door sprang open and Bosco came bounding out. Tucker turned toward the dog, ready to fire. I shoved Peter at him and the gun went off. The shot missed the dog, careening harmlessly into the baseboard. Tucker was more athletic than I anticipated. He quickly realized that Bosco was the least of his worries and fired blindly toward Peter and me. The bullet hit Peter and he crumpled to the floor.

The muzzle retorts were deafening in the small space. I dove across Shabielski's prone body, and tried to tackle Tucker. I slammed the manacle into his calf attempting to jolt him off balance, but he was too strong and wheeled the Glock around to finish me.

The kill shot never came. Instead, I heard a sickening thud followed by a squishing sound, a thick butcher's knife into ripe melon. Tucker's eyes opened wide and a torrent of blood erupted from his mouth. He teetered and collapsed, crashing to the floor like an pole-axed pine.

Behind him stood Moses Ginn. As Tucker fell, he released the golf club that he'd implanted in Tucker's brain.

66

I turned Peter over, not knowing where the bullet had penetrated. From the bloom of crimson on his white shirt, it appeared to be a through and through, creasing the left side just above the waist.

"Grab me the phone, Ginn. We need to call 911 and get an EMS crew here now."

Moses, rage still on his face, was standing over the lifeless figure of Tucker. Bosco scurried over to the corpse, sniffed once and then tried to dig his snout under Peter, his muzzle reddened by my friend's blood.

"I'll call," Moses said, as his demeanor returned to its normal placid state, as if nothing had happened.

"No. You were never here. Just give me the phone."

"What?"

"Don't argue. Give me the phone then get the hell out of here."

I was ministering to Peter as best I could, trying to stanch the flow of blood with my torn off tee shirt. I didn't have time to argue with Ginn.

But he refused to hand me the phone. He'd already dialed 911. He told the operator about the gunshot wound, which automatically triggered a police response, as well as an ambulance. I'd have to work fast.

"Ginn, I wanted to keep you out of this. Now you've blown it. They record all 911 calls and someone will identify your voice."

"What was your plan 5-0? Take the heat for me? Say *you* did Tucker? Not happening."

"Other than the two of us, no one would have ever known. Pete hit his head, he's out cold. Don't you get it? A black man killing a white police captain who was making an arrest. That's how they'll spin it. Let me take it. I've got a better chance of beating the rap."

"Ain't putting you in that position. We tell the truth. Chips fall where they may."

"What truth? Tucker told *us* about South Carolina, but he covered his tracks. His buddies down there'll scatter like flies now he's gone. They won't be lining up to confirm our story, that's for sure."

I shooed Bosco away from Peter and got up to find something to clean the wound. Soaking a clean microfiber cloth in hydrogen peroxide, I dabbed the area gently as I waited for the medics to arrive. I glanced over at Tucker occasionally, certain that he was dead. The force of Ginn's blow had been mighty.

Moses smiled. I couldn't imagine what he thought was amusing given the circumstances. Then he spoke in that reassuring baritone of his.

"We tell Tucker's truth. He was friends with Serpente. Didn't buy the Russian connection. Thought you did it. Recruited Peter to go undercover and get the goods on you."

"Then what?" I said.

"Shabielski couldn't find anything to tie you to it. So Tucker freaked and decide to blow you away resisting arrest. If Pete wouldn't go along, he'd get hit in the crossfire. That's what really happened, didn't it. The truth shall set you free."

"That's nice, but what about you? How do we explain your role?"

"Easy. Randee got hurt. Stone, too. Someone was targeting your friends and you thought you might be next. So you hired Ole Moses to cover your back. You done employed me before when you needed help, got receipts to prove it. I turned in early. Heard what was going down and got Tucker before he got you."

I found the handcuff key on Tucker's body and freed myself. The sting of the antiseptic made Peter flinch, and his eyes opened briefly. I said, "Peter. Hold on man, help's on the way. You're going to be fine."

At that point, I had no idea if that was true. People have bled out from shots to the thigh with low caliber weapons, when they graze an artery. Shabielski wasn't bleeding too heavily considering the size of the load, but I had no way of knowing what might be happening internally.

"What happened? I think I hit my head after he shot me. Where's Tucker?" he asked, his voice weak.

"He's dead. Moses nailed him with the blade putter, back of the head. His brains are all over the floor. Saved our lives."

"Holy shit."

"Take it easy now. Look, when the cops come, just tell the truth about Tucker recruiting you to get at me. Don't lie. And don't volunteer anything about Moses and the Troika. Just say Tucker wanted me to pay for Serpente."

He nodded and grimaced in pain. I found an old throw pillow to rest his head and called Stone. No answer, so I left a message telling him not to come back tonight and make sure he had a solid alibi for the evening. In his case, a lady willing to admit she was with him, a concern given his penchant for women committed to others. I said not to come back to the house, just drive directly down to Hilton Head and I'd fill him in later.

Ginn had gone back into the bedroom. I heard him talking on the phone. I hoped he was talking to a good lawyer.

Sirens closing in. I'd lost track of time, but later found out that the EMS crew arrived ten minutes after the call. They ministered to Peter, trying to disturb the crime scene as little as possible. After checking for a pulse, they left Tucker where he lay.

A minute after the EMS crew, a young Lincoln County cop arrived and ushered me into the kitchen while calling for backup and a CSI team. He told Ginn to leash the dog and confine him to the master bedroom, which Bosco didn't like. But Jaime's efforts at obedience training paid off, and he complied.

I've been through this drill before, more than once. I didn't call a lawyer. If I couldn't talk my way past these county cops, my whole career was for naught, especially since I had backing for my story.

I agreed to their request to come to the station house for questioning. I awakened Mrs. Keegish and told her that we'd had a break-in. Shortly, an officer would be bringing Bosco by and could she take care of him until I returned? She agreed after giving me the third degree about whether she should be worried about intruders in the neighborhood.

Keegish's questions were merely a prelude for the grilling the Lincoln County LEOs had in store for me. They let me drive my MDX to the precinct house, but insisted an officer accompany me. They drove Ginn separately in a squad car. I was led to an interrogation room, where I described the evening's events exactly as they occurred to the senior detective on the county force, who had been called in from home.

His most pressing issue was why a distinguished captain of the Char/Meck force would break into my house with another officer and then want to kill us both.

I said that Captain Tucker believed I had killed Johnny Serpente, a member of his club with whom he had become friendly. Whereas the higher-ups were willing to accept the easy solution about the Russian mob, he was troubled by some inconsistencies. Since Charlene and I discovered the body and she moved in with me shortly thereafter, he concluded I killed the man so I could have Charlene to myself. He researched my past and concocted a theory that I had been responsible for several other murders and had tricked scapegoats into taking the blame. Such was my criminal genius.

Frustrated that he was unable to make a legal case, he recruited Shabielski. Peter was a friend of mine, and Tucker tasked him to go undercover to try to get me to admit my role in Serpente's death, preferably while wearing a wire. Peter believed in my innocence but agreed to go along with the plan, hoping to convince Tucker that he was barking up the wrong tree.

But tonight after Peter told him that he had tried but could find no proof of my guilt, a frustrated Tucker attempted to force Shabielski into acting as my executioner. He'd stage a struggle and it would appear that I'd been shot resisting arrest. When Peter refused, he planned to kill us both --- making it look like I had killed Shabielski in the tussle.

My inquisitor couldn't fathom why Tucker would be so intent on revenge for the death of a two bit hood like

Serpente. When I was finished, I could tell he wasn't buying my story. In his place, I wouldn't have either.

We *did* have the recording, now in Ginn's possession. But the tape would lead the cops down a lot of roads we prefer they not travel. Given Shabielski's past, the agreement he made with Tucker to accept money for his services might be enough to end his career.

That section could easily be edited out. But I knew that the edit points could be easily discovered and that would render the whole recording worthless as evidence. We'd hold the SD card in abeyance unless it was absolutely necessary.

67

After two hours of interrogation, I played a card I hated to see when I was on the other side of the table. I told the detective to either charge me or release me.

After his stern admonition that this demand made me look guilty, I was about to walk out when there was a knock on the door. The Lincoln County detective left the room, locking the door behind him. Something was up and I doubted it was good news for the home team.

Through the heavy door, it was hard to distinguish what was said. But after five minutes of what sounded like a heated exchange, he returned.

He said, "I'm turning this over to the Mecklenburg authorities. The incident occurred in our jurisdiction but it involved two of their officers and Mr. Ginn resides in Charlotte. I could insist on retaining control but frankly, I don't need this on my plate right now. I'm surrendering the case to Mecklenburg. They're waiting outside and they want to talk to you."

I got a free ride to city headquarters, courtesy of the Char/Meck police. A junior officer drove behind us in my MDX and parked it in their underground garage.

The facilities were larger and better appointed than Lincoln County's but the act was the same. I told my story, they asked the same questions, registered the same skepticism. I was expecting a couple of days in a holding cell while they sorted things out, and was pleasantly surprised when they told me I could go. On the way out, I spotted Moses Ginn, sitting outside another interrogation room. He was handcuffed to a chair, but otherwise unattended.

I said, "I wish you'd have let me play this my way."

"Ain't letting you take the rap for what I done, boss."

"That's funny, you calling me boss when you just defied what I wanted you to do. I was hoping you'd lay low until we could sync up our stories."

"Nothing to sync up. You was about to get shot, I did what had to be done. Man had a gun, coulda turned it on me next."

"Black man kills a white cop who was trying to arrest a serial killer. That's how this will get twisted. I was trying to keep you and your precious Troika out of this. You *do* realize that if I have to use that recording we made, this turns into a Donnybrook and there's no end to the crap that'll get dug up."

"The truth will out. Keep the faith."

"Look Moses, I need to think this through and I'm beat. No sleep. I can't risk making a mistake that gives them a hole they can run through. They haven't booked you yet, have they?"

"Don't you worry 'bout me. And I'm telling you, don't be lying to take any heat off me 'cause I'll step up and call you on it. You ain't going down for something I done, brother."

~~~~~

Peter Shabielski had been taken to the main CMC facility off Morehead, the same hospital where Randee currently resided. Normal procedure is to separate the participants in a violent incident and question them separately. If those involved are suspects, it provides the opportunity to turn them on one another in the interests of self preservation. If they are victims, it prevents them from altering their stories to conform to a peer-shared point of view, which may distort reality. I wasn't sure how neatly Shabielski and I fit into these categories. While we were clearly victims, we weren't exactly innocent bystanders who had played things by the book.

Peter was sitting up in bed, looking none the worse for wear. There was no one on duty outside the door, so I just walked in.

I said, "How you feeling, pal? Sorry I didn't bring flowers."

"Hey, King. The shot didn't do much damage. Got stitched up. I'll be on the links next week. Worse was when I hit the floor afterwards. My head hurts like hell. They're pretty sure I was concussed."

"You'll be on the PUP list for a while. Don't push it."

"Physically unable to perform. That's how the ladies describe you."

The fact he could trash talk was reassuring. Despite the weak quip, it showed that whatever wits he had going in were still there.

"So, who's talked to you so far?"

"Detectives first, then the assistant commish dropped in, some prick from internal affairs and finally my union rep. You're a welcome break in the action, much as I hate to say it."

"So what did you tell them? You were pretty woozy last night. I wasn't sure you heard what I said or remembered it."

"You said tell the truth. I did. Didn't mention the recording. Did you?"

I looked around the room for anywhere a mic could be hidden; understanding that such precautions would be fruitless if someone had skillfully bugged the place. Any one of the group that had visited Peter might have left surveillance behind, so I tailored my comments carefully.

I said, "Not sure what you mean. The truth is the best course. Tucker used you to get to me. He was going to kill us both. Bosco jumped out and distracted him, you went for the gun. He shot you, and that gave Ginn time to hit him with that putter."

"Yeah, well, the commish already gave me shit for not reporting Tucker when he first approached me."

"What did you say to that?"

"I said he was a decorated captain asking me to do undercover work. I believed you were innocent and I was willing to go along with Tucker's plan to prove that to him."

"That's essentially what went down. You had no idea Tucker would turn vigilante and set us both up."

He rubbed the back of his head. "I guess. You sure you don't want to bring the South Carolina scenario into play?"

"Not now. It could muddy the waters. My main concern is Moses. He admitted killing Tucker. Saved both our lives and I don't want him going down for that, although he's willing to."

"Where are you going now?"

"My place is a crime scene. I can't stay there. I've already sent Stone down to the house on Hilton Head. I may head there myself soon."

Peter scrunched his brows together. "If it was me, I wouldn't let you leave town but unless they formally arrest you, I guess you could just tell them where you'll be. At most, you're an accessory or a material witness since Ginn fessed up. South Carolina is pretty good about extradition and vice versa. We sent that Charleston church shooter back to them after we picked him up."

"I don't think it'll come to that. You backed my story. You were shot by Tucker. Ballistics and fingerprints will prove that. It's self defense. The big complication is that two cops were involved. I made it clear I thought you did the right thing all along. How long did they say you'll be here?"

"Docs think one more night. They want to run some more tests on my head. Then if they find nothing, I can go home tomorrow."

"Looking into your head, they won't find anything."

"Amazing that a man over fifty still hasn't gotten out of the seventh grade."

"All bullshit aside, Peter, thanks for everything you've done. If you hadn't put your ass on the line last night, we both might be gone."

"All in the line of duty, sport."

We said goodbye, not sure when the next time we'd be able to see each other without arousing the ire of the department. Shabielski might be viewed as a traitor for helping a civilian bring down a respected captain, or a hero for busting a dark stain on the force. My guess would be the former.

68

My main desire now was to check into a hotel and get the sleep I'd been deprived of since yesterday morning. I needed to call Jaime and let her know what was happening. I was surprised she hadn't heard about the attack on her own and tried to reach me. I got her voice mail. Left a message that everything was okay and I'd fill her in later.

As I rang off, there was a call from a 704 number I didn't recognize. Ida May Wright's sweet southern voice was on the other end. Apparently Randee was starting to stir and wouldn't it be great if both of us were there when she regained consciousness?

So much for rest. I said I'd be over right away.

So I stayed on the CMC campus. For someone who hates hospitals, I was sure spending a lot of time in them. Thankfully, not as a patient. When I got to Randee's room, she was still down for the count, but resting comfortably, as they say. How anyone presumes that someone in a coma is actually comfortable is beyond me. They could be tortured by hideous nightmares the whole time and we'd be none the wiser until they awaken.

Sitting next to Ida May was a distinguished looking gentleman, wearing a worsted gray chalk stripe suit, crisp blue shirt and burgundy tie. He was deeply tanned, his weathered features exceptionally handsome. Dressed differently, I could picture him as the Marlboro Man, a rugged individualist from the old West for whom no mountain was too tall, no woman too purdy, no outlaw too ornery.

He said, "Riley King. I'm Daniel Wright. Sister, would you give us the room?"

Ida May lowered her eyes as she passed, not proud of enticing me there under false pretenses. I wondered how her estranged brother had persuaded her to carry his water and why he hadn't done it himself.

I said nothing as his gesture commanded me to sit in one of the metal chairs opposite the bed. He didn't extend a hand to shake, nor did I want him to. I had a flashback that I had been called to the principal's office for a scolding, a frequent occurrence in my parochial school days.

"I'm sure you're curious as to why I wanted to speak with you," Wright said, his smooth voice bearing a regal southern lilt.

I gave him my best blank look, modeled after the one Johnny Carson used when a female starlet spouted an unintentional double entendre. I've practiced it in front of a mirror.

Wright said, "I apologize for the deception. I thought it best we speak privately. In the event someone confiscates your phone in the future, I didn't want a call that could be traced back to me."

I still had no response.

He prodded. "So. Are you still interested in the Troika?"

He now had my interest. Early on, I had speculated that if that small assemblage was operating out of the club that Daniel Wright owned, he must be aware of it.

Shabielski had disagreed and I deferred to his greater familiarity.

I said, "I'm curious as to why you think I'd know *anything* about them. They were supposed to be a secret, weren't they, Daniel?"

Men like Wright didn't appreciate strangers casually tossing out their first name. I was sure that no one had referred to him as anything but *Mister* Wright for a long time. It showed lack of proper manners and respect. He seemed to bristle slightly, the reaction I expected, but he wasn't pompous enough to correct my insolence. I couldn't care less.

He said, "There aren't many secrets in this town I'm not privy to. I'll get right to the point."

"That's great because I haven't slept in thirty six hours and I'm not in the mood for bullshit."

I expected him to take umbrage at the coarse expression but he surprised me with a hearty burst of laughter. "A man after my own heart. Quite simply, I just became aware of this so-called Troika recently. I had a problem with them operating out of my club. But I did some investigating internally and came to the conclusion that they were harmless old men trying to do some good."

"Were they aware that you were aware?"

"Not until the last few days. I spoke to Scott Coleman about it and he said that they were planning to disband. He assured me that they could vanish without leaving a trace and that the club wouldn't suffer as a result of their actions."

"Well, now that your clubhouse attendant has admitted killing one of your members, that's down the drain."

"Well, that's one reason I wanted to speak with you. This all goes back to Johnny Serpente, doesn't it?"

I smacked my lips. "Ah yes, his name keeps coming up, doesn't it?"

"He was my mistake. As you may have heard, I keep a tight rein on the membership. I don't care how much money you have, if I don't personally approve the application, you don't get in. I'm afraid I dropped the ball with Serpente. I was away on a world tour and delegated the responsibility. From afar, his credentials looked fine and Coleman and Jackson spoke highly of him. Unfortunately, after I returned and met the man in person, I wasn't happy with the decision. He wasn't the type I wanted around the club. Read into that what you will."

"So did *you* order the hit on Johnny?"

"No. I'm not a murderer. Nor do I delegate murder. I wanted him gone, out of the club. That's all. When he died, Richard Tucker Senior swore to me that it was the Russians. His son believed you were to blame. Let me turn the tables. Were you?"

"No." I told Wright that Tucker never really believed I killed Johnny. I gave him the real reason he wanted me out of the way. When I was finished, he whistled softly.

"South Carolina, eh? Now I can add Richard Tucker Junior's name to my biggest mistakes. His father was a good man. He should have been commissioner in Charlotte, but politics intervened. He accepted the reality of the situation with dignity and never let any resentment show, at least publicly. It was largely because of him that we were so deeply supportive of the local police."

"And they returned the favors."

"In the case of Serpente, yes. They kept the club out of it as much as possible. Together with my influence with the local media, the damage to the Nat was minimal."

"So what went wrong with Tucker Junior?"

"Apparently, he didn't share his father's acceptance of the political situation in town, did he? Scott Coleman and Van Jackson were fools to let him into their little group. Again, it was out of respect for his father. He played them like a fiddle. From what you told me, he used them to further his own greed. Something his father never would have done."

"Why do you think it's important to tell me all of this?"

"Because I'm aware of your investigations. Now that Jackson and Tucker are dead, and Scottie Coleman has hastened off to parts unknown, in essence, it's over. But the club is very important to me and I don't want its reputation blackened."

I stayed calm. "Good luck with that. Do I take this as a threat? I suppose you prefer the term *warning*."

"I'm trying to help you, King. Richard Tucker Junior was a very bad man. Moses Ginn called me right after he killed Tucker and told me the story of how he was going to murder you and the detective."

"Moses had your number? He never let on to me that he had that kind of pull."

"I've known Moses Ginn for almost fifty years and no finer man walks the planet. I gave him my private cell number a long time ago and trusted that he wouldn't misuse it. He never did. Last night was the first time he called. I persuaded him to let me manage this and I will."

"So Char/Meck taking jurisdiction was your doing?"

"Yes. This whole affair will cost me plenty, but I can't let things get out of hand. After a decent interval, no charges will be leveled at Moses. The ruling will be self-defense. I've already been in touch with my media contacts. The thrust of the story will be that Tucker was an unbalanced rogue cop who had everyone fooled because of his father's impeccable reputation. His mother's dementia and bipolar nature will be cited as possible genetic reasons he went awry. They'll downplay the club's involvement. Of course, they have to mention it, but I think we'll make it through all right."

"Bully for the club."

"Sarcasm duly noted. Now, getting down to your situation, even if you're spared legal jeopardy, the fact that you were party to killing a cop, even in self defense, will virtually destroy your business in Charlotte. Plus, there are some Tucker loyalists on the force who might want to take things even further."

"So what's your plan for me? You seem to have this all mapped out."

"Moses tells me you've been talking about leaving town for a while now. May I suggest you accelerate that schedule?"

"You may suggest. What about Shabielski? I don't want him to suffer for this. He did nothing wrong."

"Your friend is a hard case. He's not looking for glory or recognition. He'll get a medal in a few months whether he likes it or not. He'll be portrayed in the press as the honest cop that he is."

"That's a pretty impressive display of power. Damn, you're a regular Vito Corleone, minus the moustache."

"I've called in a great many favors to smooth this over. The Nat will be hosting police charity events for years to come. There are some other incentives I had to provide that I won't disclose, things you're better off not knowing."

"You know, Daniel, you seem to have it all covered. I'll be moving to Hilton Head soon. As Moses told you, it was already in the works. Those friends of Tucker's will have to find me there."

"I think they'll settle for you being out of the immediate area and you won't be in any danger. That's something I can't totally control, but I'll do what I can."

He straightened his tie and went on. "But if I may say so, you've shortchanged yourself, Mr. King. I'm undermining my position now. Something I never do in business, but you *do* have some leverage. In exchange for your continued cooperation, including your silence on what you know about the Troika operations at the Nat --- there must be something I can do. I have considerable resources at my disposal, as you've observed."

"Nope. It's a wrap. We're square."

He appeared offended that his offer of untold riches and prestige was rejected so off-handedly. I'd already come to the conclusion that there was nothing more to be gained by exposing the Troika. Besides, their influence seemed minor league compared to Wright's sway over the city.

I started to leave the room, but stopped at the door. I said, "There is something you can do. I want Randee to have the best possible treatment, the finest specialists from anywhere in the world. You foot the bill."

"I was planning to do that anyway. I am a bit concerned that she won't be willing to let matters slide like you have, but between my dear sister and myself, I think we can find a way to make things right by her. As an unexpected bonus, this whole affair has re-united us as a family. She's free to love who she chooses. I won't judge. In any case, leave it to me. You are absolved of any responsibility for Ms. Blankenship's actions."

"Thank you, your Holiness." I bowed my head in reverence and beat my breast.

He smiled. "I deserve the sarcasm, I suppose."

"You do."

"You must see me as a pompous ass. But I take great pride in this city and my little club. I only want the best for it. I think Scott Coleman and Van Jackson had similar ideals. As your fictional godfather might have said, *if only they had come to me sooner.*"

His Brando impression needed work.

He said, "We could have worked together on making the city great. Johnny Serpente would have stayed in the sewer where he belonged. That may sound arrogant, but he never would have suckered me in like he did those two."

"I have no doubt of that. But as a penalty for that bit of arrogance, how about letting Stone and me play golf at the Nat during what will be our infrequent visits back to Charlotte? Promise, we'll show up in our Sunday best."

69

I booked a "Vintage Queen" room at a boutique hotel called the Dunhill on Tryon in Center City Charlotte. They boast that major literary figures have stayed there through the years and that their attention to old fashioned service is unrivaled. The building dates back to the 1920s; the rooms are smallish but elegant, with thick moldings, subtly patterned wall coverings and thick brocade draperies. The latter were particularly appealing since I planned to pull them closed and sleep forever. I had done a small job for the concierge a few years back, and upon checking in I stressed that I was not to be disturbed unless the building was on fire and please keep my tenancy there quiet.

From my experiences up North, I knew that this request would lead to a phone call to the local paper willing to pay the most for a tip on my whereabouts, but in this Southern city, I could trust the concierge's discretion. That plus the fact that no news outlet in town had the means to pay anything for a story, no matter how hot it may be.

So I slept --- through dinner, through the night and well into the next day. My phone was off and I never turned on the television. I awoke only a few times, stumbling to the bathroom and going back to sleep immediately. When I rolled out of bed for good in the late afternoon, I wasn't sure of the time, day or year for that matter. Powering up the phone, there were three messages from Jaime and a bunch of others I chose not to respond to.

After she voiced her frustration at not being able to reach me sooner, I gave Jaime the rundown and assured her that I was in good health and spirits and unlikely to be charged with anything. She listened, suppressing the impulse to interrupt with questions until I finished.

"What about the house?" she asked. "Could we ever live in it again? My dad sold the Long Beach Island house after my mom was murdered there. Can you ever see us going back?"

"I planned to move to Hilton Head anyway. This will just speed up the timetable."

"This might sound crass, but will anyone buy it after what happened?"

I hadn't given that any consideration, although I did have over a half million invested in the place. I was aware that the notoriety of her dad's LBI house where Paige White was killed actually drove the price up. In fact, there was a bidding war.

I said, "We'll worry about the house later. I'm driving down to Hilton Head tonight. Can you hop a plane and meet me there?"

"God, I want to, but it's going to be tough. The reason I missed your call yesterday and hadn't heard about what happened was that I was in a screening room all day. There's a problem with a movie they made from one of dad's early books that he wrote under a pen name. The studio hates the way it was cut and wants to fire the director, who's an old friend of dad's and the only reason he let the book be filmed. It's not a work he's particularly proud of. So I'm going to be tied up in New York for a while. Will you be okay?"

"I'm fine. Rick's already at the house on the island. You come when you can. Just call before you book a flight in case I have to come back here."

"You're sure? You sound disappointed."

"I understand. You have work to do. I'll call you from Hilton Head when I get settled."

"Love you."

"You too."

I *was* disappointed but I can't let it show --- part of my continuing effort to be an enlightened male in the twenty first century. Throughout my working life when an important case beckons, I have forsaken the significant lady of the hour, even when they ask that I stay close. I have destroyed several relationships as a consequence. But turnabout is fair play. I resent the idea that some third rate flick that even the artistically compromised John Peterman wouldn't put his name to takes precedence over my tribulations. Stone is good company but no comfort when I need a snuggle in the middle of the night.

It was just before five. I decided to treat myself to an early dinner at the Capital Grille, just steps from my hotel. After showering, I checked the Observer online and turned on the local TV news, checking to see if enraged villagers with pitchforks were awaiting me outside on Tryon Street. The incident was a lead story on channels 3, 9, 18, 36 and 46. Ken Burns had not chosen to do a documentary about it on PBS as yet.

I had to marvel at Wright's influence. It was almost as if he had dictated the copy they used. Quoting inside sources from both the Lincoln County and Char/Meck forces, each outlet got the gist of the story correct --- a rogue police captain attempted to take the law into his own hands but was thwarted by hero named Moses Ginn and a stalwart cop whose name was unpronounceable. My mug was all over the story, using a snappy ten year old photo from my website. I was described as a prominent private investigator who had been at the heart of many controversial cases.

No one took particular notice as I dined on the Capital Grille's excellent filet mignon, alone at a corner table. After dessert, I checked out of the Dunhill, retrieved the MDX and picked Bosco up from Keegish. My next stop was Hilton Head Island. I was an hour into the journey, missing my Audi, when the phone purred.

Moses Ginn.

"Where are you, man?" he asked.

"South Carolina near Columbia, on 77."

"You alone?"

"At the moment. What's up? Where are you?"

"I'm home. They got one of them leg monitors on me, case they find something that blows out our story. No charges yet and I coulda refused, but Mr. Wright tells me it's just for show. I'll be totally cleared in due time. You watch the news, 5-0?"

"I don't know anyone by that name but I did watch, yes."

"Sorry I had to go to Mr. Wright and didn't tell you about it. News already be making you out to be kinda shady. They got that right. Ha. Lookee, I do appreciate you offering to take the rap for me, but I couldn't let that happen."

I told him again why I thought it would have been better for me to take the blame. "Nothing to do with any regard I might have for you, Ginn, just trying to keep the peace. I was afraid of redneck riots if it got out a black man killed a white police captain in a particularly gruesome way."

"Makes what I got to do now all the harder."

"Moses, don't do anything stupid. Wright's got it covered."

"No man, that ain't where it's at. I been holding out on you. While you were tending to your pal the other night, I picked up Tucker's phone."

"Not wise. You know they can track those things. How are you going to explain that?"

"It's off and I took out the SIMM card. If you don't know what that is, look it up. But see, reason I took the phone in the first place is I didn't want no one tying Mr. Jackson or Mr. Coleman to anything Tucker was up to. I got his directory and the last bunch of calls he made out of the phone before I shut it down."

I said, "Cops could get that information from his carrier. I don't think they'd even bother checking that now. Cell companies don't like to give that up without a court order. But if I were you, I'd get rid of it unless there's something on it that can exonerate you."

No comment from Ginn. "Oh, by the way, Moses, Wright told me about how you were tight with him all along. I wish you had shared that with me."

"I didn't want him involved and I didn't know what he knew about the Troika. He was my hole card if I needed him and turns out I did. I woulda told you about him if things went sour. But back to the phone. There's some South Carolina numbers I found in there, people in real estate and banks. I heard through the door the other night he was fixing to start up there with his new empire."

"Right. Well now, he can't."

"Yeah, I s'pose. I'm gonna give them numbers to Mr. Wright. Maybe down the line he'll take care of it, in his own way. But see, real reason I called, there's one other number that came up a bunch of times last few days. I wasn't sure it was my place to tell you."

"Who was it?"

"5-0, I hate to be the messenger of bad news. Let me give you the number, find out for yourself and what you want to do with it."

"You know Moses, if we have any more dealings with each other, I need to teach you some lessons on how to be direct. You waste a lot of peoples' time trying to figure out what you mean, when you could just come right out with it."

"Can't teach an old dog new tricks. Hey, reminds me, you got that old boy Bosco with you in the back seat? Rub his snout for me, will ya? Listen up, here's that number."

He rattled off a 704 number, the area code for Charlotte and its immediate suburbs. After goodbyes, I repeated the digits into the MDX's voice recognition software and said "call."

Voice mail. A couple bars of a country tune. Then the voiceover that will haunt me forever.

"This is Charlene. Watch me on the CMA awards next week on ABC. And y'all can leave your message now, darlin'"

Beep.

70

I didn't leave a message but my cell buzzed seconds later. The wonders of caller ID.

"Riley, it's Charlene."

"Hi. What's up?" I said, trying to sound disinterested.

"You called me, sugar, but I was meaning to call you anyways. I know I wasn't very nice to you back when I was getting set for the show. I was a little cranky because the band wasn't tight enough. You know I like things tight."

I flirted back. "Like those cut-off shorts you were wearing."

"Funny. I had to make some changes. Not real easy to do. I fired my bass player and I'm looking out for another one."

I had the impression that the erstwhile bassist was plucking her strings as well. He had to be half her age, Stone's M.O. in reverse. The skinny, tatted kid was hardly a suitable long term match for Charlene, but she has her needs and he was convenient.

I said, "Much as I like your music, I'm not very good on bass. I'm more a rhythm guitarist and no great shakes at that. So I'm afraid if you're offering me a job, I have to decline."

"You're a barrel of laughs today, sugar."

Sugar was an all purpose term to her. It could be one of endearment, which I enjoyed for a few months while we shared living quarters, or one of condescension, which was her obvious intent now.

"Okay Charl, so you aren't asking me to join your band. But I know how you operate. What do you need from me?"

"I'm hurt that you think so little of me, Riles. I thought those months together was pretty spectacular, you wanna know the truth. I was hoping you'd remember them good times like I do."

So it was *Riles* now. It was easy to reflect back on the highlights of our relationship, which largely occurred in the sack. For all her other foibles, her skills in the bedroom are unrivalled by anyone I've ever been with. Unfortunately, I was part of a large club and I was sure that the membership had grown since our time together.

I said, "I remember that you left in a huff when you were drunk one night and sent three large men to collect your things the next day."

"There's that. I *can* be impulsive. Sometimes I do act on the spur of the moment and regret it later, darlin'."

From sugar to Riles to darlin' now. Could *Sugar-Pie, Honey-Bunch* be far behind?

I said, "Well, we all make mistakes. Jaime's doing fine, which I anticipate is your next question."

I wanted to short circuit the nostalgic pillow talk and get down to business. Like Ulysses lashing himself to the mast to avoid succumbing to the Sirens' song. With my concerns about Jaime's business activity prevailing over our time together, the chance to take some succor with Charlene would be tempting. Tempting, but wrong in so many ways.

Charlene said, "Still with that young one, eh? Well, you *will* need someone to visit with you and ladle out your gruel when they put you in the home."

She giggled at her little put-down. "Oh, did I say that? You and me are 'bout the same age, hon, I know. That's one reason Derek had to go. He was getting a little too attached to my boobies, like I was his mama or something."

Derek was the one who played bass, among other things. Talking around why I called was getting tiresome, so I got to the crux of the matter.

"Charl, much as I love catching up on your love life, we do have some issues to discuss, don't we?"

"We do. I was hoping we could do it in person."

In person? Was I being set up? The phone calls back and forth from Tucker to her might have an innocent explanation, or they might mean that Charlene was involved in the plot to kill me. I couldn't figure why she'd want to do that. I'd been out of her life for a long time now. She didn't lack for suitors. *She* dumped *me* so this could hardly be revenge.

I'm a big boy, maybe just a wee bit past the prime of my physical power. I was letting a hundred thirty pound slip of a girl worry me. Of course, if Charlene wanted me gone, it wasn't likely she'd do it herself. She'd recruit someone big. Someone like Moses Ginn. Lucky he was on my side now.

"Charlene, why now? What's going on?"

"I'm a little scared, truth be told. I can't blame ya for not wantin' to help, but we need to get some things out in the open."

"Where are you now?"

"I'm at down in Hilton Head at the condo until the weekend. Already taped my spot on the awards show."

I said, "Funny, that's where I'm headed. Free for dinner tomorrow night?"

"What, do you think I'm easy?" she said, echoing one of the lines she used when we first got together. "Let's do it. We got a lot of shit to wade through."

71

I got to the island late and slept on and off until nine. Stone's radio show on WPHX started at ten, so we didn't have time to talk. He was playing golf after that. We agreed to catch up later. I called Charlene and suggested we meet at WiseGuys at six.

She said, "I'll make the reservation. You'd be surprised how much juice my name carries these days. Or maybe you wouldn't be."

"*Juicy Jones*. Sounds like a great title for your next album."

"I can see the cover now. Me nekkid, squeezing some thick ole honey juice over my strategic parts. Sorta like that old Herb Alpert LP, *Whipped Cream and Other Delights*. I guess that little girl you're seeing taught you a thing or two about marketing."

I didn't need that vision careening around in my head all day. "Six o'clock at the restaurant. See you there."

I needed to talk to Jaime. I felt like a member of AA who urgently needs to communicate with his sponsor, for fear of giving in to his addiction.

Ms. Johansen was working in her Jersey offices when I reached her.

She said, "Hey, Riles, can we talk later? I'm kind of busy."

"Uh sure, I guess." I was stumbling a bit, unsettled by her cool tone. "I was wondering if you knew when you could make it down to Hilton Head."

"Can't say yet. Look, I need to go. Call me later today. Actually, I'm out tonight so call after eleven if you're up. I should be back by then. If not, maybe in the morning. Bye."

She blew me off as if I was an minor irritant, to be dealt with at her leisure. I suppose there was someone in the room with her, someone who, at the moment, was more important than I was.

Before heading to the Juicy Jones' lioness den, I needed to talk to Dan Logan. I told my FBI buddy my side of the Tucker saga, knowing that he must have already heard somebody else's version.

When I finished, he said, "There's some pretty powerful folks up here in the Big Apple, but the press would never let something like that stand unchallenged. Politicians and LEOs wouldn't either. I know you think you're in a big city, but in a lot of ways, sounds like Charlotte is still a one horse town. By the way, is this going to affect my Giants-Panthers tickets?"

"It's so great to have an unselfish friend like you. Someone who cares so deeply about my problems. Don't worry, you'll be sitting midfield, whether I'm there or not. I need to ask you for one thing, though."

"If it's a big favor, I may need to move down a few rows closer to the sideline."

"Ha. Listen, is there any possibility that the Russians didn't kill Serpente? Could ballistics have gotten the slugs mixed up somehow? Or could Tucker have shipped the gun up to the mob after the fact?"

"Look Riles, anything's possible. But the gun matched slugs involved in killings in Brighton Beach that pre-dated Serpente by years. Unless the weapon was on a lend-lease shuttle between the Brooklyn mob and the Charlotte police, that couldn't happen. And we took custody of the slugs from Serpente early on. Ballistics down there swore by the chain of evidence, that the seals hadn't been broken, et cetera. When we confronted the Commie shooter with the fact we had a ballistics match, and this was almost two years later, he confessed. In great detail, down to the color of the tile in the bathroom. The man's sick, he's dying in prison. You want to talk to him, I could probably arrange it but you'd be wasting your time. To me, it's a slam dunk. He did it."

~~~~~

WiseGuys is one of my go-to places when I'm on the island. Never had a bad meal there, the menu is always enticing and the service is attentive but not intrusive. I've been there many times but if anyone in the place recognizes that, it doesn't show. I like it that way. I never carry when I eat there, but tonight I made an exception.

Still a little ticked at Jaime, I entered the restaurant a little before six and saw no suspicious characters. Against my usual habit, I had valet parked the car so I couldn't be grabbed in the lot after dinner. I was leaving little to chance, given how Tucker and Charlene might have been in league with each other. In her case, I still had no idea why.

Charlene's fame was still recent enough for her to be able to travel without an entourage of toadying assistants and beefed up security, if she so chose.

Tonight, she so chose.

I asked the hostess about the reservation. The attractive young woman gave me a coy smile and led me to a table in a dimly lit corner. As my eyes adjusted to the darkened booth, they fell upon the glorious sight of Charlene Jones, nursing a chardonnay.

She was dressed the way she was when I first laid eyes on her. Form fitting stonewashed jeans, a man-tailored white shirt with French cuffs, just a hint of décolletage. A small gold cross necklace was the only jewelry she displayed, other than an expensive Piaget watch. No rings on her long elegant fingers, close cut nails, clear coated.

"Can we dispense with me telling you how great you look?" I said. "Do you ever get tired of hearing that?"

"Not from you, darlin'," she said. No air kisses were exchanged, no real ones either. "I wasn't sure if you were drinking tonight so I just ordered a wine for me. Still hooked on that single malt?"

"Yeah, but I'll wait on that."

I felt awkward. The beautiful creature sitting across from me might be the instrument of my demise. How do you bring up such existential questions without a little small talk to warm things up? So I asked about her tour, her album and how the search for a new bassist was coming along. She gave shallow answers to my shallow questions.

I said, "Well, I'm happy to hear your career has taken off the way it has. You deserve it."

"You know, for the longest time, Riley, I would have called you out on that. I thought you were fixing on keeping me in the kitchen, barefoot and pregnant, even though I'm past the age where that can happen. But now, I do believe that y'all are really happy for me."

I've never really known why she walked out on me so abruptly. I was in the middle of a case, working for a man she disapproved of. We *had* argued over that, sometimes vigorously. But Ted McCarver's influence in the music business had opened doors that led to her current stardom.

I said, "Charlene, I'm really happy you got what you wanted. But we're not here to do a post mortem on our relationship."

I felt like a politician speaking to a mixed crowd, carefully dancing around the subject so as not to offend anyone. I was dishing out clichés like pancakes at a church breakfast.

She said, "You know, Riley, ever since I saw you the other day, I can't stop thinking about us. Damn, half the songs on my last album were about you or hadn't you noticed?"

"To be honest Char, I haven't really listened to it except the snatches I hear on the radio."

We were going places I didn't want to go. I needed to know if she had collaborated with Tucker to eliminate me and why.

She said, "I hoped those songs would be healing, know what I mean. I think if you gave them a good listen, you'd see how bad I felt about the way I treated you."

We were way off topic. If I didn't know better, I'd think she was sounding me out about getting back together. As it was, it might be a diversion. Get me all lovey-dovey, then strike. Poison my scotch when I wasn't looking. Was I paranoid or what?

I said, "Look, Charlene, it's never one person's fault. I promise I'll download your album and listen sometime. Although I'm sure you can understand, Jaime won't like it."

"That's why I wanted to see you. You really think she's better for you than me? I mean, she's cute and all, so I hear, but she's a whole lot younger than you."

"Charlene, what are you trying to do here? Let's leave Jaime out of it, okay?"

"Not okay. All right, I fucked up leaving you the way I did. Two weeks after I did it I was ready to come back. But you already had that little girl all moved in with you. You don't think that hurt *me*?"

Charlene is the most unpredictable person I've ever known. She had treated me with disdain mere days ago when I warned her of the threat that Tucker posed, now she was making noises like she wanted to get back together. In spite of myself, it was a hard plea to resist. This was a woman in full, someone I don't have to explain what I mean when I reference an event prior to 1980.

I said, "So *you* walk out, send men the next day to pick up your things and you expect me to just wait around for you to reconsider? Everything out of your mouth sounded final and like it was planned well in advance."

"Haven't you ever said anything you really didn't mean and come to regret it later? Especially if you'd been drinking?"

"Enough. I didn't come here to go over old ground. I want to know what happened with Richard Tucker. Don't you dare deny you were talking to him right before he tried to kill me."

She drained her glass and signaled the server for another. The fellow looked at me and I shook my head. I planned on being gone before her next round arrived.

Charlene leaned in, affording me a peek of generously proportioned cleavage, not that I noticed. She said, "I won't lie. He'd been in touch with me several times."

On second thought, I did need a drink. "What did you two talk about?"

"It goes back to Johnny. Tucker was the point man on that investigation. He called me 'bout a week ago and said we needed to meet. I told him to talk to my lawyer. He kept at it. Said he was building a case against you for Johnny and a bunch of other murders. He wanted me to testify that you told me you killed Johnny so you could have me all to yourself."

Here we go again. "And you told him to go to hell."

"Yes, I did. The first time he broached the subject, I used those very words, darlin' and hung up. But he wouldn't drop it. He came to my house. Said that if I didn't back him up that he'd implicate *me*. That we planned it together."

"Why would you talk to him without your attorney present?"

"He ambushed me, babe. Got me all riled up so's I wasn't thinking straight. Gave me twenty four hours to get back to him before he started the ball rolling against me."

"So you agreed to lie about me."

"I never would do that, I swear. I was planning to pay him off, offer him like a hundred grand to drop it. He seemed like the type that would take it and lucky for me, I got it now. But before I could make the offer, he told me there was a change in plans. He might not need me after all and if I knew what was good for me, I'd keep my mouth shut."

I took a sip of water, wishing it was Scotch. "So why didn't you tell me, at least let me know what he was planning?"

Her second glass of wine arrived and she immediately took a nervous gulp. I asked for a Glenfiddich, rocks. I wasn't in such a hurry to leave now.

Charlene said, "I'll tell you why, but you're going to hate me forever."

She looked like she was on the verge of breaking down. I had to keep in mind that Charlene is an accomplished actress and that whatever emotion she was mustering might only be a tribute to her craft. I waited for her to finish.

She made a show of composing herself, swallowed hard and said the words I'll never forget. "You see, he was on to something. I did set up Johnny's death. Sure as if I pulled the trigger myself."

72

Shabielski had it right all along. I've come up with a lot of theories about how things went down with Johnny, but I could never bring myself to believe that Charlene was the one who had orchestrated her husband's death. Even now as she admitted it, I didn't want to accept it. I lived with this woman. Almost married her. Was her raw sexuality so commanding that it had blinded me to her true nature?

The Scotch came, along with another chardonnay for her. Her previous glass was half full but the server said that this one was on the house as well as the appetizer. Flash fried shrimp and calamari, with a sweet and spicy chili glaze, one of my favorites. This would rate a positive review in *Riley King's Culinary Times*. Although I think the special treatment was for my illustrious companion, not me.

"Okay, here goes," Charlene said, when the eager-to-please lad left. "Right after you and me met, you told me what a scumbag crook Johnny still was. How he got richer by re-using building materials that they proved cause cancer. I mean, I could tolerate our rocky marriage, but when you laid that on me, that was the straw that broke the camel's back. I really believed he left all that illegal stuff behind in Brooklyn."

I pursed my lips. "And I happened to be handy. As a place to crash temporarily."

"That ain't true and you know it. I didn't see you as transitional. I wanted to be with you bad and wasn't thinking about no time limits."

I said, "Based on what Randee and I dug up on Johnny, he was going away for a long time. Why couldn't you just be patient and divorce him when he was in prison?"

She looked at her wine with longing, and decided to drink deep again. "Here's the part you're gonna hate. He wasn't gonna be in jail right away. Remember at the time, I told ya he'd fight those charges with his every last dime. You see what I'm saying? Johnny would either beat the rap or fight it for a couple years with appeals until they convicted him. No matter which way it went, all his money would go to the lawyers and there'd be nothing left for me. And who knows if he woulda sent some goons to your place to fetch me and blow you away in the process."

"How sweet. You did it to protect me. So how did you set it up?" I knew the answer but needed to hear her say it.

"The plan was simple, my dear. I knew Johnny had been with the Russian mob. He had lots of cash that he stole from the gangs over the years. He used that as seed money to make a fortune down here as Johnny Serpente, not Dmitry Zubov."

I said, "The government wanted to put him in witness protection and make the Russians think he was dead. In addition to robbing them, he ratted them out and they never leave a debt unsettled."

"That's right. So all I had to do was let the mob know his new identity. I had no direct way of contacting people like that. But you still had friends with the FBI. I convinced you to call your old buddy up there to see if they could dig up something on Johnny."

I said, "How did you figure asking my friend Dan Logan for help would accomplish your goal?"

She didn't answer right away, staring into her wine glass. "Think about why didn't Johnny go into witness protection, sugar. Because there was a mole at the bureau. Somebody playing both sides. Johnny was sure it was his original handler. I figured he'd be the first guy your friend Logan would talk to for background. And like I thought, the sorry bastard went to the Russians and offered Johnny up. For a price."

Charlene had just confessed to using me and my FBI contacts to have Johnny killed. The irony was that the Troika re-jiggered the will and she came out with a lot less than would normally be due a widow. Karma.

I was ignoring my Scotch --- very uncharacteristic of me not to consult with my old pal Glen in times like this.

Charlene said, "So that's my story. Johnny's dead and so is Tucker. We're both free as birds. But what I can't figure is why was Tucker so hot to get you?"

"It got back to Tucker that I was poking around in Fort Mill. *South* Carolina, just over the border. There was an opportunity ripe for the taking. That was the real reason he wanted me dead. He was afraid that I'd expose him and ruin his plan to be the king of York County. Randee was gathering evidence. Tucker decided to force the issue, kill us both."

She nodded her head deep in thought, taking it all in. I moved on. "Randee regained consciousness, by the way. Docs saved her eye and she should be okay in time."

She said, "That's good. Sorry I said them nasty things about her. She's a good lady."

She took another long drink and looked up at me with those incredible blue eyes. "I guess you and me ain't got much of a future together, do we?"

My mind flashed on this: What if Bosco suddenly became a vicious, rabid dog? As much as I couldn't deal with putting him down, I couldn't live with him either. That's how I felt about Charlene. Despite the damning admissions, it was hard to close the door. I guess that means I'm still in love with her.

I said, "You've got your music. Building your career is going to take all your energy for quite a while. I'm sure you won't lack for male company."

She brushed away a tear. "You spoiled me, Riles. It wasn't for long, but you and me had it all. Didn't we?"

"That we did. You know, I'm sure I'll be on the road someday and one of your songs will come on the radio, and it'll remind me of those times. But as much as I care about you, I don't think I ever want to see that gorgeous face of yours again."

I gulped down the last bit of Scotch as I stood up to leave. Can't let good single malt go to waste.

I kissed her. Hard. I didn't catch any air.

As

a bonus

for our loyal

readers, we've included

the short story - *KING'S CHRISTMAS*

with this edition of *THE PUNCH LIST*.

This tale of the Yuletide was originally

released as a digital download in

November

of

2017.

Enjoy!

KING'S CHRISTMAS

It was the Saturday before Christmas and I was alone. And hungover.

I had spent Friday night watching my New York Rangers lose a close hockey game to the Senators. No one cared about hockey in my newly adopted city of Charlotte, North Carolina. A stranger in a strange land.

Nobody cared about me either. I knew that would change in time. I'd make friends. But that gave me little solace this Christmas. Although I held out hope for Yet to Come, Christmas Present was bleak. Christmas Past was another story.

My melancholy was my own doing. The weather, congestion and criminal activity at the Jersey shore had reached critical mass, and I finally made good on my vow to seek a warmer and friendlier clime. It meant leaving my girl and dog behind. I had tried to persuade the former to come with me, but she was running a successful business of her own and needed to be near New York. She had agreed to keep the dog until I could get settled into permanent digs down here. My golden retriever Bosco was our only link and that would be gone as soon as my house was finished and safe for the pup.

I had bought the ramshackle dwelling on Lake Norman at the end of the summer and hired a local builder to help refurbish it. The house was as incomplete as my life was. I only had power in the rooms I used most frequently --- the bedroom, kitchen and office. The rest were in the drywall stage, loose wires and rough plumbing exposed in a chaotic state. Heavy craft paper took the place of carpeting over any hardwood floors that might be salvageable.

By springtime, the place would be finished. Renewed and buffed to a high sheen --- the old painted lady would be restored to her former glory, even sweeter than she was originally. I could then reclaim Bosco and once more plead for my girl to join me. I was resigned to the fact that we both were entrenched in unyielding positions. I was totally to blame, creating this issue by moving South. As painful as it was short term, I didn't regret my choice.

But it *was* Christmas. Why not deck the halls just for me, since I had no one to share the Christmas spirit with? I'd cook a turkey with all the trimmings. Wrap a present to myself and pretend it didn't come from me. Decorate the few functional rooms I had with holly and mistletoe and top it off with a fragrant Christmas tree, straight from the forest. I'd need to find a long extension cord to light it up, but there would be no one to trip over the wire but me.

I made some coffee, boiled up some steel-cut oatmeal and dawdled over a few online newspapers and magazines. Stores were already steeply discounting their holiday items. I could buy an artificial tree for half of what they went for a few weeks ago. But I was determined to go all-in. I'd venture up to the mountains, cut one myself and tie it onto the roof of my SUV. String some sleigh bells across my bumper. Maybe have dinner at some cozy Alpine tavern on the way back.

Ring-a-ling, hear them ring! That's the spirit. Sinatra said *Ring-a-Ding-Ding*, but I think that had to do with scoring showgirls. Not very Christmas-y, or was it?

A quick web search came up with a dozen places that advertised *cut your own* trees within a two hour radius.

I settled on one called *Mary's Christmas Tree Farm*. The site had a live webcam. There was snow on the ground!

A few stops to make along the way. I needed to drop by the print shop to pick up my new business cards. I designed them myself, rather smartly if I do say so. Influenced by Richard Boone as Paladin on the old TV Western *HAVE GUN WILL TRAVEL*, the card featured a chess piece --- instead of a knight, a black king with an embossed golden crown. The face read: RILEY KING INVESTIGATIONS. On the back --- a contact number and web address. I was tempted to use 'WirePaladin.com' but nobody would get the reference.

I gassed up the MDX and headed north for the hills. The air was crisp and clean; the sunny skies in Charlotte a brilliant Carolina blue. As I neared the mountain region in the northwestern part of the state, they gave way to puffy clouds and eventually a hazy overcast. There was more snow in the forecast up there. Perfect.

Along the way, my memories drifted to past expeditions, in search of Christmas trees. The earliest recollection I conjured was as a twelve year old in Central Virginia. It was just my dad and me, trekking into the deep woods not far from our house. I had a red Radio Flyer wagon that we pulled behind us. In it was a length of rope, a saw, a small hatchet and a big thermos of hot chocolate my mom insisted we take, over dad's protestations. We'd only be gone a couple of hours, he said. She said that it was cold, under freezing, and that he'd thank her for it later. As usual, he accepted her greater wisdom in these matters.

The trees we encountered were nothing like the full, perfectly shaped ones you see today. As we trudged through a narrow, rock strewn forest path, we'd stop every so often at a likely prospect. My dad would size it up and then shake his head slowly, pointing out brown spots, broken limbs or insect damage. I didn't mind. With our frosty breath condensing in front of us, the scent of running cedar and wood smoke was bracing. Those days, my father was juggling three jobs and we had precious little time alone together, so I treasured these moments. He was dispensing bits of hard won knowledge in his clipped manner, passing along his legacy in bite sized portions for the next generation.

He was particularly wistful as he spoke of *his* dad at Christmas and how excited he was upon opening the colorfully wrapped presents that Santa had brought. A Mattel Fanner 50 with Greenie Stick-em caps. Space boots. Plastic bowling pins to be used only in the basement. A badminton set. A Davy Crockett coonskin cap. The BB rifle version of Old Betsy was too expensive, maybe next year. I discovered years later that his dad had abandoned his family when my father was nine.

We finally came upon a suitable candidate for our heavy glass ornaments, silver tinsel and multi-colored lights. It was a six foot tall scotch pine, with long needles, roughly conical in shape. A few nips in the right spots and this will look great, dad said. He started chopping with the axe, using the saw to finish the job. He was crestfallen when the tree finally toppled. The far side of it was sparse, wedged up against another tree that gave it the illusion of fullness. I said we could just leave it there and find a better one but he said that would be wrong, a waste of God's resources. He had made a mistake and we needed to live with the consequences, not punish the tree for failing to live up to our expectations. Besides, we could place it in the corner of our den, so the bad side wouldn't show.

My folks are living in Europe these days. They invited me to visit for the holidays but I had too much on my plate here and my passport had expired. That was my excuse, anyway. My only brother, now a grown man of forty seven, lived on the west coast with his third wife. He told me that he would have invited me to spend Christmas with them, but their domestic situation wasn't the greatest, if I took his meaning. Could spouse number four be far behind?

As I neared my destination, Dennis Elsas played *Happy Christmas, (War is Over)* on the sat channel. I wondered why no one ever called out John Lennon for stealing the melody from Peter Paul and Mary's *Stewball, the Racehorse*.

I branched off of I-77 North onto a two lane country highway, which wound its way higher in elevation toward Banner Elk, where Mary's tree farm was located. My ears popped several times. The GPS guided me there, something I'd never be able to accomplish fumbling with paper maps on the narrow twisting roads with little signage. Eventually, the macadam gave way to gravel up a steep incline where I spotted the tree farm. The final hundred yards was a rutted dirt trail that even my four wheel drive found challenging.

At Winter Solstice in the late afternoon, the cloud-weakened sun was barely visible. I had come prepared with axe and saw, like I had all those years ago with my dad. It was likely that Mary or whoever ran the place had elves to actually cut the trees (for insurance purposes, if some lumberjack wannabe with a chain saw sliced off a finger instead of a branch).

As I approached the main concourse, I saw a tall woman with French braided red hair, supervising a couple of Latin workers, as they were bundling a tall Fraser fir into some netting. She was wearing mud spattered jeans, a blue plaid flannel shirt, and thick leather gloves. But when she turned in my direction, I was gobsmacked. She was the spitting image of my first love, the only woman that I had ever come close to marrying.

STAVE 2

I hadn't thought about Máiréad Flannery for quite some time. I met her thirty years ago, at a Washington party for some political mucky mucks and lobbyists shortly after I had joined the FBI. I forget how I got invited to the gathering, but I was clearly punching out of my weight class. I had graduated from Georgetown the summer before, a knee injury preempting my NBA dreams. The FBI came recruiting and lacking any other prospects, I decided to give it a whirl. Looking back, it seems like a cavalier reason for joining the world's preeminent crime fighting force. But I was particularly callow then, sailing through school as a pampered athlete.

The party was held at the posh Georgetown row house of a wealthy political donor. I immediately knew I was out of place. I was wearing my best off-the-rack, Sy Syms special, while most of the men were decked out in white Armani dinner jackets or full-fledged tuxedos. Even the help had the better of me sartorially. I figured I'd spend an hour or so with the high rollers before retreating to someplace more comfortable for a rube like me. I had been invited by a teammate to another bash in Alexandria that would be more my speed.

The holiday decorations were resplendent. The twenty foot Christmas tree was dwarfed in the immense ballroom. Champagne flowed, glasses tinkled; the open bar was stocked with whatever poison struck your fancy. There were probably a hundred guests, mingling gaily, back when that word meant festive.

Máiréad Flannery was festively decked out as well, in a low cut red gown, displaying her abundant gifts abundantly. She and I were clearly the youngest in the room. I was twenty two and she was a few months shy of that, I later discovered. She caught my eye the minute I entered. She noticed that I noticed, flashing me a shy smile. I immediately began revising my plans for the evening.

She was in the company of a much older, heavyset man. Like the others, he was formally attired, a man of some importance. A group of fawning sycophants surrounded him. A large nose resplendent with the broken veins of a veteran tippler was the most striking feature on an otherwise unexceptional visage. Dark lifeless eyes, like a shark about to strike. Thin pale lips, humorless mouth. After a moment, I recognized him as the august senator from the great state of Alabama, although having been there once, I couldn't tell you anything great about it. Why was a gorgeous creature like Máiréad chained to this homely Leviathan?

Was he married, single, perverse in some fashion? Back then, there were no smart phones to instantly search the name for salacious details.

I circulated. I should say, I circled Máiréad, keeping an eye on her every move as I visited the bar and asked for a Scotch. I'd never sampled a single malt before, but it was a whisky favored by cool TV detectives. I aspired to be as sophisticated and worldly as they seemed to be. After my first sip, I told the young Irish barkeep I was in love. He said that I shouldn't get too used to it --- this was twenty one year old Glenfiddich. The expense of a bottle would consume an entire week's pay for an honest workingman. My wallet heeded his advice for a number of years.

After two Scotches, the room was spinning. I'd lost track of Máiréad. I needed to splash some water on my face in an attempt to sober up so as not to make a dithering fool of myself if I worked up the courage to approach her. One of the waiters pointed me toward a powder room, but in my inebriated state, I took a wrong turn and wound up in the kitchen. A life changing blunder.

I heard a female voice protesting "not here", coming from the butlers' pantry. The least an apprentice G-man could do would be to investigate and offer assistance. I slid open the pocket door and there was Máiréad and the senator, his hands roaming over her body as she tried to wriggle free.

She blushed at the sight of me and rushed off. The senator scowled, mumbled something about this not being what it seemed, stuck his bulbous snout in the air and started off. I put my hand on his chest to stop him and inquired if the lady had assaulted him. Since I was a federal agent, should I arrest her for accosting a United States Senator? He gave me an oily smirk and reached for his billfold. Extracting a fifty, he tucked it into my jacket pocket and strode away, head held high in indignation. Hush money and cheap at that.

I found Máiréad outside, trying to hail cabs that were speeding to other destinations, oblivious to this glorious woman. I asked if she needed a ride: my VW Dasher was parked two blocks away on a side street. It was snowing lightly and her mascara was running. She sniffled, took my arm and off we went.

We wound up going to my other party and had a great time. We spent that night and many others at my modest rental in the District. She was a student at American University, a Poli Si major. We liked the same music, cheered for the same teams and shared the same political views. I thought I was the world's greatest lover back then, but *she* taught *me* a few things.

In a word, she was perfect. I was in love. Truly, deeply, with my green eyed, wild Irish lass.

She never explained her presence at that Georgetown Christmas party as the guest of a married senator from the Southern tier. We were together for a glorious six weeks before I discovered the reason. Valentine's Day was upon us and I was thinking of surprising her with a ring. But something was nagging at me. Was it jealousy, or thinking that our love story was far too idyllic? How was she tied in with this gross looking man? It took a few calls and some digging on an otherwise slow afternoon at work to discover the truth.

She was a hooker. A whore.

That's what I called her when I confronted her. I should have used a more charitable term. A paid escort. A lady of the evening. A call girl.

In any case, I ran away from her as fast as I could. I didn't want to listen when she explained why she did what she did. She was working her way through school. No family money or scholarship aid. All she had was her most obvious asset, her beauty, and she used it to get ahead. She hadn't planned it that way, but when the opportunity presented itself at a gathering the previous summer, one thing led to another. Soon, she was not only paying her tuition but making contacts in the political world. It wasn't something she did all the time, just on special occasions for a lot of money. Senator Alabama was a one off and she never saw him again.

No matter how much she pleaded with me, I couldn't wrap my mind around being in love with a prostitute. I almost considered it my duty to arrest or at the very least, report her. As I thought it through, I realized how imprudent that would be. Federal charges for sleeping with married pols? Even the late J. Edgar would have laughed. Well, maybe not.

I was heartbroken. So was she. When I refused to take her calls, she wrote me a long letter, declaring her love for me, saying she would give it all up if we could have a life together. My cold and unsophisticated heart would have none of it. I even worried that if my association with her ever came to light, I'd be drummed out of the bureau. Dishonorably.

Selfish. Stupid. Unforgiving. That was Riley King at twenty two.

But thirty years later, here I was at a Christmas tree farm, watching Máiréad's exact double from afar, racking my brain for the right thing to say.

STAVE 3

When all else fails, go with the classic. The tried and true.

I said, "Excuse me but I have to say, you look exactly like someone I once knew."

She smiled. "I'd think a strapping hunk like you could come up with something better than that."

"I know it's not original, but it's true. It was in Washington, about thirty years ago. The resemblance is uncanny."

"You're creeping me out. I grew up in D.C. back then. Are you stalking me?"

I was afraid that was the way I'd come off. She had to be at least twenty years younger and I felt like a dirty old man. Kind of like the Senator from Alabama should have felt with Máiréad if he had a conscience.

I said, "I'll leave if I'm making you uncomfortable. It's just that this woman was special to me and I was blown away when I saw you. You look so much like her."

There were some differences, now that I saw her close up. Máiréad had green eyes, and flaming red hair. This girl's eyes were blue and her reddish hair was a bit more on the blond side. But the strong, regular features were identical, down to the freckles and full mouth. The closest I could come to describing her would be the young Ann Margret.

There was no fear in her eyes as she studied my face. "I don't imagine a handsome dude like you would need to stalk a girl to get what he wanted."

"Au contraire. It was before your time, but there was a serial killer in Florida named Ted Bundy whose victims found him very attractive."

"Are you trying to pick me up or scare me away?"

"Actually, neither. I came up here from Charlotte to get a tree. I got sidetracked when I saw you. "

"Look, mister, we're closing soon so if you want a tree, go down that aisle with Esteban and pick one out. He'll help you load it and we can talk then. Okay? My name's Mary Duncan."

She pulled off a glove and extended her right hand.

"Mine's Riley King."

"That sounds familiar. Why would I know that name?"

"I'll pick out my tree and we'll talk about it later. Maybe I can buy you dinner if you don't have plans."

"We'll see. The best trees left are about a hundred yards out on the right, two rows over."

She hadn't rejected the invitation out of hand. I welcomed the break. I had to sort out what I wanted from her. She was too young for me by a couple of decades and she wasn't the sort to be trifled with, I could see that right away. Part of the attraction was guilt over the way I had treated Máiréad. If I was extra nice to this lady, would it make up for the way I had coldly dismissed my young lover all those years ago?

I flashed on the old Dan Fogelberg song they always played this time of year, about meeting his old lover in a grocery store on Christmas Eve. I was living the song. Could this in fact *be* Máiréad, remarkably well preserved? If it was, she would have recognized me or at least the name. I hadn't aged that badly.

All the remaining trees appeared fine to my eye, given the way Christmas trees looked when I was growing up. I picked the first one Esteban suggested, and in less than a minute, we were dragging it behind us to the netting area. Mary was nowhere to be seen and neither were any other customers. Esteban's co-workers were packing up for the day and loading themselves into a rusty old station wagon.

"I help you with the tree, then I must go, señor," he said.

We bundled the tree and hoisted it onto the roof of the MDX. He helped me tie it down with heavy waxed twine. I gave him a ten and he was on his way.

No Mary. I was about to take the hint and leave when she emerged from the farmhouse porch, just up the ridge.

"Riley, hold on," she shouted, as she ran down the pathway.

"Riley, is it? That mean we're friends?"

"I Googled you, fool. So you were with the FBI? Now in private practice. Some pretty big busts in your day, no pun intended."

"You have your mother's sense of humor."

"Breaking news. You knew my mother?"

"Google works both ways," I lied. I didn't know it for a fact, but my gut was rarely wrong when it felt this strong. "Your mom's name was Máiréad. I suppose there are a few of those in DC, but not many fit the time frame. Was Flannery her maiden name?"

"Wow. Indeed it was, indeed it was. Look, I know you asked me out to dinner but I've had a pot roast in the slow cooker all day. I was planning to have an early dinner with some girlfriends but the snow scared them off. Would you like to share it with me and maybe talk a little about my mother?"

"I'd be honored. You *do* look just like her. How's she doing these days?"

"She died five years ago."

STAVE FOUR

I was at a loss for words, something that rarely happens to me. I said, "God, I'm so sorry. She was so young. What happened?"

"Come inside and warm up. I'll tell you about her then."

There was a small brass plaque on the wide lemonade porch of the Victorian farmhouse noting that it had been built in 1896 for the Larkin family. It was a dandy --- bottle glass windows cased with hunter green shutters, clapboards painted white, the steep roof topped with scalloped slate shingles. Over the years, a bit of the original detail had been sacrificed to time and insects, but the ornate gingerbread moldings were mostly intact.

Upon entering, the interior smelled of age and wood smoke, but it was bright and welcoming. The cheery openness suggested that a recent remodel had eliminated the superfluous walls so common when the place was built. I admired the craftsmanship, cognizant of the skill and expense necessary to effect such seamless changes in my own house. The fireplace was ablaze with thick oak logs, stockings hung on the mantel. Mary led me into the kitchen, where the heady aroma of pot roast filled my senses.

"Did you redo the kitchen?" I asked.

"When we first moved in. I designed the entire remodel myself."

"I'm impressed. You stayed true to the period, but you've incorporated modern amenities. You have talent. You said *we.* But you live alone now?"

"I do. The son of a bitch I married left a few years back. Moved to Florida to be with a Hooters girl. I got the house and business in the settlement. Worked out fine. I love it here and like you said, I've got all the amenities."

"Business is good?"

"As good as it needs to be. Mom left me some money. As long as I can pay the help and expenses, I'm good."

"So. Your mom. You were going to tell me what happened."

"Ovarian cancer. The silent killer. She was forty seven."

"Sorry."

"You know, I have to be honest with you, Riley. Can I call you Riley? Mom and I didn't get along very well. We barely spoke for years until she got sick and even then it was a strain. But I kind of look at her differently since my divorce. That's one reason why I wanted to talk to you about her."

She looked a wee bit apprehensive, as if I was going to tell her something she wasn't quite ready to hear. I shared the same fear. She said, "Hey. I need to take a shower and change. I've opened a nice cab. I won't be but a few minutes. You're welcome to look around and start the wine without me."

She flashed her glorious smile and walked off. The snow was shifting from flurries to large gentle flakes. I checked the weather app on my phone. They were calling for 3-5 inches in the mountains. The roads were treacherous enough while clean during daylight hours. I could only imagine how daunting they'd be covered in snow and ice on a dark night. I'd worry about that later.

I was eager to hear about Máiréad and why she had been estranged from her daughter. I busied myself exploring the ancient house while I waited for her to emerge from the bath. I didn't have to wait long. Like her mom and unlike any other woman I had known, she was in and out of the shower within ten minutes, dressed in a cleaner version of her previous outfit. Canvas jeans, green plaid flannel shirt, auburn hair loose, finger combed and still damp.

I said, "I waited for you to sample the wine." She poured us both a generous measure.

"So, Mary, tell me about your mother. I knew her when she was a student at American. She wanted to go into politics back then. Did she?"

"More like politics got into her. Or politicians, more accurately. That was a big part of our problem. Mind if I put on some music?"

"Not at all. As long as it's not Christmas music. The radio stations in Charlotte started playing carols wall-to-wall right after Halloween. Much as I like them, it's too much of a good thing."

"Me, too. I have satellite radio and there's a traditional jazz channel I like that's not too intrusive. Good background for conversation."

"Your call. I'm good with whatever. So what did you mean about the politicians?"

"Makes for strange bedfellows. Literally, in my mother's case. I hope I'm not disillusioning you about her if you harbor sweet memories of poor innocent Máiréad Flannery. I'm not sure you'll want to have your bubble burst."

I left her mother because she was sleeping with prominent Washingtonians for money. To me in those days, that was the biggest sin she could commit, short of murder. Now, I'd experienced enough of life to be more forgiving. I said, "In my line of work, I've seen most everything. Fire away."

"All right, here goes. Mom never married, but I didn't know that until I got married myself. There was a man that I thought was my stepfather. He was a

Congressman from our district in Northern Virginia, and he was away a lot. Came with the job, I thought. I was a kid, I didn't understand these things. Turns out he was married. He supposedly was separated from his wife, but he only lived with us part time. Probably had a couple of others on the side."

She took a deep pull on her cabernet and ran her tongue over her lips.

"I called him dad. He was older, died when I was ten. Apparently left mom a good chunk of money. Then she raised me herself, pretending to be a widow. To me. I'm sure everyone else knew the truth."

"Mary, that's not an unusual story. The guy might have loved your mother, but back then, messy divorces were enough to get you voted out, so he led a double life. But for her part, she gave you a dad in your early years, then took the responsibility on herself. She probably loved him, but she understood why they couldn't marry."

"Yeah, that sounds nice except this wasn't love. Even as a kid, I could see that. I never witnessed a tender moment between them. She was doing it for the money. After he died, there was a string of what she termed 'gentlemen callers.' Most of them had something to do with government. A couple of them came on to me when I was a teenager. The last one succeeded and I married him."

"How old were you?"

"Eighteen. My ex was closer to my mother's age. He was the one who told me the truth about her. How she whored herself out to gain favor with politicians. I admit, I was a rebellious teenager. I saw him as my salvation. My escape from a wicked libertine. His parents were rich. This farm was a tax shelter for them. They let the Central Americans run it. When his folks died, they left it to him along with a lot a cash that he gambled away. As it turned out, he was worse than my mother was. He did me a favor by leaving. If I hadn't hidden it, he would have run through my inheritance as well."

"You've had a tough go of it. But I hope you see now that your mother wasn't some wicked libertine, as you put it. She raised you as a single mom. Hooked up with a man she apparently didn't love to provide for you. There were other ways to do that to be sure, but she did what she thought she had to. Your marriage should give you some perspective, at least."

Her eyes were a million miles away. "I suppose that's why we're here talking now. Why I trusted a complete stranger in my home. You know, mom did do *something* I'm really proud of. After I left, she got into performing her music. Did cover versions mostly but she wrote a few songs of her own. She played small clubs. Got some nice notices."

"You know, I wondered if she followed through with that. She had the voice of an angel and she could really play guitar."

"She had a cult following in DC. Like a lower case Eva Cassidy. Even put out a CD on her own. I'll burn you a copy, if you're interested."

"I'd like that. I get it, Mary. You've had a tough life. But you seem happy now. You have your own business. Sounds like money isn't a problem. I'd just say, don't be too judgmental about your mother. She got caught up in the game in DC. She was a pretty progressive lady when I knew her, wanted to do good. Big on women's issues. She figured the best way to change things was from the inside."

"You make her out like she was some kind of feminist, but her actions fly in the face of that, don't they?"

"It sucked for women back then. Still does, but it's a lot better now, maybe due to people like your mom. But it's not fair to impose today's standards on yesterday's people."

"You're not the first person to bring that up. I've thought about it. I've softened on her a lot since she's been gone. Before she died, she told me a little about my real father. Seemed like he was a great guy."

Did she know about me all evening? Had she been stringing me along, just waiting for the right moment to call me on my secret? "Did she tell you his name and what happened with him?"

"Never told me his name, and believe me, I tried. Now, I'm not so sure I want to know. I'm not sure what purpose it would serve. He'd be old now, a family of his own. Maybe grandkids. He'd be embarrassed about me."

"Don't assume that. That's all she told you about him?"

"She said he was the love of her life. He left her to serve his country. It sounded like he might have died in combat but she never said that in so many words. The reason they split was all her fault according to her. He left because he was a straight arrow, a real righteous man, and she was a corrupting influence. Made him sound like Captain America."

My mind was racing through the math again. I had met Máiréad thirty years ago, almost to the day.

"How old are you, Mary?"

"I turned twenty eight in October. Why?"

"Just wondering if I knew your real dad. I knew a few of your mom's friends."

I'd been considering the possibility since I first laid eyes on her. The timeline synced up. My eyes are blue, my hair was blonde then, speckled with grey now. A strong case could be made that our combined genes had resulted in this lovely mixture. Although Máiréad had slept with other men during our relationship and any one of them might have been the father. Did *she* even know?

I couldn't share any of this with Mary until I was a hundred per cent sure. I excused myself to fetch more wine and when I got back, I changed course. I told her about myself and what Washington was like back then. How I joined the FBI, then started my own investigations business.

She responded by telling me about some of the other good things her mother had done. It turned out to be quite a long list. As she went on, I could see that she missed her mom more than she had ever admitted to herself. Especially now, at Christmastime.

The snow was piling up outside. We drank wine and ate pot roast. We talked deep into the night. The more we talked, the more I liked her. Despite all the drama, she had an amazingly positive outlook on life. And she loved Christmas, much as her mother had. She was planning on venturing down the mountain Christmas morning to serve food at the local homeless shelter.

There was no man in her life and she was lonely. When she looked at me, there was that unmistakable gleam in her eyes, the same look that her mother and I shared thirty years ago.

What a terrible position fate had put me in.

This beautiful and talented woman was mine for the asking. And if she was just a new friend seeking some warmth and comfort over the holidays, we could have had a wonderful night together. And she might be just that --- a lonely lady whose mother I had known briefly three decades ago. There would be nothing unseemly with letting nature take its course.

But she *might* be my daughter. If that were so, I couldn't think of anything more abhorrent than giving in to my desires this night.

Midnight came and it was Christmas Eve. She brought out homemade eggnog, laced with a healthy portion of rum. She said, "Riley, the roads are bad and we've both had a lot to drink. I can't send you out into the night like this."

"And baby, it's cold outside," I sang. I was a bit tipsy.

"One of mom's favorite holiday songs, too. She sang it once with James Taylor in a club. He happened to be in town and caught her act."

"Wow. I wish I had a recording of that."

She reached across and touched my hand. "Riley, stay with me tonight. They're great about clearing the snow up here. The roads should be good by morning."

Awkward.

"I did notice you have a comfy guest room. I roamed around the house exploring while you were in the shower."

There was that look in her eye again. "You don't have to stay in the guest room."

"I do. You see, I really like you, Mary. A lot. But I'm in a strange place now."

I almost told her the truth. Actually, I did tell her the literal truth, but not the real reason I couldn't be with her. "My life is complicated now. I just moved down here. Left someone behind in New Jersey. That's still unresolved. I respect you too much to make this a one-nighter. I'll bunk in the guest room and leave in the morning."

"Wow. A faithful man with old fashioned principles. And loyalty. That's a first in my experience. Hey, even if we never see each other again, you'll always be my Captain America."

If she only knew. "You'll see me again. You have the best trees I've ever seen. Worst case, I'll be up here every Christmas. And best case? Well for now, let's stick with visions of sugarplums."

"You got it. Only thing is, the hot water heater on the second floor isn't on so if you want to clean up before bedtime, you'll have to use the bathroom in the master. I won't peek, much as I'm tempted to."

"Don't be naughty, tonight of all nights. Or Santa may leave coal in your stocking."

Given her flirtatious manner, there was no way she could have traced her family history as I had done. When she awoke in the cold light of day, would she piece together what I now believed to be fact? Her naiveté had a lot to do with my deliberate omissions. I never said exactly how well I knew Máiréad. I didn't tell her how and when we met. And at my age, as fit as I may be, I bear precious little resemblance to Captain America.

She showed me into the master bath. It was as well appointed and period correct as the rest of the house, right down to the claw foot tub. I didn't need a shower, so I just eliminated some of the wine and washed up.

My detective instincts kicked in. I rummaged through a vanity drawer and found a plastic zip-lock bag. On the countertop, there was an electric toothbrush. I put a new head on it and dropped the used one into the bag, along with some strands of hair from her brush. My old friend Dan Logan at the FBI could get me DNA results by New Years. I tucked the bag into my shirt and said good night to Mary. She was sitting up in her canopy bed, wearing jammies and reading glasses, holding an old leather bound book. Dickens' *A Christmas Carol*.

I fought hard against my masculine instincts. I merely smiled and nodded as I departed her warm boudoir and mounted the stairs to the cold and lonely guest room. After a fitful night of sleep marred by ghostly dreams, I got up at sunrise. I left a note and one of my newly printed business cards on the kitchen table, thanking her for the wonderful evening. After warming up and brushing snow off the car, I turned back one last time and saw her standing at the window, looking all sleep-tousled and innocent. She waved as I drove down the snowy path toward the highway.

A few minutes later, at an overlook just off the road, I stopped to take in the *Currier and Ives* scene below. A snow crested town in the distance, with proud white church spires towering over the low slung redbrick village shops and houses. The serene beauty of it caused my throat to thicken and my eyes to mist over. At least, I think it was the beauty.

I took the glassine bag from my jacket and considered tossing it away, into the gorge.

I didn't. I never sent its contents to Dan Logan, either. They remain in the top drawer of my desk at home. Maybe someday, I'll have the courage to find the real truth. Beyond a reasonable doubt.

Until then, I'll be content to buy a freshly cut tree every year and have Christmas dinner with my daughter.

The End

For more information about ovarian cancer and how you can help fight this terrible disease go to the Ovarian Cancer Research Fund Alliance
https://ocrfa.org/

ACKNOWLEDGEMENTS

Many of the locations cited in the books do exist, although as usual, I made a good many of them up. The Charlotte Police headquarters was one such fabrication, as was Riley's perfect house on the lake. But Four Mile Creek in South Charlotte is a great place to enjoy nature *and* watch people. The Dunhill is a fine old hotel and WiseGuys is a favorite restaurant on Hilton Head Island. To my knowledge, there is no Mary's Christmas Tree Farm.

So many people have been helpful in encouraging my written work. On the radio side --- Mark Chernoff, Bob Gelb, Mark Mason, Ryan Chatelain and Harris Allen. Friends like Peter Larkin and Michael Harrison.

From a literary standpoint, there is always the world's number one Mets and Jets fan, Reed Farrel Coleman.

And of course, my wife Vicky who not only designs the covers and handles the business end of publishing, but is unfailingly supportive and a great source of inspiration. Camine Pappas was a tremendous resource during the design process. Erin Mitchell has been invaluable at spreading the word.

A nod to Duncan, (aka Auregrande Monarch of the Glen), who always knows when his dad needs a break from writing and insists I take him for long walks to return to reality.

"The Punch List" is Richard Neer's fifth novel, following the success of "Something of the Night", "The Master Builders" "Indian Summer" and "The Last Resort". The books feature detective Riley King and his talk radio ally Rick Stone as they fight crime along the eastern seaboard.

His work of non-fiction entitled "FM, the Rise and Fall of Rock Radio", (Villard 2001), is the true story of how corporate interests destroyed a format that millions grew up with.

Neer has worked in important roles at two of the most prestigious and groundbreaking radio stations in history --- the legendary WNEW-FM for almost thirty years, and the nation's first full time sports talker, WFAN, since 1988. Early in his career, he and Michael Harrison started the first suburban progressive rock station, WLIR on Long Island.

He currently is completing the next Riley King novel.